PRAISE FOR
LESLEY A. DIEHL

DEAD IN THE WATER

"How can you not love a cheeky Yankee-chick-consignment-shop-entrepreneur who's willing to fight alligators, the Russian mob, and treacherous blackmailers to avenge her uncle's murder? Eve Appel is strong-willed and sassy and will stop at nothing to save her kidnapped friend and learn the truth, even it means putting herself in danger or ruining her Jimmy Choos. Eve does it all with class and a gaggle of smitten lovers and quirky friends. *Dead in the Water* is a laugh-out-loud cozy with just the right balance of suspense, plot twists, romance, and airboat rides."
—Sharon Potts, author of *South Beach Cinderella*

"Lesley Diehl has outdone herself with *Dead in the Water*. She still has her carefully drawn characters you enjoy knowing and the sense of humor that makes you laugh out loud. But in *Dead in the Water*, Diehl has developed her most involved plot. With murder, kidnapping, the mob and alligators, you won't want to put the book down. This second Eve Appel Mystery is a must-read."
—James R. Callan, author of *Cleansed by Fire* and *A Ton of Gold*

"Like the biblical Eve, Eve Appel, the main character in Lesley Diehl's *Dead In The Water*, is an impulsive, curious, and determined woman who doesn't always live by the rules. Those

characteristics place her in extremely dangerous situations and add to the intriguing plot in this second book in the series."
—Patricia Gligor, author of *Mixed Messages*, U*nfinished Business*, and, *Desperate Deeds*.

A SECONDHAND MURDER

"Lesley A Diehl is a very clever writer. Most of the time I can figure out the murderer in a book but this one kept me guessing right until the end. The characters all have one thing in common, trying to solve the murder .... *A Secondhand Murder* is a cozy mystery, and is part of a series called An Eve Appel Mystery. Hopefully all the other ones will be just as good as this one."
—Sharon Salituro, Fresh Fiction Reviews

"Fun from Page one! .... Not only is *A Secondhand Murder* filled to the brim with entertaining characters, but the mystery contained in its pages is also well crafted. Everyone, even Eve, seemed to have some sort of secret. I enjoyed peeling back all the layers of this story as I tried to figure out what was related to the murder and what wasn't. I absolutely enjoyed reading A Secondhand Murder. The web of murder and deceit is well spun, but the characters Ms. Diehl has created are truly the shining stars of this book. Anyone looking for a laugh out loud, fast paced mystery would do well to pick up *A Secondhand Murder* today."
—Long and Short Reviews

"A full cast of zany and dangerous characters makes this cozy mystery a fun read. With laugh out loud scenes and some scary moments, this book is so hard to put down and when the end did come, I found myself wondering what madcap adventure awaits the reader in the next book. I loved it!!"
—Kathleen Kelly, Celtic Lady's Reviews

"I'll have to personally recommend this book to all of my friends who love cozies. It's a great mystery, with a little suspense, a little romance, some slapstick, and most of all, characters who feel like family. I read it in one sitting. Is it one sitting if you stop to put another log on the fire, pour a tall glass of apple pie vodka and let the dogs out? At any rate, I didn't want to stop reading, and stayed up late to finish. It was worth it."
—Ryder Islington, author of *Ultimate Justice*

"Thrift with a murderous twist ... vivid Florida setting with lots of suspense and humor."
—Kathleen Delaney, author of the Ellen McKenzie Mystery Series

"Author Lesley A. Diehl blends humor and suspense into a delightful tale of intrigue. Diehl has created likable, realistic characters that will have you laughing as you try to guess who the killer is. *A Secondhand Murder* flows at a steady pace with some interesting twists along the way. The setting is inviting and the story will draw you in."
—Mason Canyon, Thoughts in Progress Blog

"An extremely fun and wickedly entertaining cozy mystery. The quirky characters and the complex entanglements each of them have with the deceased and the protagonist is the best part of the book. The author creates a well-plotted, light-hearted mystery that has some really good laugh out loud scenes. Cozy mystery lovers will thoroughly enjoy *A Secondhand Murder*; it is an outstanding read from beginning to end."
—Robin T. for Manic Readers

"Humor, adventure, mystery and romance are all blended together to make this a fun few hours of reading. The book

kept me guessing until the end—I kept changing my mind about who the killer was and I guessed wrong. LOL—This was a good thing. I enjoyed this one. This is the first book in the series and it's already off to a great start."
—Yvonne, Socrates Book Review

"[A Secondhand Murder] will delight you. It has a little bit of everything that you want in a murder/mystery, complete with romance!"
—Mary Bearden, Mary's Cup of Tea

"I am absolutely in love with this story. Lesley Diehl has created such a fun character in Eve Appel! She was funny, sassy and smart. She's a great protagonist. The story has a great mystery and there's so many different things going on that I was definitely surprised by the ending. I love a good mystery dashed with humor."
—Brooke Blogs

"I really enjoyed the page turning action that even involved getting help from a Mob boss. The story was complex but very easy to follow. The quirky characters including Eve lead the reader through lots of excitement…. I wholeheartedly recommend this cozy for all cozy mystery readers."
—Carol McKinney, Carol's Reviews

"There were so many characters that I really enjoyed everyone from Eve's crazy ex-husband Jerry to Alex the Private Investigator to her grandmother and grandfather. They all had their quirks that I loved. Definitely a great new refreshing series that I can't wait to read more of when the author writes more!"
—Community Bookstop Blog

Dead in the Water

Dead in the Water

AN EVE APPEL MYSTERY

LESLEY A. DIEHL

CAMEL
PRESS
Seattle, WA

Camel Press
PO Box 70515
Seattle, WA 98127

For more information go to: www.camelpress.com
www.lesleyadiehl.com

Cover design by Sabrina Sun

Dead in the Water
Copyright © 2014 by Lesley A. Diehl

ISBN: 978-1-60381-937-4 (Trade Paper)
ISBN: 978-1-60381-938-1 (eBook)

Library of Congress Control Number: 2014937928

Printed in the United States of America

Acknowledgments

—

Eve owes her taste and courage to two women in my life, my paternal grandmother, Minnie Appel Diehl, who inspired me to be frugal, and my aunt, Fern Diehl Stouffer, who invented retail therapy.

CHAPTER 1

IT WAS so hot in my closet I could feel my makeup running down my face, and so dark I couldn't see where I was going. I wasn't crazy about the smell, either. Mostly leather and dirty socks. I reached out, searching with my fingers for …. I touched something furry. *Yikes*. There was some animal in here with me.

"Find them?"

I jumped at the sound of my friend's voice and hit my head on the shelving in the back of the closet.

"You scared the hell out of me."

"I don't know who's worse, you or your uncle. He's tied up on his cellphone, and you're exploring your closet. Let's get going." Madeleine sounded irritated, and I couldn't blame her. I'd been crawling around on the floor for close to a quarter of an hour and still hadn't located my boots.

"I can't think where I might have put them. They've got to be in here someplace."

"Then wear a pair of sneakers. We're going to be late."

Sneakers? I didn't own a pair of sneakers unless you counted those high heel wedgie ones. I guessed I could wear them, but I had no idea where they were either. My closet floor was a mess. The hunt was made more difficult because I'd failed to replace the burned out light bulb in the closet.

I hated to give up my quest. Madeleine was right. It was cold and windy today and wearing boots on the airboat ride was the smart thing to do. I pulled back my hand, holding the furry object between my thumb and index finger. What was this? I held it up to the faint light coming through the open closet door. Oh, right. It was one of a pair of slippers made to look like two moose heads, complete with antlers and large noses. They'd been a Christmas gift from Madeleine.

I tossed the slipper over my shoulder and continued to explore the floor. My hand landed on one of my boots. I could tell by the feel of the leather, ostrich skin. Pricey, but I'd found them at a consignment shop on the coast. One had a small scratch on the toe, not noticeable unless I bent over and touched my nose to the damaged area, something I had no intention of doing and every intention of discouraging anyone else from doing. *Ah*. The matching boot was right beside its mate.

"Got 'em." I exited the closet, pulled them on, tucked my jeans into the tops and examined myself in the mirror. Nice. Airboat and swamp chic.

Madeleine did not share my opinion.

"You're wearing stiletto-heeled boots? How practical is that?"

"I couldn't find my hip waders. Look, I'm only trying to keep my feet warm. I don't intend to take a walk through the swamp, you know."

"Hip waders, huh? They'd probably have heels too." Madeleine had my number as no one else did. I loved her like a sister, so she was the only person I never sassed. Well. Almost never. I followed her out of the bedroom and into the living room.

"That's my gal, my little Eve." My Uncle Winston flipped

his cell closed, got up from the couch, came over and threw his arm around my shoulder. "You look fantastic, honey." He gave me a squeeze and looked at the woman seated beside him on the couch. Darlene Banks, introduced by Winston as his "domestic partner", wore sneakers, jeans and a sweater that screamed, "I'm a Gucci or Pucci or some other designer brand, and this woman stupidly paid full price for me."

Darlene wrinkled up her nose at my attire. "I agree with Maddy. How can you walk in those things?"

I caught Madeleine's look of disapproval and knew she wouldn't say anything, but I would.

"Her name is 'Madeleine.' She hates being called 'Maddy.' "

"Well, I'm real sorry, but she looks too small to have such a large name." Darlene was as outspoken as I was, a trait I found quite acceptable in myself and just plain irritating in others. Especially Darlene.

Uncle Winston, my favorite uncle from childhood, had given me a surprise call last week asking if it was convenient to come visit. I was surprised to learn he'd bought a condo in West Palm, less than two hours from Sabal Bay, Big Lake country where cows and cowboys rule. "We'd like to see rural Florida. I hear they have cowboys there. And lots of gators."

I'd insisted on putting them up rather than allowing them to stay in a nearby motel. The accommodations in the Sabal Bay area have more character than luxury unless you think a gator skull on the bedside table is de rigueur. Tourists usually choose to stay in a motel on the coast and cruise by here without stopping on their way to the other coast. As they speed by, they complain they can't see the lake. Of course not. If they looked at a map they'd know a canal and a dike surrounded much of the water. You have to drive over the berm or levee and park on the other side to see the lake. I'll admit there's not much to see, mostly brown water. You don't go there for the view. It's for fishing. And for alligators to play water games in.

Looking back on my offer to serve as their bed and breakfast,

I conceded it was a mistake. As I ushered them and their luggage into the guest bedroom, Darlene wrinkled up her nose in distaste.

"We prefer a king-sized bed," she said.

"Really. So do I," I said.

That was just the first of her many complaints. The restaurants didn't offer enough fish items. She was shocked that anyone ate catfish. Or turtle. Or frogs' legs. I could forgive her the dislike of our dining establishments. It's a bit of a culture shock to drive from the sandy beaches of the coast and find yourself in a world populated by gators, cowboys, and cattle and then see fried catfish bones on the menu. And I'd tolerate her because it was clear that she adored my uncle. She hung on his every word and hustled to get him whatever he wanted.

"What's the deal with the boots and the cowboy hats?" she asked. Again she wrinkled up her nose. If she continued to do that, her nose and forehead would join together in a blanket of wrinkles.

"This is a ranching community." I know I sounded defensive.

"So?" She did not understand the concept of working the range.

"Honey." Winston encircled her waist with his arm. "This place has got real character."

She looked at Winston as if he'd lost his mind and should be locked up. "I want to go back to West Palm."

Oh, good idea.

I responded to most of her criticism with a breezy, "We consider this a quaint place, traditional, old Florida."

To which she replied, "It's just not civilized here."

Well, no it wasn't, and that's why I liked it around the Big Lake. Slower paced than either of the coasts, this area of Florida was like walking back in time. I was a sucker for nostalgia. I even preferred to call my Capris pedal-pushers, and some of them were. I frequented vintage stores to find many of my clothing items. Madeleine and I even carried a line of vintage wear in our consignment shop. *Très* great.

I adored Winston, had ever since I was a kid. I would put up with Darlene if it meant I could be with my uncle again. I hadn't heard from him since I was in my early teens and lived in Connecticut. I remembered him as the fun uncle, the guy who was up for any adventure, including riding the tilt-o-whirl at the county fairs, entering a jalapeño eating contest and sharing downhill ski lessons with me after he was well over forty. He also coaxed me back on a sailboat for the first time after my parents' boat had been caught in a storm, and they'd been lost in Long Island Sound. I guess he was actually a great-uncle, the youngest son of one my grandfather's brothers. The other uncles in the family just seemed the same as most adults to a nine-year-old, boring to me, spouting lots of rules and regulations and admonitions about what a girl should and should not do. For Winston there were no boundaries on fun regardless of your age or sex.

We hadn't been in touch for years, but he was as I remembered him: tall and lanky with a boyish mop of hair, now turning white, that flopped over his forehead. He certainly seemed to have kept his zest for adventure. I took them to the rodeo the first day of the visit and had to hold him down when it was announced that anyone could enter the bull-riding contest. I'd seen the size and surly temperament of those huge creatures at the past several rodeos I'd attended and discouraged Winston from trying his luck. The guy had to be on the far side of sixty. To my surprise, Darlene egged him on. What was she, the beneficiary in his will? She seemed disappointed when I persuaded him it was too dangerous, unless you were a bona fide cowboy. She seemed to like living dangerously, or at least she liked *him* to live dangerously. Maybe she liked her danger secondhand.

At one time she might have been judged to be beautiful, and she still was a looker in the over sixty set. She had a full figure which she showed off to good advantage, choosing to wear tops that revealed enough cleavage to make Winston's eyes twinkle when she leaned into him. Her breasts seemed a bit too bouncy to be anything other than enhanced. Her red hair was teased into a style reminiscent of the late sixties. Of course, the red was a shade never found in nature and achieved with the help of Lady Clairol or one of her color-in-a-bottle cousins.

Darlene took an instant dislike to Madeleine, whose red hair was home grown. Where I was tall and flat-chested, Madeleine was short, tiny, and although I usually hate 'perky' as a description, she was definitely perky. If we had been guys, we would be called Mutt and Jeff. I guessed it was jealousy that made Darlene call her "Maddy."

Madeleine smiled at my intervention on the name issue. "It's fine if Darrel or Darren wants to call me whatever."

"It's Darlene, missy."

Madeleine opened her blue eyes wide in a look of absolute innocence. "Like I said, 'whatever.'"

Winston rubbed his hands together. "Let's get going, girls. I'm anxious to see what the swamp has to offer. Think we'll see any gators, Eve?"

"I've pointed out the gators on all the canals around here. I can't see why you think they'll look any different from an airboat."

"Maybe we can get real close. I got my cameras with me." Winston held up his duffel bag. In his other hand, he carried another duffel. They both looked heavy.

"How many cameras have you got in there?"

"Enough to get some great pictures. And I've got snacks, water and several sweaters if it gets too cold. I've got to look out for my ladies."

"It's an airboat ride, not a weekend cruise." I chuckled and unlocked the door to my car, then moved the seat forward so Darlene and Madeleine could get into the back. After a round of intense barbecuing last year, during which my little red Miata had suffered irreparable burn damage, I replaced her with a blue Mustang convertible.

Darlene looked at the small backseat with skepticism but she struggled into it and dropped the huge purse she carried on the floor. Winston hung back a moment before he got in.

"C'mere a moment, Eve," he said.

He took my arm, and we walked a few feet from the car.

"I know you were surprised I called you after all these years and I'm sorry, but things came up." He seemed about to explain, but instead he simply shrugged, as if embarrassed. "I won't fail you again."

"You didn't fail me." I touched his arm and leaned into him with a half hug.

"Anyway, you know how important family is, don't you?"

I nodded, thinking of the loss of my parents and how my grandmother and Winston made me feel I was still loved and had family to take care of me.

"Family comes first. Don't forget that."

I looked toward the car, seeing Madeleine's dismal expression at being cooped up in the back seat with Darlene.

"Madeleine's like a sister to you, isn't she?" he said. "Sometimes family is more than blood relatives. It's those we love."

"Sure. I know. I'm just glad I have you in my life again."

The serious look on his face was replaced by one of happiness. "Now, let's go get us some gators."

He threw his two duffel bags on the floor on the passenger's side and folded himself into the seat. Twisting around, he winked at Darlene.

"I guess there's no room back there for these with that purse of yours, huh?" he said.

"I could put some of those bags in the trunk," I said.

"Nope. We're good." Winston positioned his feet next to the bags and slammed the door.

DESPITE THE WIND blowing cold and hard out of the north,

the Mustang held the road well as I maneuvered her around the curves leading to the airboat facility.

"We could wait until tomorrow to do this. It's so windy today they may decide not to operate." I wasn't keen on riding one of those machines anyway and certainly not in this weather.

"No, today is fine. I called ahead to make sure they were running." Winston's tone was firm, but there was almost a note of desperation in it.

"You gals wimps?" Darlene seemed as keen on the ride as Winston, an attitude I found odd since she'd pronounced every gator I'd pointed out "ugh, so ugly." What did she think we'd find in the swamp? Gators wearing lipstick, mascara, and blush?

"Absolutely not." Madeleine shook her head. "We love this weather. We get far too much sun, heat, and humidity down here. This is a pleasant change."

I caught Madeleine's eye in the rearview mirror. Maybe she was planning to push Darlene off the boat. I shook the idea from my head. Madeleine was too polite for that, and I knew it. Maybe I'd push Darlene off the boat. Or was that little talk I had with Winston all about how he considered her family and so should I? I re-adjusted my attitude toward her. If he liked her then I'd try to tolerate the woman.

Only a few cars were parked at the airboat landing. We purchased our tickets inside the building, where they also sold fruits and vegetables and displayed small alligators in an aquarium. The man behind the counter was short and skinny with the face of a weasel, an unfriendly sort until he got a look at Madeleine. Her flaming red hair, small stature, and feminine clothes made her look like a fairy queen. The girl never failed to draw men to her, as they say, like moths to a flame, at least until they got burned. Madeleine's dating history was heavily punctuated with unfortunate mishaps. The vegetable, fruit and baby gator guy pointed us down a path leading to the dock where a boat was tied up fifty yards from where we stood. He offered to show us the way.

"We don't want the little lady to get lost." He looked directly at Madeleine and waggled his bushy eyebrows.

"This is it, right?" I pointed to the well-worn dirt path. He nodded. "And that's the boat, right?" He nodded again. "I think we'll manage. You can keep an eye on us, and if we stray, go ahead and call the emergency search and rescue."

He gave me a dark look and returned to unpacking strawberries.

At the landing, we settled ourselves on the airboat's bench seats. It wasn't a private boat, so we were glad to be the first to arrive and claim the choice seats. Winston sat in the outer seat with me on the bench ahead and put the two duffel bags on the floor in front of his feet. Darlene pulled a paisley-print scarf over her teased-to-submission and lacquered hair and settled in beside Winston. He put his arm around her shoulders and she leaned into him. Madeleine sat beside me in the front. Neither Madeleine nor Darlene wanted an outside seat, so this seemed the best arrangement. Wimps in the middle, the brave ones inches away from the water and whatever chose to live in it. *Maybe I should rethink my seat.*

Two couples from Montreal took the unoccupied seats, one couple in front of us and the other next to us. A teenage boy and girl belonging to the first couple took the seats in the far front. There was room for two more riders next to the kids, but no one showed up.

The airboat pilot seemed friendly enough, but like his partner who sold us the tickets, he took one look at Madeleine and got friendlier, directing most of his attention to her, helping her to put on her ear protectors to muffle the sound.

"I think I can do it myself."

He ignored her and leaned over the couple next to us to clap them on her ears. "Don't want the little lady to hurt her hearing now, do we?"

In this part of Florida attractive women of normal or shorter height are always "little ladies." Close to six feet without my preferred footwear, I've never been called anything but "hey you, lady." Men rarely offered me help with anything, but I thought I'd test this theory.

"What about me?" I held my ear protectors out to him.

"You'll be fine." He continued to adjust Madeleine's, and I held my breath just as I'm sure Madeleine did. Whenever it came to men and Madeleine, something bad always happened. The last time a man took an interest in her, my car blew up. I'm not saying it was her fault, but things seemed to always go awry when she was around.

I sighed in relief as he stepped back and checked the red containers of gasoline on the dock. He shook his head, added gas to the boat, then flipped open his cell. I couldn't hear what he said, but the call was brief. Good. I was anxious to get going. I was cold enough just sitting here in the boat. I couldn't imagine what it was going to feel like flying down the canal with that wind whipping at my face. I wanted the ride to be over before it began.

The pilot took his high seat behind the passengers. The boat leaped forward with much rattling, roaring, and shaking. He increased the speed, and the roaring grew louder as we flew out to the main waterway. Soon we were cruising down the wide expanse of the canal surrounding the Big Lake, its waters on the other side of the high berm to our left. The vibrating was so strong that I thought I'd chip teeth if I clenched my mouth closed. Mouth open, I risked bugs flying in.

I was surprised at the number of boats on the canal—other airboats, canoes, bass boats—heading toward the locks and the lake beyond. Even a few kayaks. As chilly as the air was, I hated to think what it would be like if a person went overboard into the water. Instant hypothermia.

Winston tapped me on my shoulder. I turned to look at him.

"Having fun?" The skin around his eyes crinkled with humor as he grinned at me.

He'd turned his cap around so that the wind couldn't catch

the bill and flip it into the water. I pulled the hoodie on my sweatshirt up over my head and tied it under my chin.

"Uh, sure." I smiled back.

The cold wind rushed at us, flattening my face and making my eyes water. If there was anything to see, the tears in my eyes obscured the view. The boat raced through the water, swaying back and forth over the surface, making me worry it might swerve and capsize. Once I got used to the rocking from side to side, I settled back to enjoy the ride, noisy as it was. Abruptly the boat slowed and we pulled up to the shoreline; then, as suddenly as we'd lost speed, we took off again.

"Hey," the pilot called, "nothing here. We'll go into the swamp and chase us some gators there."

Oh goodie, I thought. *Here's where we get lost.*

As we sped down a small waterway, the vegetation on either side closed in around us. The pilot took an abrupt turn to the left and almost mowed down two kids fishing in a small motorboat.

The pilot cut the engine. "Hey, get the hell out of the way." The wake from the airboat washed toward their tiny craft and rocked it.

"Damn Indians. They think they own these swamps. Always in the way." He shook his fist at them.

"Well, they really do own this land, don't they? Isn't it part of the Miccosukee Tribal Territory?" I didn't like the pilot's arrogant attitude. The kids weren't in anyone's way. They were just fishing.

He gave me a dark look and revved the engine. We headed back across open water with reeds and swamp grass, then into a small canal.

We slowed, and the pilot again shouted, "Hey!" The boat headed toward the bank—dense with cattails, reeds and fallen logs—then nosed into land. Before us, not six feet away, was an alligator. It didn't move, merely lay there eyeing us. The pilot stepped down from his seat and onto the front of the boat. He grabbed an overhead branch and shook it. The gator opened its mouth and hissed. Close encounters of the reptile kind. We all jumped. Cameras snapped pictures. The captain reached for Madeleine's camera and got a close-up. She smiled her gratitude and her friendliness seemed to stir his need to show off. He grabbed the knife that was in a sheath at his belt and brandished it as if he was about to take on the creature. Some of us oohed. I yawned.

"You're not going to hurt that alligator, are you?" Madeleine's eyes flashed a mixture of anger and concern.

"No, ma'am, little lady."

Oh, for heaven's ....

"Sir, you need to get back in the boat."

Distracted by the scene of our macho pilot entertaining both us and the alligator, no one noticed Winston step off the boat onto the shore and wander back into the overgrown island.

"Sir," the pilot called again, "Come back here."

"Uncle Winston!" I said.

"Oh, let him go. He's just curious." Darlene grabbed my shoulder as if to restrain me from getting off with him.

"Did you miss something here? That's an alligator right in front of us, and I'm sure it has friends and relatives out there." I called Winston's name once more.

"Go get him." Madeleine looked up at the pilot as if he was an action hero.

"I'm right here." Winston appeared once more out of the thicket of brush and stepped back onto the airboat, settling into his seat. "Nothing much out there, and it's too thick to walk far."

The pilot gave Winston a stern look. "Don't do that again, sir. If you want to help, grab that pole and give us a shove off. The boat don't have reverse."

Winston complied, the engine started again, and we were off for another alligator sighting. I turned my head to look back at where we had been, wondering how that gator felt about airboats invading its sanctuary. I caught a spot of red just to the right of where we'd seen the gator, but before I could crane my neck for a better view, we turned a bend and started across a watery area, chasing mud hens as we flew across the surface. When I looked down I could tell the swamp was only inches deep here. Water flew at us and deposited leaves and other debris on our faces and in our hair. I pulled a small caterpillar off Madeleine's sleeve. Looking down, I spotted a few of the crawly critters on my shirt.

Okay, we got up close and intrusive with a gator. That should be enough.

Three more gator sightings and a few more races at the poor mud hens and we turned back toward the dock.

"Hey."

Hey yourself, I wanted to yell at our pilot. He said something I did not understand, but Madeleine translated for me.

"He said to grab onto something."

What was this crazy man up to now? He throttled the engine up, and we raced by the dock at top speed; then he cut the engine and abruptly cut to the left, making the boat slide sideways through reeds.

"When the water's lower, I can do a 360 degree turn."

Oh gosh. What a shame we had to miss that.

I was about to share my thoughts with Madeleine when I noticed her face had taken on a decidedly green tinge.

"You okay?" I asked.

"Ulp." She nodded, but not too convincingly.

We headed back for the dock at a sane speed. The wide bow wave pushed the water lettuce and water lilies away from the boat. They seemed to duck under the surface as if they were trying to get away from us. I could understand why.

"First airboat ride?" The pilot held his hand out to Madeleine once we were tied up. She got up from her seat and wobbled a bit, then took his hand. For the first time today, I was grateful he was behaving like a gentleman and helping her debark.

His attempt at gallantry would have been successful, had Madeleine's sneaker not come untied. As she stepped onto the dock, she slipped backwards into the boat, pulling the pilot with her. He let go, his foot missed the boat, and he plunged into the water. I looked at her, and she at me. Yep, she still had it.

"It was bound to happen, honey." I pushed her onto the dock and joined her there. The pilot floundered around in the three foot deep water for several minutes before he was able to pull himself out. One water lily in full yellow bloom perched on his shoulder, while other plants trailed their watery roots along his arms. He shook himself like a wet dog and smiled.

"Have a nice day, folks." He waved as we took the path back to our car.

Darlene removed her scarf and patted her hair back into its helmet shape. "I'm gonna buy some strawberries. I love Plant City berries. And I gotta pee." She started toward the building, catching up with the other passengers.

"Oops, forgot." Winston turned and started back to the boat. "I didn't give him a tip."

I shook my head in disgust. "Here's a tip. Stay away from 'little ladies.' "

A hurt looked crossed Madeleine's face.

"You weren't really interested in him, were you?" I asked.

"Of course not. It's just that I feel as if all men who show any interest in me are cursed."

"In this case, it might be for the best. Think how you'd handle dating someone who smelled like swamp water even after he bathed and whose idea of fun is to do wheelies in an airboat."

The sound of raised voices drew my attention back to the dock. Winston stood with his back to us, the pilot in front of him. It looked like the two men were arguing. I made out the words "money" and "owe." Was the pilot arguing about the amount of his tip?

"What's happening? I'm going back there." I started toward

the dock, but stopped when I heard a loud pop. I watched the two men drop to the ground. As I ran toward them, one man got to his knees, looked toward the opposite bank of the canal and rose to his feet, waving at me. It was the pilot. My uncle lay on the path. He wasn't moving.

CHAPTER 2

——

"CALL 911!" I yelled to Madeleine. I kneeled, gently touched Winston's cheek and placed my fingers on his neck. I could feel no pulse. Winston was dead, his eyes staring up into the blue sky but seeing nothing. *How could this be?*

"A heart attack?" Madeleine stood over me. I blocked her view. There was a dime-sized hole in his forehead and blood pooled under the back of his head. I shook my head, afraid to turn and look into her eyes, afraid she would see my horror, my grief.

I took a deep breath and a sob worked its way up my throat. I swallowed it before it escaped my lips, but tears poured down my cheeks. I wiped them away then stood and turned toward Madeleine.

"Don't look. C'mon. We need to let the police handle this."

Madeleine's face blanched, her tiny freckles standing out like dots on white paper. "Oh, Eve, Eve, Eve. What happened here?"

"Go on back to Darlene. She'll need someone, and you're better at offering words of comfort than I am. Those kids ought not to see him either. Keep them away."

"Take charge Eve" did not feel anything like in control. I

looked down at my shaking hands.

Madeleine must have seen them too. She reached out and pulled me toward her in an embrace neither of us wanted to end. She drew back first. "Okay." Her shoulders heaved, and she seemed to pull herself together. She headed back to Darlene, who appeared not to have heard the shot or noticed what was happening. She was still in animated conversation with the other airboat passengers in front of the building.

I knew better than to tamper with anything around Winston, but I yearned to throw my jacket over his body. I wanted him to have privacy, even though I couldn't say how I thought that might help.

The pilot of the airboat had moved away from Winston's body and boarded the boat. He seemed to be looking for something on its floor. The pilot's movements drew my attention. What was he doing? I leaned down and touched Winston's shoulder, then walked toward the boat.

"What are you doing?"

He jumped, too intent upon his search to hear me coming. "Ah. I just wanted to see if there was a hole in my boat."

"That's your only concern? Your damn boat? I only heard one shot. What about you?" I looked around at the boat and the dock, then directed my gaze across the broad canal to the sabal palms lining the other bank.

"Sorry. Is he …?" The pilot now looked embarrassed.

"We called 911."

Fear drained the expression of shame from his face. "I could have been killed."

"You think someone was trying to shoot you?" I was no expert, but the bullet entered my uncle in such a precise location, he had to be the shooter's target, not merely someone who got in the way.

I shared my thoughts with the pilot, but he didn't look reassured.

Then it hit me. Who would want to kill my uncle? And why?

I sensed someone behind me and spun around.

"You're supposed to be comforting Darlene." But it wasn't Madeleine. It was my friend Frida, a detective with the Sabal Bay police department. Frida's brown eyes, usually so warm and soft, were flinty and hard. She was almost as tall as I was and slender. She dressed for the job—slacks, white shirt, and low-heeled shoes. She wore her dark hair pulled back and fastened in a tortoiseshell clip to keep it out of her face. As well-tailored as her jacket was, it didn't totally hide the shoulder holster she wore as part of her detective's gear.

"I got the call on my way out to Deer Mound to check on a robbery there. And Eve, I can read your thoughts. Whoever is responsible for this, it's my job to find them. Not yours." She knew me so well. No wonder I couldn't bluff her at girls' poker night.

"Of course. Why would I think otherwise?"

Frida gave me one of her looks, the one that said she couldn't trust me. Of course she couldn't. When I'd gotten involved in a murder investigation last year—Frida's first as a detective on the force—I'd almost gotten myself killed and nearly botched the case she'd been so carefully working. Yet the voice in my head kept repeating, *my uncle, my uncle, my fault, my fault.* I should have insisted we take the airboat ride another day. I knew it was too windy. I knew something would happen ….

Frida and her new partner, Detective Tooney—Linc was his first name—bent over Winston's body. I heard the wail of an ambulance in the background. Crime scene technicians arrived and were soon swarming the area. Frida turned her attention back to me.

"You need to get out of here, Eve. This is a crime scene. We've got to seal it."

Detective Tooney took my arm and steered me away from Winston's body and toward Madeleine and Darlene. Several emergency personnel had seated Darlene on the rear bumper of the ambulance and were talking with her.

"She's in shock, I'd guess." Madeleine tucked my arm in hers. "How are you doing, hon?'"

"Why would anyone want to kill my uncle?"

"You don't know he was the target."

I kept seeing the bullet hole planted neatly in the middle of his forehead.

Darlene shook herself free of the EMTs and walked on wobbly legs toward me.

"It was the mob. The Mob." With that, she sank to the ground in a faint.

AFTER THE AMBULANCE took Darlene off to the hospital, and yet another arrived to remove my uncle, Madeleine and I stood behind the yellow tape strung around the airboat dock, the boat itself, and the spot where my uncle fell.

"When you guys gonna be finished? I got a business to run here." The airboat pilot and his weasel partner stood far to our right with Frida and Linc.

"Hey!" The yell had worked on the ride, so I tried it on our pilot. It caught his attention. "Someone died here, you know. Maybe it could have been you. I'd think you'd want the authorities to do their job and the hell with your business, especially if you're in danger." I really didn't think he was, but the man irritated me, playing macho with the wildlife and with my friend Madeleine. Or maybe it was death—violent death— that made me surly.

Frida gave me another of her stay-out-of-this-Eve looks, finished walking the crime scene, then approached Madeleine and me.

"You don't like him?"

I shared with her what I knew of the fight between him and Winston and his intense interest in the airboat following the shot.

"Anything unusual about the ride? I mean aside from him?" Frida nodded over her shoulder at the pilot.

"Winston tried to take a walk through the swamp." I explained about Winston's debarking when we spotted the first alligator.

"Tourists sometimes think they can go where they want."

"I saw something odd when we left there." I told Frida about the spot of red.

Frida verbalized what I was thinking. "Winston left something there and marked it. We need to take a look at that place."

"I have no idea how to get back there."

"He does." Frida signaled to the airboat captain. "Let's take a ride."

When I started toward the boat, Frida reached out and placed a restraining hand on my arm. "Not you, Eve. You wait here."

I waited, and not with any degree of patience. I hated being left out, my brain eager to map out a plan of action and get—

"You're thinking loud enough to be heard across the canal." Madeleine put her hand on my arm and tried to lead me back to the building where we'd purchased out tickets.

My attention was diverted to the trees on the other side of the canal, where a patrol boat was pulled up on the shore and men in uniform were milling about. Soon I saw the airboat return from the swamp and turn toward the opposite shore. Frida debarked and talked with the deputies, who pointed out something on the ground. They marked it, took a picture and handed it to Frida. It was too far away to see what she held. She got back into the airboat and headed toward us.

"Well?"

I could tell Frida didn't like my imperious tone, but she hesitated only a moment. "It looks like a number of people took a walk in that area of the swamp. And not too long ago, maybe just after the airboat ride left there."

"And ...?" I wanted more.

"And there was a shell casing over there." She nodded toward the opposite bank.

"One shot, only one. Some marksman," I said.

"It's a doable shot if you've had some training." There was something else on her mind.

I waited.

"It just seems too easy," she said.

"Easy?" I asked.

Her gaze traveled back over the canal to the palm trees there.

"You'd think whoever fired the rifle wouldn't leave a shell casing behind. It's evidence. A beginning. Now we need to find out who wanted your uncle dead."

"You think he was the intended target."

"Don't you, Eve?" Frida took my arm and steered me toward her car. "Let's talk. Tell me about him."

I told her all I knew about my uncle, which wasn't much. I hadn't seen him in over twenty years.

"Then, out of the blue, he called you? Didn't you think that was strange?" Frida scribbled in her notebook.

"Of course, but I was so eager to see him again that I didn't think twice about it once he was here."

"How did he act? Was he nervous?"

"I really couldn't tell because I haven't been around him for so long. I thought he seemed quite happy. In a good mood, although he did make a lot of calls on his cell."

"Could you hear what he said?"

"No. He usually went outside to make the calls, but then that's normal around my place. Cell reception is better out front of my house."

"We haven't found his cell. Do you know where it is?"

"No. The last time I saw him use it was at my house, but I know he took it with him. He had it in the car."

"We'll look there." She signaled one of her men to check out my car. He returned with a cell in his hand.

"And his girlfriend?" Frida asked.

"Don't know her."

Frida caught something in my tone of voice. "What you do know you don't like. Right?"

I hesitated, then nodded. "I think he was lonely. Who knows why men pick the mates they do? I do know he cared for her. He didn't have any family, just Grandy and me." The words stuck in my throat. Just the two of us and I hadn't been in contact for years. It was as much my fault as his for not keeping in touch. Now he was gone forever.

I WATCHED FRIDA drive off in her cruiser with her questions about Winston still in my mind. The truth was, I didn't know him at all. All I had were my childhood memories and a few days' experience squiring him and Darlene to local events. The conversation we'd had about family kept running through my mind.

I had two things on my agenda. First, I wanted to see what Frida had seen, revisit the place where Winston walked onto the island and take a closer look at the spot where the shooter had taken the shot. The second item was a call to Grandy—my grandmother, who knew more about our family than anyone. She'd tell me about Winston, about the Winston I hadn't seen for two decades. What had happened in that period of time?

Madeleine and I walked back up the dusty path toward the parking area. As we got into my convertible, I spotted Detective Tooney questioning the airboat pilot and weasel man. They did not look like happy entrepreneurs. A horrific thought, but I could have told them what I knew from experience: murder could be good for business. The one in Madeleine's and my shop last year brought customers in for a time, but when the macabre curiosity roused by the event wore off, it was business as usual. Noting the angry looks they both shot at Madeleine and me, I decided not to play business advisor.

I remained quiet in the car as I drove home.

"I suppose we should check on Darlene," Madeleine said, not

sounding the least bit enthusiastic about her Good Samaritan instincts.

"Uh-huh. Right. I guess so." My gaze was glued to the road but I drove on autopilot.

"Eve, you are a million light years away. I hope you're not thinking what I know you're thinking."

"Of course not." When I lied to Madeleine I always kept it simple. Yes or no. Once I opened my mouth with anything more, the truth was likely to spill out like, *Yes, my dear friend, I'm totally wrapped up in this crime, and I'm working on a plan to solve it, one certain to get me into trouble.*

We continued to drive in silence.

"Pizza?" I said. I hated pizza, but it was easy. And fast. That I wanted to unload her so I could begin my quest did not sit well, but I could handle the guilt. For now.

"But first we should go visit Darlene." Madeleine may have disliked the woman, but she sympathized with Darlene's loss of my uncle.

"Oh, do we have to?" I knew Madeleine was right, but I groaned at dealing with Darlene again. She was a reminder of my uncle. "Okay." I took the left to head into town and north to the hospital.

DARLENE WAS IN a curtained-off area in the emergency room.

"What kind of joint is this?" She lay on the bed, cranked into a sitting position.

"I see you're recovering from the shock. You should be able to get out of here soon and go home." And I did mean her home, not mine.

"You should tell the police what you said about Winston's death," I said.

"You have something you want to tell me?" Frida shoved aside the curtain and leaned over Darlene's bed. "Sorry it took me so long to get here."

Darlene shot a look of anger at me, then settled back onto

her pillows. In a flash her expression changed.

"I'm sorry, dearie. I don't blame you. Really, I feel a little sorry for you when I think of it. Winston led you to believe he was coming here to visit you."

"Wasn't he?" I asked.

"Well, sure, but he had another reason why he wanted to be in these parts." She wiggled around in the bed, then sank back, a look of exhaustion on her face. "This is going to be hard for you to hear, Eve, but Winston was a bag man for the mob. He was here to make a drop-off."

"Not to see me?" I stared at her for a long time.

"To see you, of course, but for business purposes also."

"Winston was a bag man?" I couldn't believe it. My uncle had mob connections. Of course I had mob connections, too, but they were not job-related. They were ex-husband related, I guess you'd say. I met Nappi Napolitani—purported to be a mob boss from Connecticut—through Jerry Taylor, my former squeeze by law, now no squeeze at all. But I didn't work for Mr. Napolitani. In fact, he sometimes did work in the form of favors for me. It was a complicated relationship.

Darlene leaned forward and reached out for me. I didn't take her hand. "Honey, this was going to be his last job. He was retiring."

"He was dropping off money. Well, now his walk in the swamp makes sense." Frida looked almost joyful. Her case must have appeared a lot easier to crack.

"So he leaves the money in the swamp and then they kill him." Frida flipped her notebook closed.

"Maybe they found out he intended to retire. I don't think anybody gets out of the mob. I warned him there might be trouble." Darlene fidgeted around in the bed. "Where's my purse?"

"It's here on the floor by the bed." Madeleine reached down and picked it up. "Wow. This thing weighs a ton. You rob a bank or something? It feels like gold bullion in here."

"Gimme that, Maddy." Darlene yanked it out of Madeleine's hand.

Madeleine shot her a look of contempt.

"If you girls don't mind, I have a few more questions to ask Mrs. Banks. About the mob connection."

Frida had given us our cue to leave. I don't think either of us minded. Another "Maddy" out of Darlene and Madeleine would have tossed the bedpan at her.

Madeleine and I waited to talk until we had left the hospital. "Do you believe your uncle was mob-connected?" she asked.

I didn't answer her.

"Eve, are you there?"

"Winston had two satchels with him. Do you think both of them contained money?"

"Why?"

"Because if the money for the drop-off was in one, what was in the other?"

"More money?"

"They both looked heavy. That would be a lot of money. And I think it unlikely the mob shoots their bag men for doing the job right. That's what Winston did. He dropped one or both of the duffels off in the swamp and marked the spot. A perfect location for the money. Frida didn't bring back the satchels. Did he do his last job right? And if so, why kill him?"

I needed to confer with someone who was more conversant with the mob rulebook than I. Was it true a man never left the mob, or did he have a retirement plan? Make that three things on my to-do list: visit the drop-off and shooting spots, call Grandy, and get in touch with Nappi. My current boyfriend and PI, Alex Montgomery, wouldn't like me hobnobbing yet again with my mob friend, Nappi. Neither would Madeleine. That was a problem only if I told them.

CHAPTER 3

———

THERE WAS NO way I would use our old buddy, the airboat
pilot, to visit the place where Winston took his walk.
I didn't trust the alligator agitator on general principle. Too
much loose testosterone in that one. I'd have to find another
airboat company.

There weren't a lot of tours around here. Most operated
farther south and explored the larger area that fed into the
Everglades. After dropping Madeleine off with a promise to
keep out of this investigation—I had my fingers crossed so it
did not count—I pulled off the road to think. To be honest,
tears filled my eyes and blurred my vision. I found Winston's
death so hard. How could I not be involved? This was my
uncle, my favorite uncle. And he was killed visiting me. I didn't
care if that wasn't the primary reason for his trip here. If he was
dropping off money, I was certain he chose this place to make
contact because of me; that made it my problem to solve. Also,
he was family, and I had so few relatives still alive.

I wiped my eyes and punched a query for airboats into my
cell. It came back with one listing for "The Hardy Brothers
Deluxe Airboat Rides". So our airboat pilot and his weasel

companion were brothers, or called themselves brothers. I gave a cackle at the name, then tears welled up again. I sopped them up with my soggy tissue. Hmm. I thought I remembered another place several miles beyond the Kissimmee River and north off the highway. I needed to take the trip back to that spot today before all the clues were gone. *What clues?* I asked myself. I was no crime scene investigator. What did I think I might see?

I pulled back onto the road and flipped a U-turn. On the way I called Grandy. It rang eight times and went to voice mail. I didn't want to leave a message about Winston. I'd get back to her later. Getting in touch with Nappi Napolitani would be more difficult. He'd always contacted *me*. I had no number for him and a search of West Palm and Hartford, Connecticut directories provided no listing for him. That meant I'd have to get in touch with my ex-husband Jerry, who worked for Nappi. I hated the thought of talking with Jerry. I'd leave that task for later.

I crossed the bridge over the Kissimmee River, drove on past the park entrance and into a small community beyond the river. I was certain I saw an airboat business just past the Legion. Ah! There it was. A small, hand-lettered sign nailed to a fence post announced, "Airboat Rides. Here." An arrow pointed toward a large chickee, a thatched roof building supported by wooden cypress posts. These were common structures in this part of Florida, built by the native Americans in the area. Beyond it I could see a small vessel parked in the grassy water. It looked as if it had seen some rough days in the swamp. The camouflage paint had worn off and the metal hull was dented. A flap, flap, flap caught my ear. The leather on the pilot's seat hung off in strips which the wind caught, blowing them against the framing around the engine. *Maybe I should rethink taking this ride.*

A tall man with massive shoulders leaned against the center support of the chickee. He had long black hair, which fell loosely down his back. His jeans looked as if they had been laundered so often the once blue color had faded to white. His cotton shirt was of a pattern I'd seen often in the shirts, blouses, skirts, and dresses worn by Florida Indians. But his eyes were what made me stop short. They were the eyes of a bird of prey—sharp, intense, missing nothing. They seemed to change color from the gold of the setting sun to the brown of the water of the Big Lake. They almost snapped with electricity as he watched me approach.

"You need something?"

"A ride on your boat. How much?" Why else would I be here? Not for the polite conversation.

He uncrossed his arms and stepped forward. "It's kind of late in the day. And it's cold. You sure you wouldn't want to come back another time?" He looked me up and down, then settled his gaze on my boots. His surly attitude swept my hesitation to one side. I was determined to have a trip on that boat today.

"I need to go now."

His sweeping visual assessment of me made me feel as if my clothes hid nothing.

He nodded. "Emu?"

"I'm sorry. I don't understand the Seminole language."

"I'm Miccosukee. I wondered if your boots were made of emu."

"Oh." I gave a nervous laugh. "Ostrich."

"Well, we were both wrong then, I guess. That'll be twenty bucks." He held out his hand for the money.

I extracted the bill from my jeans pocket. When he took it, he held onto my hand just a moment too long. The touch was electric. When he let go, I felt as if my hand had been branded. The heat of his touch remained. He gestured to follow him to the boat.

I walked behind him, marveling at his height. He had to be at least six feet six. I'd never seen a native this tall. Most were shorter, rounder.

As if he could read my thoughts, he turned and stopped. "My mother was white. Tall like you, but she had more up top." He then continued down the path.

"Listen, you—" I began.

"What?" He stopped and walked back toward me. "You want to go someplace in particular." It was a statement, not a question.

How did he know that?

IF THE FIRST airboat was like being on a carnival ride, this smaller boat slipped and slid over the surface of the water like a toboggan on ice. I hung onto the side of the boat as if expecting to be thrown into the water at any moment. Just when I told myself I had adjusted to the swaying motion and could move with it, the boat made a sudden jerk to the left. I gripped the side with both hands. I could almost feel the pilot smirking at my fear.

I had told him where I wanted to go, simply describing the place as the one where the other airboat company visited the resident gator. I didn't have to provide anything more in the way of directions. My guide nodded. "I know the place. It's the one where the Hardy boy likes to annoy Mathilda."

"Mathilda?"

"Mama gator."

"He told us they were all mamas."

"Yeah, well, he's dead wrong or will be when he chooses one of the big ones to hassle during mating season. What that boy knows about gators wouldn't fill a shot glass."

We flew down the canal and took a sharp left, coming upon the place where Winston had done his swamp walking earlier.

"I don't understand how you knew this was exactly where I wanted to go."

"It was where the cops were not long ago. From your attitude I guessed you had similar business."

He stopped the boat and pulled up to the shore.

"Is it safe to get off?"

"What are you looking for?"

"Clues, I guess."

"Of course. Like the cops."

"Maybe." I was beginning to rethink my trip here with my pilot. Was I being too trusting? He seemed to know a lot about what had gone on earlier today.

He scanned the area, then stepped off the boat and held out his hand to help me. "I think our mother gator is gone for the day."

Not only was Ms. Reptile gone, but so was much of the other swamp traffic. No kayaks, canoes or airboats here. When I glanced back in the direction of the rim canal I could see few boats there also. It was getting late. Shadows lengthened over the small path leading into the vegetation. I hesitated.

"Scared, are you?"

"Not at all." I hopped off and my boot slipped a bit on a rotted log, but he caught me from falling. I looked down at the brown hand holding my arm. It was huge. I looked up at his face. His expression was masked in the deepening twilight.

I steadied myself and withdrew from his hold. I thought I caught him smiling, just the flash of white teeth in the deep purple of the swamp as he turned and led the way.

We walked several feet into the still, deep green vegetation. The path came to an abrupt end, a downed palm tree blocking our way farther in.

There were no duffel bags, no hat. What did I expect to find? Some clue about why my uncle was murdered. If anything had been here, Frida and her deputies would have taken it.

"Nothing."

"Well, that's the second time you're wrong."

"What?"

"If you know what to look for, there's a lot here."

"Okay, Mr. Know-It-All. What do you see?"

"You hired me as an airboat pilot, not a tracker."

I was about to offer him more money when I bit back my words. This was a test, a kind of right-of-passage for me, the white woman in his world.

"How foolish of me. Take me back. I'll need to find someone who can read sign." I turned to retreat to the boat.

He crossed his arms and blocked my path, then stepped closer to me, so close I could see his black eyes clearly and smell a mixture of sweat and something primeval, not unpleasant, but unsettling somehow.

He pointed to an indentation in the ground. "Something heavy was there."

"Like duffel bags?"

"I can't tell you that."

"Can't or won't?"

He ignored my jab. "Many people have been here. You can see their boot prints have disturbed the ground. And the branches overhanging the path are broken." He moved back toward the boat and touched a branch at eye height. "Something hung here."

"Like a cap?"

He smiled.

"I know. It's just something else you 'can't tell me.' "

"Most of the tracks have been wiped out by something heavy traveling across the area."

"You mean, someone tried to intentionally wipe out these footprints?"

"Probably not. I think the gator came in here after everyone was through tossing the area. She was curious. Hardy boys bothering her has given her an attitude. Usually she keeps away from people, but I think she's mad. And unpredictable. She's probably watching us now."

I barely caught his last words. I was back down the path in a flash and sitting in the airboat, shaking, when he sauntered out of the brush. It was difficult to tell from his expression whether he was just fooling with me or serious. I didn't care.

I'd had enough of swamps, airboats, murder, and Seminoles, er, Miccosukees for one day.

Before we parted company at his dock, I decided to pry some information out of him. It was clear he didn't like me much, but I also got the feeling he liked the Hardy brothers even less. I was pretty certain he just plain didn't care much for white folks, but I thought, what the heck.

"You've got a small operation here. Just you? No one to help you?" I circled my way into the subject.

"My grandfather sometimes comes by."

"And he helps? I mean, you certainly could use someone to give out information and let folks know when you'd be back if you were out on a tour."

He just stared at me.

"The Hardy brothers have quite a business going, but there must be room for more rides around here. People come in from the coast looking for a tour of the swamp." I waited. He simply looked at me. Or through me. I wasn't sure.

"Why are you asking so many questions about what I do here? You some kind of inspector from the state?"

"Me? Gosh, no."

He smiled, his teeth showing white against his brown skin. "Someone you knew was on that airboat ride, right?"

"My uncle. He got off the boat. I think he left something. I wanted to find it."

"The cops already looked for it. I thought I pointed that out to you." Now he sounded contemptuous as if I weren't paying attention or didn't believe him.

"I know. I had to see for myself."

"Now are you going to investigate the place where the killer took the shot?"

Ah, so he knew about that too.

"Of course. I would have had you take me by, but it's the other direction on the canal from here."

He crossed his arms and leaned back against the chickee

support. "I guess you could always use the Hardy brothers. They're right across the canal from the spot."

Why did he know so much about what went down earlier today? It made me suspicious. And uncomfortable.

"I'm not real crazy about the two of them," I said. He continued to stare at me. Again I waited for him to say something. He didn't.

"And you. How come you know so much about what happened to my uncle?"

"I didn't know he was your uncle." He shifted his weight then leaned back against the support once more.

This was like having a conversation with a stretch of concrete. Maybe I'd play at the game too. I leaned against the counter, my head propped up by my fist.

He looked beyond me toward the lake. Was something out there more interesting than I was? He probably found most of his world more interesting than me.

"Sun's getting low." He shifted his eyes back to me.

I gave up. The man could out-silence a mime. I needed to move this along or move on. "I get the feeling you don't think much of them, either. You know, the Hardy brothers. Am I right?"

He turned his gaze again on the canal then raised it to the lake beyond. "Time to close up for the day."

Ten minutes of a one-sided conversation, and I get tossed out of the place.

I moved around the counter and stepped up to him. "I think you've got lots to say about their operation, things you'd prefer saying to someone like me."

That got a laugh out of him. "You? Why you?"

"Because I think you can tolerate me better than most folks, most non-native folks, that is."

"You could be wrong." He reached into a beaten-up bait bucket and pulled out the metal box where he'd put the twenty dollar bill I'd paid him for the ride.

"Good hiding place. I didn't even see you put the box there before."

"Of course not. You're about as observant as the other white folks that come in here."

"But it's true what I said. So talk to me. I'm a quick learner. Maybe I can learn to be more observant."

He extracted a single twenty from the box and held it up before he stuffed it into his pocket. "You were my only ride today."

"I know."

"So you saw the box was empty when you paid me?"

"Nope. I'd say you haven't had a tour out for some time. The pathway to your boat is overgrown with grass, and it would have been packed down if people had walked it recently."

"So I guess you can learn."

It was a lucky guess based upon my concern when I walked to the boat about what might be hiding in all that grass. I'd only braved the journey because I had on my high boots. *And Madeleine thought the boots were too fashionable for an airboat ride. Silly girl.*

He closed the already small distance between us and stared long and hard at me. Then he seemed to have decided something. He grabbed me and spun me around. "C'mon. You look as if you could use a drink."

We walked side by side toward the small parking area, but just as I headed toward my car, he took my arm again and steered me down a path running parallel to the water. Soon the palm trees and small live oaks closed around us. "Where are we going?"

"For a drink."

"There are no bars around here."

We stepped out of the trees and into a clearing, where a small house stood on cinderblocks. Its siding was unpainted and made of roughhewn lumber. A porch ran the entire front of the building. Several chairs and a rocker sat on the porch.

"My house. It's about time for tea. My grandfather usually brews a pot about this time. I think he'd like to meet you, and you might find him interesting."

"Oh."

" 'Oh.' That's all you have to say after chattering on all afternoon like a mockingbird in mating season?"

"I do not chatter like some bird."

"I hope not. Since you asked about the Hardy brothers, I thought I'd give you their résumé according to me. You won't like what you hear."

As I prepared to step up onto the porch, an elderly man, his long white hair plaited into two thin braids, stepped into the doorway. On his head he wore a red hat. It was familiar.

"That hat!" I spun on my heel and looked back at my guide. What game was he playing with me?

CHAPTER 4

———

THE OLD MAN swatted a fly away from his face and gestured for us to enter the house.

"Just a minute. I'm not going a step further until you explain about that." I pointed to the cap on his head.

The two men exchanged looks too opaque to read. It might have been caution or merely amusement at my anger.

"Well, she's kind of skinny, got no shape whatsoever, but I guess she's a woman. That might account for her lack of manners." The old man's eyes twinkled as he spoke.

"Hey, I'm as much a devotee of Miss Manners as anyone. I just don't like to practice my skills with someone who's stolen from me. Or taken advantage of one of my relatives and then …." The memory of my uncle lying on the dusty path dead overwhelmed me once more. I tried to choke back my grief, but tears spilled from my eyes. "Oh crap."

"The person killed today was her uncle." My Miccosukee airboat pilot said these words with reverence in his voice.

The older man came forward and held his hand out to me—the gesture so filled with sympathy and care that I grasped it and held on. He put his arm around my shoulders and walked me up the steps and into the tiny house. The room I entered was high-ceilinged with the supporting beams and roof rafters reaching upward toward a central peak. They were made of logs stripped of their bark. A kitchen was to our right, table and chairs in the center of the room, couch and two upholstered chairs across from one another. Simple but welcoming. He pulled out a kitchen chair and helped me into it. I felt comforted by his touch.

I suddenly remembered I did not know the name of my guide or his grandfather.

"My name is Eve Appel." I held out my hand to him.

My guide stooped over and took my fingers in his. "I'm Sammy Egret. This is my grandfather, Harold."

Grandfather Egret had by now placed cups and a tea pot on the table and cut slices of thick brown bread, which he spread with jam from a canning jar.

A sip of tea and bite of the bread allowed me to recover my usual sassiness. "I don't want to abuse your hospitality, Mr. Egret, but could you explain about the cap?"

He took the chair across from me. His eyes met mine. "I'm not sure I can in a way someone not born in these swamps could understand."

"Try her." Sammy surprised me by this vote of confidence.

"The swamps are ancient, and they have ways that humans find difficult to accept. The swamp takes things—people, animals, objects—and loses them. Sometimes they appear again. Most times they do not. Whatever enters these waters becomes the possession of the swamp." He stopped talking and looked down at his hands. He seemed to be off on a tangent, yet in a way, his words did provide some explanation of what happened to the cap.

"Thank you, Mr. Egret."

He smiled at me, and I felt encouraged. Maybe I could ask some more questions to clear up the matter of how he got the cap.

He shook his head as if reading my mind. "I'm tired now." He got up and walked to the back of the house and into the room beyond. I watched him close the door behind him. The room seemed somehow empty without him, and I felt like an interloper in a world I did not belong in and did not understand.

Sammy broke into my thoughts. "I'll walk you back to your car now that you have what you came after."

I did?

BACK AT MY Mustang, Sammy opened the door for me. His gallant gesture surprised me. It was as if some of his grandfather's manners rubbed off on him.

"That was my uncle's hat. I'm sure of it."

He said nothing. Great. We were now back to the Sammy I'd met earlier in the afternoon.

"You know it was, don't you? The cops would be very interested to find out how he got that cap." I knew I'd made a mistake the minute the words slid out of my mouth. His earlier friendly expression disappeared in a flash, replaced by the darkest anger I'd ever seen.

"You should leave now." He slammed my car door and stalked off toward the house.

The words he didn't speak couldn't have been clearer or louder in my head. "And don't come back."

I drove out of the small parking area and turned toward home. The sun was at my back and about to slip behind the western edge of the Big Lake. The traffic heading south around the lake was already beyond the Kissimmee Bridge and moving toward their homes in Moore Haven. The waters shone peach and violet in the light from the sun. This was the time of the day I liked the best, when the colors of sunset became true night and washed the land in serenity.

I sighed and slid down in my seat, thinking again of my uncle. It was time to make some calls. I pulled up my contacts on my cell. Grandy first. I hit "connect." Instead of her comforting voice, I again got the machine. They must have had a charter today. I hated to do it, but I tried my ex-husband Jerry to see if he could get me in touch with Mr. Napolitani, who knew more about mob stuff than anyone. Maybe that was because he was the only gangster in my life, and I sure didn't need more. Again I got voicemail. And again I decided against leaving a message. My current boyfriend, a private investigator named Alex Montgomery, was away on a case in the Panhandle. I should have called him sooner, I chided myself, but things came up. I wondered if he would buy that excuse when he found out I was again at a murder scene, this time of someone I loved.

I sighed so deeply I felt as if my diaphragm would reposition itself somewhere near my Adam's apple. My gaze left the road, and I focused for a moment on the last rays of the sun reflected in my rearview mirror. It hid behind a cloud bank, reappeared for an instant, then dropped beneath the horizon, leaving a streak of silver over the water. As beautiful as the sight was, I knew I couldn't put off calling Alex a moment longer. I swiped his name in my list of contacts and raised the phone to my ear.

Something hit me from behind. The wheel was almost ripped from my grasp. The cell flew from my hand onto the passenger's seat. I struggled to get control of the car as it headed toward the right side of the road and the small canal at its edge. I glanced in the rearview mirror and saw the grill of a large black pickup behind me. It roared up closer as I wrestled with the wheel, then it hit my rear end again, pushing me closer to the water. I stood on the brake and jerked the steering wheel hard left. The rear tires spun on the gravel but held. The truck stopped several feet behind me and sat there for a minute, then I heard its engine rev, and it headed for me again. I stomped on the accelerator and fishtailed back onto the road. When I rechecked my mirror; the truck was still there and gaining on me. This time it popped me with such an impact that the car shuddered for a moment and slid sideways across the road. I saw the palm tree coming for me, but I couldn't do a thing. The front end hit. The airbags deployed and enveloped me in white plastic. I heard the truck drive up behind me and worried he might again ram my car, making me the bologna in a tree and truck sandwich. It didn't happen.

I heard a door slam and footsteps on the gravel. *What new hell is this?*

"You stay right there," a voice commanded.

Like I could move. I was so wrapped in airbag I couldn't see or speak. When I turned my head to try to look at my visitor, a hand reached in and pushed my head toward the passenger's side of the car. *And damn, that hurt my neck.*

"Where is it?" The words were muffled as if he or she was holding something over their mouth to disguise the voice.

"Wha—"

"This is just a small taste of what can happen if you don't tell us where the money is."

"Ugh … guff." I tried to tell my interrogator I couldn't talk, but how could I? I had a mouth full of airbag.

The hand pressing against my head let go. Thank God. When it returned, I felt something cold and steely against my jugular. A knife.

"Maybe some persuasion will help."

The blade touched my neck. *Yikes.* The pressure against my throat increased, then disappeared. *That felt better.* Or maybe I was dead and couldn't feel anything. In case I was still alive I waited for my life to flash before my eyes. All I saw were shoes on sale followed by an image of my credit card being cut in half.

"Let's get you out of there." Someone reached in as the airbags deflated, and a strong hand on my arm jerked me from the car.

Okay, so I was still alive and now the guy would kill me. And why not? I had no idea where any money was. Did he mean Uncle Winston's money? Must be.

"Open your eyes."

"No, just do it. I don't want to watch."

There was silence for a moment.

"You are one strange woman, Eve Appel."

I recognized the voice. My eyelids opened. Sammy Egret stood in front of me.

"You. I should have known. Are you and your grandfather in on this together? And here I believed that crazy story about the swamps taking things. You're taking things. First the cap, and now you're trying to get my uncle's money. That was for the mob, not for you. And I have no idea where it is now." I was babbling out of fear.

Sammy continued to stare at me. "What are you talking about? Maybe you've got a concussion. I'll call an ambulance. I assume you have a cell. I don't."

None of this made any sense. First he tried to run me off the road, then threatened to kill me and now he wanted to take me to the emergency room? Maybe I did have a concussion. Or perhaps he was calling his grandfather for backup.

Sammy still had my arm in his strong grasp. I'd play along with him. Once he let go, I could run and flag someone down on the road—although no cars had come by since mine kissed the tree.

"The cell's on the seat." I gestured toward the Mustang with my head. Gosh it hurt when I moved my neck.

He let go, but my knees gave out from under me.

"Whoa there." He walked me to the offending tree and propped me up against it.

Good, now let's get these legs going. They refused to obey my command to run. I dropped to the ground and tried to crawl to the road.

"Where are you going?" Sammy bent and put his arm around my middle, lifting me again to my feet as if I weighed no more than a heron's feather.

"Here. It's for you." He handed me the phone. I had a vague memory of connecting with someone before the truck hit me, but who?

"Eve? Who's the man I just spoke to, and what was all that noise in the background a minute ago?"

Now I remembered who I'd called. Alex was on the other end of the call, and he didn't sound happy I'd gotten in touch.

"Hi, honey. That's Sammy. My Mustang is a wreck." And then I began to cry.

SO HERE I was at the hospital for the second time today. This time I was the patient. Sammy had been kind enough to follow the ambulance to the hospital, a gesture that convinced me he was telling the truth when he insisted he had come upon the accident after it happened. He said he saw the back end of a pickup driving off as he arrived but was too far away to get the license number. I believed him.

Frida was here too, and she was not happy with Sammy's description of the vehicle that had rear-ended me.

"A black truck? Everyone around here drives black trucks or SUVs. Anything else you remember that might help to identify it?"

I sat at the end of an examining table, a large plastic collar around my neck. I wondered how I was going to make this fashion accessory work with my wardrobe.

"Guys?" I tried to get their attention, but Sammy and Frida ignored me.

"Guys?" I tried again.

"Hey!" I banged my foot against the leg of the table. They turned toward me, annoyed looks on their faces, as if I was disturbing something important.

"Here's something that might help. How about …."

Frida flapped her arm at me. "How could you see anything? You were slammed against the seat by the airbag. You just rest a bit. The doctor said you have whiplash."

"The truck smashed into my Mustang so—"

"Yeah, sweetie, we know. Another car bites the dust. Looks like the accident totaled it. You're lucky you sustained only minor injuries. Cars can be replaced. Well, I guess you know that, don't you?" Was she making a snide remark about my Miata that blew up last year?

"That wasn't my fault," I said.

"Nobody said it was, although two cars in less than a year? You sure are hard on transportation."

"Wait. 'Minor injuries'? I was almost killed."

"Not really. Those airbags saved your life."

"Not the accident. The guy held a knife to my throat."

Frida turned her attention on me. Finally. "Did he? What did he look like?"

"How could I tell? I was enveloped like a mummy in plastic wrap. You said so yourself."

"What do you mean? Did he try something funny with you?" A look of anger crossed her face. "Attempted murder and sexual assault? I'll have his butt."

"No, I meant I was shrouded in airbag plastic. I couldn't see a thing."

"Right." She patted my hand and directed her attention back to Sammy.

"Not just hit and run, but attempted murder. I've got to get this guy. And Eve said he asked about the money. This has to be related to her uncle's murder. Can't you be more specific about the truck?"

I grabbed the bedpan sitting on the counter next to the table and banged it against the wall.

"I'll find a nurse." Sammy left the examining room.

I took a deep breath and tried for a reasonable tone of voice. "What I've been trying to say for the past five minutes is that the front end of that truck now has blue Mustang paint all over it. And despite its size, it has to have sustained some damage."

"You're right. I guess we didn't think of that, but we were just so worried about you."

I arched my eyebrow in a look of skepticism.

"The doctor gave you a solid going over. I apologize for not seeming more sympathetic, but I can do the best for you and your uncle if I find out who killed him and then tried to kill you. I want to get this guy." Her tone was both defensive and determined, a friend and a cop.

"Yeah, well, what I don't get is why Sammy was there. When I left him some minutes before, he was furious with me. Then he says he came to my rescue. He did call the ambulance, but why was he following me?" Correction. He called the ambulance after telling Alex to get off the phone. I wondered what Alex was thinking right now. On cue, my cell warbled.

"Can you find my purse? I hear my cell."

Frida rummaged around the cubicle, poking her head into the cupboards above the counter, then left, returning with my bag. "It was on the bed next door. Check to make sure nothing's been taken."

I held up one finger to signal her I'd do that after I answered.

It was Alex, and this time he was hotter than a bed of ancho chilies.

"Don't hang up on me, or let that guy hang up on me. I need some answers, and I need them now, Eve."

I mouthed, "It's Alex," to Frida.

She grabbed the phone out of my hand. "She was rear-ended, a guy tried to kill her, and an Indian came to her rescue."

Alex said something else, to which Frida replied that I was fine.

I lunged for the cell. "I am not all right. They put this ugly thing around my neck and said I have to wear it for a week. And my car is ruined. And my uncle is dead."

"You're not making any sense. I'm calling Grandy. She'll take care of this."

"Don't, please. She doesn't know about Uncle Winston's murder yet."

"He was murdered?"

I could almost feel him shaking his head. "I'm so sorry about your uncle, Eve, but not *again*. Not again with a murder."

"Again? It's not like my relatives get killed every day."

"No, but it seems like people who associate with you do."

"One person. Last year. I hardly knew her, so how can that count?"

There was silence for a moment.

"Put Frida back on," he said.

I knew when I was beat. With Frida, Alex, and probably Madeleine savvy to what I had done to find the killer and correct in thinking I'd do more, there was no way I'd be able to find out who did in Uncle Winston.

Someone pulled back the curtain. Yep, here she was, Madeleine, her round blue eyes filled with concern, and of course, anger.

"I thought you were dropping me off and then going home. What have you done now?"

I held the phone out to her. "Something came up. Here. Try to talk some sense into Alex. You can see I'm fine, except for the wardrobe they gave me here."

She took it, but didn't allow Alex to say much. "You'd better get back here. The Indian is gorgeous."

The score was now Frida, Alex and Madeleine, 3; Eve,1. Would Grandy side with me? Maybe. She had a real sense of adventure and justice. She'd want Winston's killer found, and although she respected Frida, she wouldn't trust anyone other than family to do the job right.

Madeleine handed the phone to me. "There's another caller on the line. I disconnected from Alex. He was using a lot of words with a minimum of syllables."

I slid off the table and walked to the other side of the room for some privacy. "Hello?"

"I heard something about an uncle and some stolen mob money. Can I help?"

"Mr. Napolitani. Of course you can help."

CHAPTER 5

———

FRIDA AND MADELEINE tried to take the phone back from me, but I held it above my head, the advantage of being almost six feet tall, even without my stilettos.

Nappi Napolitani's voice, smooth as cannoli cream, came through my cell. Thank heaven for mobsters. "I just happen to be at my condo in West Palm. I could run up to see you today if you'd like."

Oh, yes. I would like. Now I had someone who was on my side. I ended the call after arranging to meet Nappi at the Burnt Biscuit Bar and Grill, the place where we'd first gotten acquainted a year ago. I gave Madeleine and Frida a defiant look.

"I think we pushed her too far." Madeleine's mouth curved in a smile of apology, but Frida shook her head and stalked out of the cubicle.

"I'm going home. Where are my clothes?"

Madeleine pointed to the chair. I struggled into my clothes and shoes, then grabbed my purse, slid the curtain back and walked smack dab into Darlene. Oh gosh. I'd forgotten all about Darlene. This couldn't be what everyone meant by my being irresponsible in the face of murder, could it?

"How are you doing?" I tried to fill my voice with concern, but I know I failed.

"Not well, thanks to you. I've been trying to reach your house. They released me an hour ago. I need a ride to get all my stuff. And Winston's too." She blew her nose vigorously on a tissue.

"Sorry. I assumed the hospital would keep you overnight. I guess we should talk about Winston's funeral."

"All taken care of. I called the funeral home in West Palm. He'll be cremated as soon as they're finished with the autopsy and release the body. And services will follow the day after."

I was a little taken aback by the speed with which she'd arranged everything, but then, she was his partner.

"What happened to you?" Darlene indicated my collar.

As I started to explain, she interrupted me. "Can we leave now? I'm tired, and I have a long drive back home."

Sammy returned to the cubicle and came up behind me. "There's a nurse coming to check on you. How are you going to get home if they release you, Eve?"

"I'll take them." Madeleine jingled her keys at me. "I'll wait for you in the car. Maybe you should check with the desk to be certain you can go."

"I'm not checking with anyone. I'm out of here."

A nurse approached us as I started down the hallway.

"The doctor clear you to go?"

"Yup." I gave her my most winning smile and strode by the emergency room desk, Darlene struggling to keep up with me.

At the doorway, I turned to find that Sammy was right behind us.

"I can follow you home to make certain you're safe, if you'd like." Sammy's dark eyes conveyed his concern for me

I almost took him up on his offer—looking into those chocolate eyes nearly melted my cynical heart—but somewhere in the back of my head I heard Alex's voice cautioning me about men I'd just met and did not know well. Alex should know. He was one of those when we met.

I turned to him and placed my hand on his arm, his muscular arm, my gesture a peace offering for my snappish words. "We do need to talk." My tone was almost a purr, and I saw Madeleine give me a questioning look. "I'll be in touch. And thanks for the offer of a ride." I was sending mixed messages to the man and I knew it, but he made my toes curl.

He looked confused for a moment, then smiled and shook his head. "Later then."

In the car Madeleine helped Darlene into the back seat and left me to struggle into the passenger's seat. The collar got in the way of everything.

She adjusted the rearview mirror and started the engine. "I'm so sorry about Winston."

I smiled forgiveness at her earlier anger at me. "You already said that."

"I'm not talking to you, Eve. I'm talking to Darlene."

I opened my mouth to say something, but let it go. Probably murder trumped attempted murder in the social concern rule book. Madeleine would know that.

We drove in silence for a few minutes.

"And I'm sorry for what you had to go through today, Eve. I'm relieved you're fine," Madeleine said.

I was about to give her a snarky "thank you," but she interrupted.

"How do you think Alex is going to feel about Sammy?"

I should have given her some of my sass after all. "Why should he feel anything about him?" Gosh, there were a lot of rules about relationships I didn't understand.

Darlene leaned forward. "Oh, you mean that hunky Indian who was in the hallway? He sure was handsome."

"Right. We're all agreed he is handsome. I don't want to have this conversation," I said.

"You were off in the swamp playing detective when you

should have been contacting Grandy and Alex and checking up on Darlene. You can be so irresponsible when it comes to murder."

There it was again. The mention of my irresponsible streak.

"I don't intend to be judgmental, but I worry about your sense of adventure, Eve, especially your tendency to go off on your own in dangerous situations. You're going to get yourself into trouble you can't get out of." There was no anger in Madeleine's tone now, only worry.

"You mean she's done this before?" Darlene asked.

"You don't want to know. And she gets others in on the action. Like mob bosses."

I heard Darlene gasp. "You're connected, too, like your uncle?"

It wasn't worth denying, then explaining, so I simply nodded.

MADELEINE HAD GONE home, and Darlene had packed everything and headed for West Palm and the condo she shared with my uncle. I mixed myself a Scotch and water without the water and used my cell to connect to Grandy.

The front door banged open. Grandy. The light from the street lamps illuminated her white hair, and she appeared to be bathed in some heavenly fire. I looked at the Scotch bottle. Nope. The level of liquor indicated only my one drink. I wasn't drunk. It was just my Grandy's way of appearing in my life when I needed her most. She was better than a guardian angel. She'd been my guiding star since my parents died.

"Grandy. What are you doing here? I mean, who called you?"

"I got calls from everyone. Alex, Madeleine, even Frida. They told me about Winston. I wondered why you didn't call, but I figured you got yourself into some kind of mess. Are you okay?" Grandy dropped the overnight bag she was holding, strode over to the couch and enveloped me in her arms.

"What's this?" She touched my cervical collar.

"Well, it's not a fashion statement. They told me I had to

wear it for a week." I burst into tears.

"Honey, it doesn't look that bad."

But I knew it wasn't just the collar. "Winston's dead. And, how could he? How could he get involved with the mob?"

She sighed and sank back into the couch. "I know he seemed perfect to you, but Winston always had shady contacts. That was the way he led his life. I worried he'd get in over his head, but he assured me he only worked as a bag man. No hits."

"Instead he gets hit. But I'm sure he delivered the money." I told her about his swamp walk, then my accident. "Frida's certain the two are connected, and because of Winston's mob job, she's thinking they're mob connected."

"It doesn't make sense. We need someone who knows more about this than we do." She picked up her cell.

"Are you going to call Max?"

She shook her head. "Max only knows boats."

"Alex?"

"He's a law and order freak."

"If you're contacting Nappi, he's already on his way here. It seems the mob telegraph is up and running. He called me." I looked at my watch. "It's time we set out to meet him, unless you'd like to stay here?"

She rolled her eyes and pulled me off the couch.

"Now, ABOUT YOUR Indian ...." Grandy and I were sitting in the Burnt Biscuit at a table in the back corner. On the small stage in the opposite corner a cowboy strummed his guitar and sang about some gal who'd done him wrong. Cowboys seemed to have the worst luck with women.

Before I could tell her anything about Sammy and his grandfather, we were joined by Mr. Napolitani. Tonight he was dressed in a most unusual manner—well, odd for him. A black cowboy hat with a silver band sat on his head. The rest of him matched the hat: blue shirt with cowboy yoke, tight jeans, and boots made of some kind of lizard.

He reached out for Grandy's hand and bent over it, his lips not quite touching her fingers, Poirot style.

I jumped out of my seat and threw my arms around him. "You fit right in."

It was a lie, of course. No matter how the man dressed, his style was always head and shoulders above the rest. His clothes screamed money and taste. No tacky shiny polyester-blend suits for this mob guy.

He kissed me on both cheeks and smiled, allowing me the little fib, pleased I would notice his attempt at dressing the part of heehaw in the wilds of Florida.

"My two favorite women." He sat down and signaled to the waitress. "A Scotch for me and the ladies will have …?"

The waitress bought our drinks in record time. Nappi got great service no matter where he dined.

"How did you hear about Uncle Winston?" I asked. "It couldn't have hit the news. It happened only today, early afternoon."

"There's news, and then there are contacts who know the news. I use the latter."

Well of course he did. That's why he was here, because of what he knew and what we didn't.

"There's a 'family' in Boston who's not very happy with your uncle."

"What do you mean?" I tied my plastic swizzle stick into knots and chewed it into shreds.

"This family sent him here for one last job. He didn't deliver. The money never showed up and now they're angry."

"I guess they're angry. They tried to kill me." I explained my odd choice of necklace and my encounter with a tree and a knife.

Nappi listened without interrupting; then he shook his head. "Your detective friend may be right that the two incidents are related, but the family doesn't kill someone who owes them money, at least not until they get it back."

"You're saying somebody took it before it reached the right hands. This is something Frida should know."

He nodded. "I'll let her know."

Grandy shook her head. "I knew someday Winston's mob connections would do him in."

We all sat back, thinking.

"Could some rival family have nabbed it?" I wanted it to be that simple. Nappi could find out from his connections

"That idea is now being explored, but I don't think it likely." Nappi signaled the waitress for another drink.

"The swamp took it." I explained to Grandy and Nappi about the story Grandfather Egret told me.

"So you think an interested party made off with the money, perhaps the Indians? But how did they know it was there?" Nappi leaned forward with interest.

"They know stuff, believe me. Yet something tells me, as shadowed as their actions were, they weren't responsible."

Grandy picked up the menu and scanned it. "Solving murders makes me hungry."

NAPPI PROMISED HE'D continue to monitor the mob grapevine for information. Grandy and I dove into a large helping of ribs and a pile of slaw. Like Grandy, I never let anything interfere with my appetite. She was right. This sleuthing stuff made a gal peckish.

Grandy left the next morning to return to Max, her husband and partner in their fishing boat charter business out of Key Largo. They were a small operation and ran half-day trips—no frills, just good fishing. A Keys easy lifestyle.

Grandy said she and Max would see me at Winston's funeral.

MADELEINE AND I attended the funeral together. Alex couldn't get away from his PI assignment in Pensacola, but I could tell from our phone conversations he wasn't happy to miss it. And not just for romantic reasons. He knew I'd be up to my spiky blonde hairdo in this murder investigation if someone didn't rein me in. That someone wasn't Grandy. Much as she liked Alex, her need to intrude was about as keen as mine. And Madeleine? Well, she never could control me and was too tiny to carry out any physical threats. She did keep glancing at me as we drove the Bee Line to the turnpike and south to West Palm.

"Keep your eyes on the road or we'll hit something," I said.

I was in a crummy mood. The cervical collar made my neck itch, and I couldn't see anything except what was straight ahead. I reached up and yanked it off. That was better.

Madeleine made no comment. She knew I'd do what I wanted, but she continued to glance from the highway to me. "I know you met with Nappi, and I know Grandy was there. That's just bad chemistry. The three of you could get into trouble. Last year you broke into a house trying to find clues to a murder."

"You were with us, so technically you're a felon also."

"It wasn't voluntary on my part. Alex made me do it."

"Whatever." I turned my head to look out the windows as we breezed by the subdivisions outside West Palm. I didn't want to pursue the conversation. It was bad enough Alex was suspicious of me and mad, too. I didn't want Madeleine to worry.

"I wonder if anyone has threatened Darlene the way they did me, with a truck grill in her trunk or maybe a sharp instrument at her throat. She was Winston's partner. She had to know what he was doing." I paused to let my line of reasoning sink in. "I believe Darlene will be holding the after funeral get-together, and I was wondering—"

"What? No. Don't you think Frida already considered all of this? Can't you let her do her job?" Madeleine gripped the wheel with white knuckled fingers as she blew by a sanitation truck going the speed limit.

"That damn purse of hers the day of the murder? I wonder

what she had in it. I'd like a chance to look around the condo. Maybe you could distract her for a bit while I—"

"What?"

"Really. There's nothing illegal about this at all. I'll just wander off looking for the bathroom while you engage her in talk."

"Talk about what?"

"Clothes or something like that. Or makeup. Or hair."

"This is a funeral, Eve. Not a kaffeeklatsch."

"Okay. Never mind. I'll think of something else."

"Please don't. And put that collar back on before you do permanent damage to your neck."

AT THE FUNERAL parlor, Darlene wore huge dark glasses and a Jackie Kennedy pillbox hat to match. The black dress she chose was elegant, although the neckline showed more cleavage than was appropriate at a funeral. Although the glasses hid her eyes, her mouth was turned down in an expression of fatigue. She was flanked by two people, a man and a woman, also sporting sunglasses but looking more like the president's secret service people than mourners. They too wore black— the man a black suit, white shirt, black tie shoes. The suit and shirt looked expensive, but the shoes might have been made of shiny cardboard. As for the woman, she was thin, thin, thin, but muscular, stringy muscular. The cords in her neck stood out like tendons on a stripped turkey leg. I guessed the dress to be Ralph Lauren. Their bearing was ramrod straight, and they surveyed the room as if scanning for possible assassins.

"These are Winston's children, Sophia and Boris. His niece, Eve, and her friend, Maddy." Darlene's look defied Madeleine to correct her.

"I had no idea Winston had children." I shook hands. Well, strictly speaking these weren't children. They were adults, adults whose military bearing suggested that, given the choice, they would have preferred marching through Lenin Square than standing in the receiving line at Winston's funeral. They certainly didn't look anything like my uncle; no evidence of his fun-loving nature on their stern faces. They both seemed more uncomfortable in the setting than saddened by it. Sophia held Darlene's arm as if she feared the woman would topple over.

"There's a lot you don't know, my dear. You were absent from his life for many years. Never called or visited. It just broke his heart. I can't imagine why he …. Never mind."

I hated it when someone guilted me even when they were right and I deserved it, but I sucked in my angry reply and patted Darlene's shoulder.

"I'm so grateful he tracked me down in Florida and came to visit, so I could see him once more."

"Lot of good that did. It got him killed, didn't it?" Darlene dabbed at her eyes.

So much for guilt. Now I was mad. She made it sound as if I was responsible for his death. I was about to snap back at her, but Madeleine interrupted me.

"You were as gung ho to go on that airboat ride as he was, Darlene."

Darlene snatched the dark glasses off her nose and leaned toward Madeleine. "What are you saying, little girl? You take that back. Make her take that back, Eve."

Madeleine might be a sweet person, but saccharine lies are not part of her character.

"Now, Maddy, let's play nice." I loved it when Madeleine got attitude. I couldn't resist kidding her for her comment. She delivered a withering look in my direction. But her eyes twinkled so I knew she didn't take my remark seriously.

Someone tapped me on my shoulder.

Grandy. And Max.

"Oh, honey, we're sorry we're late. This must be Darlene." Grandy took Darlene's hand and held it. "Sorry, my dear."

"Thank you. You're so kind. It's nice to see someone around here has manners." Darlene shot a look of defiance at Madeleine, who smiled her angelic smile in return. The exchange was interrupted by the appearance of the minister, who signaled for us to take our seats.

Darlene, Boris, and Sophia moved toward chairs in the front while the rest of us followed. Grandy's hand on my shoulder stopped me before I could sit down beside them.

"Who are the toy soldiers next to Darlene?" Grandy whispered so they couldn't hear.

"Oh, I thought you would know. His children, Sophia and Boris."

Grandy rocked back on her heels for a moment, then leaned forward.

"Winston never married. He had no family aside from you and me, Eve."

CHAPTER 6

I CAUGHT MY breath.

"Maybe you just didn't know about his kids. He was a pretty closed person, and neither of us saw him for many years." I couldn't believe Winston would hide his family from us, from me, but it was a possibility.

"Those kids are as old as you, Eve. Maybe they're stepchildren," Grandy said.

"Will you two sit down and stop chattering?" Darlene gestured toward the minister, who was staring at us. Everyone was staring at us.

"Sorry." I took my seat beside Darlene with Grandy, Max and Madeleine to my right. I turned my head to look around the small room. There weren't many people in attendance. A few older folks, probably from the condo complex in which Winston lived, took seats behind us. Standing at the back of the room were two beefy fellows wearing suits cut too tight to hide bulges beneath the jackets. Ah. The mob was here to check out the situation. To their right, Frida was standing and checking them out. Madeleine was correct. Frida was doing her job. A well-built man dressed in a dark sports coat stood at her side. He leaned over and said something. She smiled up at him. Had Frida brought a date? Her work schedule must have been rough if she had to tuck a social life into attending the funeral of a murder victim.

I was surprised to see the airboat captain and his brother slip in and take chairs in front of Frida and the goons. They were pretty far from home. Hmm. Maybe I should revise my opinion of the Hardy brothers. They did have some social graces. Of course, they were wearing ball caps with their suits, so no fashion sense, but I was impressed they'd attend. I also wondered why they were here.

The minister had just begun speaking when the back door opened. We all turned to see who was arriving now. Well, well, Sammy Egret and his grandfather. Were the folks around the Big Lake just nosy or did they have some hidden agenda? I shrugged. Maybe they just had more manners than I gave them credit for.

The minister took up his canned speech where he'd left off.

"You'd think he could have embellished some on the information I gave him." Darlene sniffed and waved her hanky in front of her face. "I paid him good, too, and he's just reading what I wrote."

Finished with the scripted eulogy to Winston, the minister asked if any of us wanted to speak.

Darlene stood and approached the podium. "He was a wonderful man. We'd only been together for a year, but no one was closer to him than me. He mentioned marriage, but we never got around to it." She paused and gave a dramatic sigh, choking on her tears. "And now this."

After the minister's droning monologue about my uncle, I thought I should say something more personal about him, but his children gathered round Darlene and tried to comfort her with awkward pats and mechanical-looking hugs. From her tears and shaky sighs of grief, it was clear Darlene wanted her comments about Winston to be the final words of the occasion.

I looked at the urn of ashes sitting on the table in front of the podium. Winston was in no shape to care if I spoke about him in public. I let it go. His visit made me regret the years we'd been separated. We should have tried harder to stay in touch. *I* should have tried harder. I loved him. Words wouldn't bring him back, but tracking down his killer might bring me some sense of satisfaction. I owed him that.

DARLENE AND WINSTON'S condo wasn't far from the funeral home. Most of the mourners piled in their cars and followed Darlene and the children to the gated community where it was located.

"Nice digs." Frida came up behind me on the walkway in front of the two-story building.

I agreed. My gaze travelled over the complex behind me. Tropical landscaping, brick walkways, not a weed in any lawn, and I could just make out a large building at the end of the block, which must have been the club house. Behind it, the blue waters of a pool sparkled in the sunlight. Very classy. Winston's unit was an end one—more lawn, more windows. Mob money must have been good over the years.

Darlene certainly had the event under control. Catered, no less. Young women and men in white shirts and black pants carried trays of champagne glasses and finger foods and roamed the large living area that opened into a small garden beyond. From the abundance of libations and snacks and the number of servers, she must have expected at least a hundred guests, yet there had been only twenty or so at the service.

In the next hour the room began to fill with people, most of them men, all dressed in suits tailored to accommodate guns in shoulder holsters. Tasteful silk blends in muted colors. I almost believed they were business associates. They were, if you counted family with a capital "F" as a corporation. They gave Darlene warm hugs and began to mingle with the other guests. They appeared relaxed, comfortable with their roles as mourners, and appropriately sympathetic to Darlene. She knew them all. Several of them took my hand and offered their condolences. These had to be the men Winston worked with over the years, and because of their friendly demeanor, I gathered they were not the bosses for whom he worked. The bosses would send less accommodating representatives, more like the two who appeared at the service, their intention clear. They'd be looking for their lost money. I glanced around the room, but the muscle from the funeral home was not here.

It was just an after-funeral event like any other—food, drink, a few tears, no guns in sight. I caught Frida's eye. She bit into a stuffed mushroom while keeping an eye on all the firepower in the room. She gave me a "nothing to worry about" wink. Darlene was busy talking with Winston's friends. I spotted the others I knew in the garden. It was time for me to take a closer look at the place.

"Excuse me, but I have to find the powder room." I nodded to the man I'd been talking to—the one in Bermuda shorts, white socks and wing tips—and spotted the staircase to the second floor. He smiled and waved his empty champagne glass at one of the servers as I headed off.

There were four doors leading off the upstairs hallway. One was open—the bathroom. The others had to be bedrooms or perhaps an office and two bedrooms. I opened the door on my right. As I guessed, it was an office, but there was no point in searching it. It held a chair and a desk—no filing cabinets, no laptop on the desk, no other furniture. I opened the desk drawers and found them empty. It was as if no one had ever used the room. Odd.

The second door led to a small bedroom. Like the office, it was sparsely furnished: two twin beds, nightstand between them, and a small bureau across the room. I opened the closet door. It too was empty, with the exception of a single wire hanger swinging abandoned on the clothes bar as if someone had just pulled a garment off it. When I tried the drawers in the nightstand and bureau, they yielded empty space. It appeared that Winston's grown children did not live with him, or if they did, they traveled light.

The third room had to be the master bedroom—my last chance to find anything of interest, my final attempt to unearth Darlene's purse or the remnants of my uncle's life.

I opened the door. This time the room was not empty. Instead I found someone with the same idea as I. The Hardy brothers turned in surprise as I entered. Their search techniques were sloppy. Clothes lay strewn around the room, drawers pulled open, their contents tossed on the bed.

"Here I thought the two of you were being sensitive, attending my uncle's funeral like civilized people. Instead you came here to rifle through his stuff, seize the opportunity to steal whatever you could find. You're just common thieves."

"We're here to find—"

The smaller brother, the one who managed the produce stand and sold us the tickets, was cut off by his brother.

"Shut up, Digby."

Digby? His name was Digby Hardy. I almost laughed at the thought of it and would have, but the airboat captain pulled a snub-nosed revolver out of his suit pocket.

"That's improper attire for a funeral," I said.

"Look who's talking." He gestured at my cervical collar.

"Let's boogie. There's nothing here anyway." Digby headed toward the door, but before he could walk out, Sammy Egret entered and blocked Digby's exit. His body language was loose, arms hanging at his sides, as if he had wandered into the room by accident; yet his mere size seemed to threaten the brothers. I was certain the subtle threat was exactly what Sammy intended. It worked. Digby backed up. Captain Hardy eyed him warily. Behind Sammy stood Frida.

"Having trouble, Eve?" she asked.

"These two were searching the place. Arrest them. They're thieves."

Airboat captain Hardy lowered his gun.

"You have a permit to carry that, I assume." Frida crossed the room and took it out of his hand.

"You bet. And we're not thieves. We was just lookin' around." The airboat brother allowed Frida to take the weapon, but the defiant look on his face said he wasn't afraid of the law. Digby was less sure of himself. His eyes darted around the room. I thought he might jump through the window.

"Empty your pockets, you two, and let's see what you've got in them, unless you'd prefer to have me arrest you here and do a thorough search down at the station."

Both brothers complied with her request, dropping change, a few dollar bills and a set of truck keys on the bed.

"See? Nothing."

"You're right, Mr. Hardy. You got a driver's license in the truck?" Frida tried to hide her smile, but one side of her mouth twitched as she watched the brothers' jittery expressions.

"What's going on here?" Darlene stood in the doorway.

Frida took a set of cuffs from her belt and clapped them on the bigger brother.

"Here, let me help you with that." The man I'd seen Frida standing with at the funeral came up behind us. He reached under his jacket and withdrew a set of cuffs, which he snapped on Digby.

"What did they take?" Darlene watched Frida and her companion lead the men from the room.

"They didn't take a damn thing, Darlene. They just made a mess of this room searching it. Curious. There's nothing much in this place to steal. Why is that? I think you've got some explaining to do," I said.

By this time, Madeleine had joined our little group and heard what I said to Darlene. She nodded her head in agreement, but unlike Frida, she made no attempt to hide her smile of satisfaction.

"So why are you arresting them?" Darlene followed Frida into the hallway.

"Driving with no license."

Pilot Hardy stopped and faced Frida. "You're arresting us for that? That's no felony."

"I didn't finish. And for vandalism."

"You don't have the authority. This is not your jurisdiction."

Why did he not sound so much like a good ol' boy now?

A look of concern crossed Frida's face. "Oh gosh. I forgot. I guess I'm just a cop abusing my power."

He smirked, which did nothing to improve his looks.

"But my friend here has authority." Frida gestured to the man leading Digby down the stairs. "Meet Detective Murphy of the West Palm Beach Police Department."

"Thanks for the help, Frida. Let's get these two out to my cruiser, and I'll do a check on them for outstanding. I'm guessing it'll be interesting reading. If you want to accompany me to the station, I'll return your cuffs." Detective Murphy continued down the stairs with his charge.

"Don't worry, Dig. Our lawyer will get us out by dinnertime." The airboat captain shot me a dark look. "I was just paying my respects. Nice company you keep."

His southern accent seemed less pronounced, and his comments about felonies and a lawyer didn't sound so down home in the swamps now. Maybe he just watched too much television.

The appearance of Frida and her detective companion leading two men in cuffs out the front door erased the mourners' need for snacks and drinks. Everyone except for those I knew found a reason to leave. I sat Darlene on the couch, handed her a glass of water, and looked down on her, my arms crossed. With my height and porcupine's hair, I can be very imposing.

"Okay. Now spill it." I tapped my foot as an additional threat factor.

It was as if Darlene just gave up. Her face fell into a picture of utter despair. She shook her head and looked up at me, tears rolling down her cheeks. "I just couldn't bear it. I couldn't stand the memories. I got rid of everything of Winston's."

Boris and Sophia repeated their earlier, to my eye, ineffectual attempts at comforting her. Hand pat. One-armed hug, not so close that one body touched another.

Darlene fended them off. Being around her swift changes in emotions was making me dizzy. "You wouldn't understand. You didn't care like I did. You don't know what it's like to lose someone you love."

Well, actually I did know. It was an insensitive remark on Darlene's part. If she was so close to Winston, he had to have told her about my parents. I also couldn't relate to her form of mourning. When I lost Mom and Dad in the boating accident, I wanted to keep everything as it was so I wouldn't lose the memories.

"There's not much of yours here, either. What about that?" I asked.

"It's the house. The memories of how happy we were in our little place. I moved in with his children." She wiped a tear from her cheek and held out her hands to Boris and Sophia. They, too, looked confused by her emotional U-turns, but with a heave of her shoulders, Sophia dropped onto the couch beside her. Boris remained standing yet distant.

"She's having a hard time with this." Sophia put her arm around Darlene, this time hugging her close, genuine concern for Darlene on her face.

I shook my head. None of this made much sense to me.

"I'm—" Before I could say the word "sorry," Grandy interrupted me.

"Since we're on the subject of mourning Winston, I have a question."

"Go ahead," Darlene said.

"I don't remember Winston having a family, and I kept pretty good track of his life, even though we rarely saw each other." Grandy's gaze settled on Sophia and Boris.

There was silence for a moment before Sophia spoke up. "We are the children of Winston's wife. We're stepchildren. Winston helped bring our mother over from Russia, and we followed the next year. Our younger sister is, uh, up north right now. Mother died several years ago, but we think of Winston as our father. He took care of us."

"Well, that's news to me." Grandy still looked skeptical.

"I hope you don't want us to prove it." Sophia shot a look of anger in Grandy's direction. Those gray eyes were like a wind out of Siberia.

"Of course not. Grandy just means it's odd he kept the marriage a secret from us. I mean, from Grandy and me. We're family too."

"He did not get around to telling you, but he would have eventually," Sophia told us.

I glanced at Boris. He'd been so quiet. "Would you like to say anything?"

He didn't look back at me, merely shook his head.

Madeleine leaned in close. "Does he not speak? Or is it some kind of a tradition in Russia that the women do all the talking?"

"I don't think it's tradition anywhere that women do the talking," I whispered back to her.

"I HATE LEAVING you here alone, but the shop needs attention. We're down in new arrivals. I'll stop by some of our clients in West Palm on the way back from the lawyer's." I'd taken off the cervical collar with Madeleine's blessing, so driving was possible again.

It was the day after the funeral and Madeleine and I were taking stock of our store's merchandise. The rounds and racks were only half-filled.

"What are we going to do if the stock market continues to climb? Those women trying to make a little money by selling last season's fashions here won't be interested." Madeleine looked as if she was going to cry.

"Don't worry, honey. They've found a way to take in some money without their hubby's knowing. The easy money is too inviting for them to quit us now. Besides, they like the idea of slumming in the swamps of Florida, eating BBQ at the Burnt Biscuit and dancing with cowboys. It's addictive. Even the very rich like to have fun, especially if it's on the sly and not too fattening. Doing a little two-step can really burn off those beer and barbecue calories."

POOR MADELEINE, I thought, as I drove my rental car down the Bee Line Highway. She worried so much. Maybe that was the source of her clumsiness. I'd read somewhere that tension made your muscles cramp up and your movements jerky and awkward. I hated leaving her responsible for the store today, but Winston's lawyer had summoned all of Winston's family— including Darlene—for the reading of the will. I had no idea how much money Winston had accrued over the years, but it had to be a substantial sum if his condo was any indication. The source of his income was from working for the mob, of course, but how should one view mob money, once it was invested and became stocks, bonds, treasury notes, and real estate investments?

Well, I wasn't worried that I'd have to consider what to do with anything Winston might leave me. It had been so long since we'd been in touch—as Darlene had pointed out many times—that she and his children would have to make a judgment about whether they wanted tainted riches or not. If Madeleine had heard me say any of this, she would have snorted and told me Darlene wouldn't refuse money hidden in a pig wallow.

I don't know what I expected, but Winston's lawyer looked quite respectable, not as if he had any "connections" of an unsavory nature at all. Grandy had driven up from Key Largo again today. I'd asked her and Max to stay with me last night, but they wanted to get back to the boat. A storm was coming in overnight, and they needed to check lines and ready the craft for a hard blow.

Mr. Sandimore, the lawyer, seated all of us around a conference table in his office and proceeded to get right to the point. He explained that the will had been updated less than a year ago. I assumed the only reason I was here was Winston had left me some small remembrance, a piece of jewelry or statuary. The sooner this was over, the sooner I could get out of here and visit my clients to see if they had any apparel for the shop. My mind wandered away from the immediate company, and I mused about the days Winston and I skied together, went horseback riding and .... Suddenly I realized the room had gotten very quiet. The lawyer had stopped reading, and all eyes were turned on me.

Attorney Sandimore removed his glasses and set them on his desk. "I guess you didn't know anything about this? Your uncle said nothing to you on his recent visit?"

"What?"

"Ms. Appel. Did you know your uncle left his entire estate to you?"

No, I did not.

CHAPTER 7

———

GRANDY WALKED ME to my car. "Can you drive?"

"Of course. Why would you think I couldn't?"

"That was quite a surprise."

"Yep. Now I have to decide what to do with money made in ways even I can't imagine, not even in my worst nightmares."

"You'll figure it out." She hesitated. "I could follow you home."

"Go take care of your boat. And Max. I'll call you as soon as I get there."

I didn't remember much of my drive back to Sabal Bay or of my conversation with Grandy because I was still focused on the astonished looks on the faces of everyone in the lawyer's office. And then there was my own shock. Of course Winston has left money to Darlene and a small sum to his stepchildren. Grandy received some pearls that had been in the family for a few generations, but the bulk of the estate—estimated at over one point five million dollars—went to me.

I did recall the children and Darlene stalking out before Grandy and me, their faces purple with rage. Mr. Sandimore told me he'd be in touch about the details, but I didn't want to know any details. I worried they might outline how each dollar had been obtained. *This one was part of the payment delivered to Big Donnie Giovanni for the hit on Sonny Capri, but this one came as the result of the Rigatoni family's burning of Sal's pizzeria in Bay Side. We deliver, Winston seemed to be saying. Yipes!*

I didn't feel like going back to my empty house to be further haunted by Winston's voice describing his career path. I checked my watch. Madeleine should still be at the store.

"I'm cleaning. This place needed sprucing up." Madeleine wore a bib apron and had covered her hair with a white scarf. "So what did you get?"

"I got a migraine headache, the undying enmity of at least three people and a lot of money obtained mostly through illegal ventures."

"What?"

I tossed my purse on the counter and told her about the afternoon.

"So, no clothes?"

"Come on, Madeleine. The last thing I was thinking about was the shop."

"Sure. I get it. Now that you have all that bread, you'll probably quit our business and take Alex on some fancy vacation and then retire to the Caribbean."

I was shocked she would think that. Then it hit me. She was scared—worried I'd do just that, leave her alone with the shop.

"Do you really believe I'd abandon this business after what we went through to build it up? And do you really believe I want that disgusting moola? I'll find a way of giving it back."

"You can't return money to a dead man."

She had a point there.

"Don't be too hasty in throwing it away. We'll figure out something to do with it," she said.

"Like what? Who would want the money if they found out how it was obtained?"

She sneezed. "Let's get out of here. It's time to close anyway, and I'm sick of breathing in dirt and dust. We can work on this better if we have a cold margarita, don't you think?"

Madeleine always had the best ideas, and when she had a little booze in her, she could problem-solve like a corporate CEO.

THREE MARGARITAS APIECE and some salsa and chips in the local Mexican restaurant didn't yield much in the way of good ideas. But we felt better. I insisted upon sitting near the window so I could keep an eye on my rental car. I'd lost my red Miata to a fire bomb last year in this very lot, and I wanted to make certain no one tampered with this car. Besides, I hadn't taken the extra insurance when I rented it.

Madeleine watched me survey the lot outside. "When do you get your convertible back?"

"The repair garage said sometime the end of this week."

My cell trilled.

"It's Sophia," I mouthed to Madeleine.

"Is she calling to warn you she's about to trash your car?"

I signaled Madeleine to hold her comments.

The call was brief. In what I had come to recognize as her customarily brisk manner, Sophia asked to meet me, well, she *told* me she'd meet me later tonight and recommended the canal lock at the Ridge. I thought about the isolation of those locks late at night, the tall, cold concrete walls and the dark water beneath. Creepy. I countered with the Burnt Biscuit. Something about Sophia made me uneasy, and I wasn't going to take a meeting in an isolated location with someone who thought I'd stolen the family's money

"Come alone." She hung up.

"The general has issued her orders." I reported her words to Madeleine.

"I don't know. I think she's weird. You need someone to watch your back."

"Well, how many cowboys do I know who hang out at the Biscuit? I think I'm safe."

"No. You need to call Nappi or Alex," she stopped in mid-sentence, "or someone closer, someone around here." She looked at me with expectation in her eyes.

"I'm not calling on Sammy."

"Why not? He likes you. A lot."

"What would Alex say? Weren't you the one who thought Alex might be upset about Sammy's interest in me?" *Or my fascination with him?*

"Sure, but this is an emergency. No one else can get here in time."

"She's just a girl."

"I'm not so sure." Madeleine signaled the waiter for another margarita. "As for you, you're not having another one. You need to be sober."

Well, that was no fun.

I CHOSE A table in the back, the same one Grandy and I had taken when we met with Nappi. The Biscuit's light was dim, but I thought Sophia's eyes looked red-rimmed. Had Ms. Grim and Stoic been crying?

She sat down and began talking. The waitress approached the table, but Sophia waved her off. Good thing I had my libations earlier.

"We were upset when we heard Winston gave you all the money that he should have given us, but now we're over it."

Wow, talk about a quick bounce-back.

She held up her hand to prevent me from saying anything.

"No. Do not interrupt. This is hard for me to say, but we need you, so I must apologize for our bad manners leaving the lawyer's office in, what do you say here, a 'huff'?"

No, not a huff. It felt more like a bomber circling to take another run at the target. Why did I feel like the target?

She still held her hand up, palm toward me. I didn't want to risk her working herself up into yet another huff, so I listened.

"So I am forced to apologize and ask you for that money."

What? I could not comprehend where this conversation was going.

Tears spilled out of her gray eyes. Here was a woman unused to showing emotion and forced to divulge family secrets to someone she felt had cheated her out of her inheritance. I began to feel for her.

I reached across the table to pat her hand. She removed mine. Now I wanted her to hurry the story along so I could say no and get the hell out of here and never see her again.

"My sister, my little sister, I think Darlene told you she was up north?"

I nodded.

"She is in the United States, but some bad people, actually part of the Russian Mob, have kidnapped her and are holding her for what you would call ransom. They contacted Winston, and he took money out of his accounts. He was supposed to leave it in the swamp."

"He did, but I thought that was for the mob?"

"There are two mobs, the one that Winston worked for and the Russian Mob. I don't know about the mob money. I just know someone took the ransom money. When the Russians were sent to pick it up, it was gone. Now they are saying they will kill my sister or," she paused and gulped, "something worse. We need your money to get her back. So you'll give it to us." She hesitated, then reached out and touched my hand. "Please?" A tear worked its way down her cheek.

The storyteller didn't do the tale justice. I'd read about the Russian Mob, and I knew they were ruthless. This was just the sort of thing they did—kidnapping young women and bringing them to the United States or other countries to be sold into slavery, used as prostitutes. Killing this young woman would be more merciful than the life she would face as a sex slave.

So yes, as much has I didn't like Sophia, I would try to help her. Her stoicism made sense to me. She had to hold herself together until she found a way out of this dilemma. Winston was dead, so who else could she turn to? Winston had tried to help. I could honor his memory by following through on his plan. What better way to use his money?

I knew not to suggest Sophia contact the police. But guess whose name jumped into my head? Nappi was a contact I'd keep to myself until I discussed the situation with him.

We were both silent as we stepped out of the restaurant and headed to our cars. Heavy clouds obscured both the moon and the stars, leaving the night inky black. The smell of sugarcane fields lit on fire earlier in the day in preparation for harvesting made the air smell burnt and sour. I coughed once to clear my throat. Sophia lit up a cigarette as soon as she hit the parking area.

She grabbed my hand as I opened the car door to leave.

"Why can't you give it to me now?"

"I don't have it now. The will takes time, legal stuff and all. I'll get in touch with the lawyer and try to hurry things along, but—"

"She might die."

"Delay them. Tell them what's happening," I said.

"They won't listen to delay."

"Then you'll have to go to the police."

Her face turned white. "No, no. They said no police. Okay. I'll delay. Somehow."

I got into my car, rolled down the window to ask her how I could get in touch, but she did an about-face and marched across the parking lot to a car sitting underneath the large cypress tree. Sophia got in the passenger's side and the tires threw gravel as it sped out of the lot.

I assumed brother Boris was driving. I was so intent upon watching the car I wasn't prepared for a touch on my arm. I whirled around, the sound of my racing heartbeat loud in my ears.

"Sorry, Evie."

The only person who ever called me Evie was my ex-husband, Jerry.

"What are you doing here? You almost scared me to death."

"Nappi sent me. He's tied up with another job, so he asked if I would drop by and give you an update. I was more than happy to." He smiled at me and stroked my shoulder.

"Okay, Jerry, here's the thing. Don't call me Evie, ever. Don't smile at me like that. Don't stroke me, anywhere. And say what you have to say, then leave. Quick."

Jerry and I had a relatively amicable divorce. I signed the papers willingly, thinking he had gotten Nappi's daughter pregnant. Not knowing Nappi well at that point, I didn't want to make things difficult for Jerry or me by delaying the wedding of a mobster's daughter. As it turned out, there was no pregnancy and no wedding. Everyone seemed relieved, except perhaps for the daughter, who seemed to love him for reasons I couldn't fathom after having been married to him for ten years. I guess it was a matter of taste. I'd demonstrated mine by divorcing him and she hers by wanting to trap him in marriage.

"Let's go back to your place and get ...." He stopped when I gave him a look of warning. "We need someplace to talk. This could take a while."

"Okay, Jerry. Where's your car? You can follow me back to the house."

"I don't have a car. One of Nappi's men dropped me here when I didn't find you at home. I figured you might be having a drink or something."

"No car? How are you supposed to get around in town?"

"Taxi?"

"There are no taxis in this town. You should know that."

"I'll rent something."

"In the morning you'll rent a car. Until then, where are you staying? I suppose I'll have to drop you off."

"Uh, I haven't gotten a place yet."

"Have you thought any of this through? There's a big bass tournament in town. There's probably not a room for fifty miles around here."

He shook his head and plastered what could only be interpreted as a hopeful, save-me look on his face.

That was Jerry. When we were married he counted on me to bail him out of dicey situations. I guess divorce hadn't changed that.

"Okay. You can crash on my couch for the night; then I drop you by the rental place early tomorrow, and I do mean early. You're on your own from then on."

I muttered under my breath the entire way to my place.

When we got there, I tossed my purse on the coffee table and headed for my liquor cabinet. The margaritas had worn off, and after my day, I needed something. Scotch or chocolate. Scotch and chocolate.

Without asking, I also poured Jerry a shot of Scotch.

"Cheers." He lifted his glass.

"We'll see about that. Talk." I threw myself onto the couch.

"Tough day, huh?" He set his glass on the end table and moved my feet off the couch, then sat there. "I could give you a foot rub. Remember when I used to do that?"

"I do remember. And don't do it now." I sipped my Scotch. It felt like fire going down and like velvet in my tummy. *Ah*.

Jerry remained on the couch and tossed down his drink in one gulp. It seemed to light the fire of important conversation under him.

"Nappi looked into Darlene's past and found some interesting things. It seems Winston wasn't her first mob connection. She was the long-time girlfriend of Fingers Bucoli." Jerry paused and gave me an expectant look.

"So? This is supposed to mean something to me?"

"You never heard of Fingers?"

I wiggled mine at him and shook my head.

"Fingers Bucoli died several years ago, supposedly hit by a rival family vying for control of an area of Philly."

"Darlene likes mobsters. That's all you've got?"

"Nappi says there's a rumor going around that the hit wasn't by someone outside the family, but might have been the work of one of Finger's closest associates." He sat back on the couch with a look of satisfaction on his face.

"Maybe Darlene?"

"Maybe Darlene."

I thought about this. "Perhaps it was a lover's quarrel?"

"Then she's a real smart dame. It looked like a legitimate hit."

I wondered about using "legitimate" as the way to label having someone killed off, but I let it go.

"What does Nappi think?"

"He's still talking to his contacts, but regardless of whether she's involved or not, his feeling is that Darlene lacks good girlfriend potential."

Some might question whether such a judgment coming from a mob guy carried any authority, but I trusted Nappi to protect my interests, regardless of the ethics he adhered to in his own business relations.

"What do the Philly authorities think about Fingers' murder?"

Jerry shrugged and held up his glass. "Got any more of this?"

"I'll run this by Frida and see what she says." I ignored his request for more Scotch.

"Oh, and Nappi says to remind you again. Mob folks don't kill people who owe them money. It's just bad business."

"I get that."

He set the glass on the end table and reached out to pat my shoulder.

"God, Eve, you're tight as a corset on an overweight hooker." He grabbed my feet and lifted them into his lap, then slipped off my Ferragamos—the ones with the snake skin straps and three inch heels, of course—and began to rub my toes.

It felt so good, I let him continue.

"Did you hear a car pull up?" I slid forward on the couch.

The doorbell rang.

I swung my feet onto the floor and went to the door.

"Am I interrupting something?"

It was Sammy Egret. He eyed Jerry with suspicion.

"No, of course not." I gestured him into the room.

Jerry rose from the couch and approached Sammy. He stood a good six inches shorter than the Indian. Both men seemed to square off as if they intended to engage in combat in my living room. It looked like a toy poodle had wandered into the fight ring with a pit bull.

"I'm her husband."

"Ex-husband." Why did it seem so important I make it clear to Sammy that I wasn't attached to Jerry?

"Same difference. Who are you?"

"He's my airboat pilot, tracker, and bodyguard."

For a moment Sammy looked doubtful about the titles I'd given him, but he nodded anyway.

"You won't need him tonight, since I'm staying over," Jerry said.

I could tell Sammy wanted to laugh at this, but he made polite and didn't.

"In your house? With you?" Sammy seemed puzzled at my choice of sleep-over companion.

"By the way, Sammy, what are you doing here?"

"Madeleine sent me. She wanted me to check on you. She said you had an appointment tonight, and she was worried you might not be safe. I followed you from the Biscuit. You really want this guy in your house?"

"Not really, but he's not the one she was worried about."

The two men stood in the middle of the room, still squared off, as if waiting for the starting bell to signal round one.

"Let's all of us sit down. Can I get you anything, Sammy? We're having Scotch."

"I'll take a beer if you have it."

"In the fridge." I gestured toward the kitchen, grabbed Jerry by the arm and shoved him onto the couch. I stuck my feet back in Jerry's lap. He was too good at foot massages for me to let this one go.

Sammy got his beer and sat on the arm of the couch farthest from Jerry.

Jerry paused mid-massage. "I think I heard another car. Are you expecting someone else, Eve?" Jerry nodded toward Sammy.

Was I expecting anyone else? Not really, but there's no accounting for who might come through my door. This was a friendly community, and people dropped by. Maybe Madeleine decided to check up on me and Sammy. Maybe Sophia decided to get pushy once more. And there were Grandy and Max ….

Nope. Wrong on all counts.

The front door banged open and Alex stood there, backlit by the street light and looking like an avenging angel.

"What the hell is going on here?" Alex asked, and not in a friendly way.

Now there were three men in my house. The level of testosterone circulating in the room rose astronomically, my tingling from tip to toe not simply the result of having my feet rubbed.

CHAPTER 8

━━━

I INTRODUCED ALEX and Sammy and explained that Sammy was here at Madeleine's behest and Jerry at Nappi's, information I hoped would calm him down. I hadn't seen him for several weeks, and I missed him. I assumed he missed me, too, and that was why he was here. I also considered another reason for his visit: he didn't trust me and was checking up on me. Putting myself in his shoes, I might have had some concerns if I entered his apartment to find his ex-wife and a comely bronze-skinned Indian maiden on the couch having cocktails.

Sammy seemed to sense he should leave. He was quick to pick up that Alex was more than just a friend. He offered to give Jerry a ride, but Jerry, being the insensitive lout he was, declined. Jerry knew Alex, knew he was my boyfriend, so it was classic Jerry that he would hang around to make things difficult for us.

"Wrong, Jerry. You do want a ride." I gave Alex a look I hoped he would correctly interpret as a hankering to get cozy together. Alone. It seemed to miss its mark. He appeared fixated on Sammy.

"I don't have any place to stay. You know that, Evie." Jerry wrung his hands and looked helpless.

I bristled at being called Evie, especially in front of Alex. I considered simply throwing him out onto the lawn but worried the neighbors might object to trash in my front yard.

"That's not my problem." I appealed to Sammy's knowledge of the area. "Is there any motel around here that won't be filled with bass tournament people?"

"Sure. I'll get him a place." Sammy smiled his enigmatic smile, and I wondered for a moment where he would put Jerry—maybe a hammock in a chickee—but as I'd said earlier, that wasn't my problem.

I closed the door on the two of them and turned to Alex.

"You don't know how happy I am you're here," I said.

"No, I don't. It looked to me as if you had plenty of company to make you happy. Two men, one massaging your feet, the other sending smoky signals of desire."

"You know Jerry and you know there's nothing between us. Well, nothing on my part. As for Sammy, don't you think your remark is kind of racist? Besides he's Miccosukee. They don't use smoke signals."

"This one does."

"Okay, I get that you're perturbed with me. But for no reason."

He stood there for a moment, then moved across the room and took me into his arms. *This was more like it.*

We settled on the couch and began talking. That's when I made my mistake. I told him about everything that was happening, and he did what I should have expected him to do.

"You've got to go to the cops. You know that. You think kidnapping by Russian mobsters is something you can solve by giving this woman money? Maybe it's just a scam and there is no kidnapping."

"I've already thought of that. I have a source—"

"Source?" He snorted the word. "You mean you're going to

use Nappi's connections to find out, don't you?"

Well, sure I did. "It's a damn reliable source."

"And then you'll owe him." He got off the couch and moved toward the door.

"Hey, where are you going?" I thought by getting rid of the other guys I made it clear to him that he and I could have some time together, like the entire night.

"I'm leaving."

"You're punishing me for using my friends to help me find my uncle's murderer?"

"This is not finding his murderer. This is blackmail. With the Russians. Are you crazy?"

"I think it's all related."

"How?"

Well, he had me there. I didn't know how. I spread my arms in a gesture of helplessness. You'd think a guy who loved a gal might sweep her off her feet, carry her into the bedroom and forgive her all her recklessness, wouldn't you? Maybe not.

"I can't stay."

"You are punishing me. How can you? You were simply checking up on me, weren't you?" I knew I was going overboard with what I said to Alex, but I couldn't help myself.

Alex looked exasperated at my outburst and threw up his hands.

"Just go then." I pointed at the door.

Alex got very still and silent for a moment.

"That's what you really want?"

"Absolutely." I crossed my arms in front of my chest and tapped my bare toe.

"Fine, but I think you should know I drove here from Pensacola just to make sure you were all right. I can't stay because I have to get back for an important meeting tomorrow."

Oh, no. I rethought the drama queen act.

"I'm sorry. I didn't mean what I said."

He turned away from the door. "Sometimes you are a

challenge, Eve." He put his arms around me, this time pulling me so close I thought he might break something. "Listen to me. Stay out of this investigation and stay away from the blackmail thing. The Russian mob is nothing to get involved with. Even Nappi will tell you that."

THE NEXT MORNING I rolled over in my empty bed. Alex had left as he promised, but he'd stayed until early morning. I didn't envy his long drive back to the Panhandle. The evening wasn't what I'd envisioned for us, but work sometimes gets in the way of romance. Murder is even more intrusive. I grabbed my cell off the bedside table.

"I hate to do this, Madeleine, but can you tend the store alone this morning? I've got an errand to run."

"Sure, but what errand?"

"I'll be in around one this afternoon with some clothes from our clients on the coast. Promise. We can talk then." I clicked off before she could ask any more questions.

Before I went to the store I had the morning to accomplish two items of business. I wanted to find out where Sammy had stashed Jerry so I could make contact with Nappi. And then I needed to hire Sammy to take me on another airboat trip. Oops, three things: I had to make a quick trip to replenish our dwindling supplies of designer items in the store. If I forgot that, Madeleine would have my head. Or worse yet, she'd tell Alex and Grandy and maybe Frida what I was up to. Then I'd have an entire posse on my trail.

The sun was inching its way over the eastern edge of the lake, sending pink light onto the water's surface. It looked like a fine day, despite that old sailor's warning rhyme. I turned onto the dirt drive to Sammy's chickee, thinking I'd have to walk to his house and roust him out of bed. I was wrong. He stood leaning against the center post to the chickee, his eyelids half closed as if he was just awake enough to hold his body upright but not so alert he welcomed another human interfering with his morning meditations.

I smiled, thinking I'd caught him off guard and almost napping. I was wrong. In the few seconds it took me to get out of my car and approach him, he'd moved out of the chickee and was walking toward me. His lids still hooded his black eyes, but when he got close I noted they were sharp as a raptor's.

"I guess your boyfriend left early. And you got lonely and came to see me. Should I be flattered? Had your coffee yet?"

Before I could decide which comment I wanted to address, he moved away from the chickee and headed down the path to his house, gesturing with a lazy sweep of his hand that I should follow. "Grandfather's been up for hours. He figured you might show up looking for something."

He did?

The smell of coffee welcomed me into the house. Sammy pulled out a chair for me at the table.

"When I drove past the Hardy brothers' place, it was closed. I guess they're still in jail," I said.

I sipped my coffee. For having been made in an old enamel pot, it was surprisingly good, the flavor deep and full. The world's most experienced coffee barista couldn't have improved on it.

"Don't stir the grounds. Let them settle. An eggshell keeps it clear." Grandfather Egret slipped a fried egg out of the pan onto a plate and handed it to me.

"No, really. I don't eat breakfast."

"If you're going to stake out a varmint's nest, you need to keep your stomach from growling or they'll hear you and run off." Grandpa gave forth a throaty chuckle.

"I'm hoping the, er, varmints won't be home." I ate the egg with gusto.

"If you're saying we should be careful, I know that, Grandpa. I'm always careful. You raised me to be." Sammy stood and offered me his hand.

"We haven't agreed upon your fee."

Both men exchanged looks.

"Never mind. Whatever you charge is fine. With me."

"Because you've got money, right?" Sammy glanced at his grandfather and then back at me. "Smoke signals. Indian telegraph."

"I'm not that stupid. How did you find out about the will?"

"Voices came in on the wind last night." Grandpa gave me a sly look. However they found out, it was clear they wanted to keep their sources to themselves.

"SPEAKING OF WIND, it's sure kicked up since sunrise." We were in Sammy's airboat speeding down the Rim Canal toward the Hardy's Swamp Tours.

Sammy looked at the whirling clouds overhead. "Let's get this done fast. Weather's coming in. There's a tropical storm brewing in the gulf."

"Will that be a problem?"

"Not if we beat it back, but it can get treacherous on the water if the wind starts shifting around on us."

Sammy roared past the Hardy landing, then made a sharp turn. The boat slipped sideways in the water, and we headed back the way we'd come. "I just wanted to come in with these reeds as cover in case someone was around the place. I don't think you're going to find anything, Eve."

"Maybe not, but I can't believe the Hardy brothers were at Uncle Winston's funeral to pay their respects. It wasn't mere curiosity that made them search through the condo. They were looking for something, and I don't mean the silver and crystal. They were looking for the same thing I was."

"And that would be?"

"Winston's money or some of it. He was carrying two satchels. One he certainly left on land when he got out of the boat in the swamp. The other had to be somewhere on the boat or near the landing. Or someone took it. Perhaps Darlene secreted it in that huge purse of hers."

"Fits."

"It does?"

"Sure. The Hardy brothers took over their airboat operation about a year ago. From what I've seen, they know little about the swamp and aren't interested in learning. They seem like displaced city boys to me."

"Why do you say that? What have you seen?"

"Nothing much, except they like to go out in the airboat at night. I thought they might be poaching gators, but I've watched them. They come back with an empty boat, no sign of hunting. I know most of the people around here who buy alligators and the Hardys aren't selling to them." Sammy pulled up to the landing.

"So if they aren't hunting alligators, what are they hunting?"

"People."

"What?"

"They're in the transportation business."

Sammy knew more than he was telling me, but I couldn't get it out of him. He'd said all he wanted to. His suspicions about the Hardys, as unclear as they might be to me, fit with my assumption that the brothers were doing something illegal— and that included knowing about Winston's work as a bag man.

We tied up Sammy's airboat and began our search. Nothing turned up in the Hardy's boat. I didn't expect it to, but I thought perhaps we might uncover at least a clue to where Winston's other satchel went. We carefully scoured the area around the dock and up into the field we'd walked through that day, but turned up only a few lizards and one black snake. I was beginning to feel foolish. Frida and her team had to have covered the area days ago.

The wind whipped around us and gained in intensity as we searched the grassy area. The gusts were so strong they took my breath away.

"How do you feel about breaking and entering?" I asked.

Sammy shrugged and walked toward the produce stand. He leaned hard against the back door, then shoved his entire body against it. The door banged inward.

"Door's open. How about that," he said.

It was clear the Hardy brothers hadn't been here in several days. The smell of overripe strawberries, rotting peaches and onions past their prime was all-pervasive. In their glass cages, the baby alligators looked at us expectantly, as if hoping to be fed. I opened the top of the aquarium and looked around for their food.

"What do alligators eat?"

"Other alligators." Sammy grinned at the look of shock on my face. "Fish, turtles, birds, sometimes people."

I snatched my hand back from the cage.

A shadow fell over the tank.

"These guys aren't ready for a diet of sassy Yankee gal and Indian yet. But there are plenty of hungry big ones in the swamp." Captain Hardy stood in the doorway with that revolver in his hand.

Beside him stood Digby, sneering but unarmed. Despite his angry squirrel demeanor and short stature, I wasn't going to underestimate him. He had stringy muscles, and being the smaller of the brothers might make him meaner.

Revolver Hardy approached Sammy, who stood his ground. I expected Sammy to reach out to try and grab the gun, and I guess Hardy thought the same thing. He swung the weapon at Sammy's head. Sammy groaned and fell to the floor, limp.

"Tie her up and search both of them," the bigger Hardy brother said.

Digby grabbed a rope out of a storage closet and tied my hands behind my back; then he did the same to Sammy. He poked through our pockets and shook his head when he found nothing.

"Now how we gonna get him to the boat? He's dead weight," Digby said.

"You're going to drag him."

"Me? Why not you? He's a big one. I'll handle the gal."

Hardy gave his smaller brother a look of contempt. "Do it."

Digby grabbed Sammy's tied hands and began to pull.

"Not that way, you stupid weasel. Pull him by his legs."

Big Hardy and I walked out of the building and headed down the path toward the water. Behind us the wind banged the door against the siding.

"Damn Indian broke my door." Hardy shooed me ahead of him. I considered running off the path and into the grass, but that would give me no cover, and I was certain he wouldn't hesitate to shoot me. And then do the same to Sammy. Or worse.

He pushed me into the boat and onto the seat, then took his dirty handkerchief out of his back pocket and tied it over my eyes. The odor of Hardy coming from it made me want to retch. Imagining how he had used that handkerchief only made the nausea worse. A few minutes later I felt the boat sink with the weight of Digby and Sammy.

"You sure took long enough. If this plan is going to work, we need to get out of here. Now. Storm's coming on us. Fast." Hardy started the engine, and we took off.

The motion of the boat through the water, its slipping from side to side made my stomach churn even more. I was sure I'd throw up all over everything. For a moment that sounded like a good idea, and I wanted to laugh. Ha. He'd have to clean it up. Then I wondered if he'd do that before or after he killed us.

I began counting off seconds by using the one-one hundredths, two-one hundredths approach. It took my mind off my queasiness and our fate.

I lost count after ten minutes, aware that we had turned off the Rim Canal into smaller channels more protected from the wind. *Good*, I thought, then realized we'd never find our way out of this maze of smaller canals.

The boat slowed, and I felt it touch land. A big hand pulled me out of my seat and tossed me onto the shore. I heard both men grunt and then felt something warm next to me. Sammy. The boat engine started up and soon its sound dissipated into silence as it left us. A bull alligator roared somewhere nearby, and the wind gathered in intensity.

"Sammy? Are you conscious?" I rolled over toward him and placed my face on his shoulder. "Sammy. Wake up."

I had to get this blindfold off my eyes, but I couldn't do that without help. A guy could die from getting slammed across the side of the head by a pistol, couldn't he? I shoved my face nearer his, hoping to get close enough to feel him breathing. I turned a bit so my mouth was almost on his nose. Did I feel anything like warm breath?

"If you're trying to kiss me, we Indians like to do it mouth to mouth, not mouth to nose."

"You're alive. Thank God."

"Takes more than a pistol whipping to do in this hard skull. Not that I don't like this closeness, but I want you to roll onto your side and I'll do the same."

"Spooning? Now?"

"No. Our backs toward each other. I can untie you and then you can get me free. The spooning comes later."

After several minutes of struggling with the knots, Sammy freed my hands. I pulled off my blindfold and worked on his ropes. It took me more time to free him, but soon we were sitting side by side on the edge of a small canal. Overhead the wind whipped the trees around, toppling dead branches and palm fronds onto the ground. The water at our feet began to rise.

"We need to move back before we get soaked. Watch the branches." Sammy took my hand, and we started into the jungle-like growth behind us. I mentally kicked myself for leaving my purse in Sammy's airboat. My cellphone was in it.

I was lost. Only the sun told me what direction was west.

Still, I was unafraid because Sammy knew these swamps. He was Miccosukee, after all.

"Where are we, Sammy?"

"I have no idea."

We were lost, hopelessly lost in the swamps.

CHAPTER 9

——

"**Y**OU'RE KIDDING, RIGHT?"

He shook his head, then looked upward at the sky. "We need shelter before this storm comes in. I'm worried about hypothermia. I can always build us something to keep most of the rain off us, but not here. There's an animal trail leading off there." He pointed to a small break in the undergrowth. "We'll follow that. It'll lead us to higher ground."

"How do you know that?"

"This is where they come to the water to drink, then go back up the path to higher ground into that hammock to bed down for the night."

"They who?" I thought of a herd of alligators trudging along the trail marked, "Water this way and also food."

"Deer. Let's go."

"What are we looking for?" I was out of breath from keeping pace with Sammy. For once I'd worn fashionable footwear with lower heels, but his stride was much longer than mine on this rutty trail.

"My people used to live in these swamps, you know."

"So what? You said yourself you're lost."

"I said I didn't know where we were. That's different from being lost. You think being lost is hopeless. It's not. This was once our home."

"Your home, not mine. So now you're going to call upon your ancestors to rescue us?" I almost believed he could do that.

"In a manner of speaking."

"You said you could make a shelter for us. Out of what?"

"Vines, palm fronds, small saplings."

"With your bare hands?"

"No. I'd use this." Sammy stopped for a moment, bent over and extracted the biggest, meanest looking knife out of his boot. Déjà vu Crocodile Dundee. He chuckled as he held it up for me to see. "They searched me, but not very well."

The blade of the knife glittered in the waning sunlight.

"You sure you don't have some matches, kindling, wood and a side of beef hidden on you?"

"Nope. But look." Sammy pointed ahead of us. The trail opened up into a clearing. A shack stood there. To me it looked like the Taj Mahal.

"You think the people who live there will mind our dropping in?"

"The place is deserted, Eve. Nobody's been there for years. It's all ours."

That sounded quite homey, especially as the first raindrops began to hit. He grabbed my hand, and we ran for the building.

Only part of the roof was intact, and that's where we sought shelter. Sammy searched the inside of the shack, found several pots and stuck them outside the sheltered area so that they would catch the falling rain.

"We've got water now. In the morning, I'll look for food." Sammy sounded positively cheerful as I examined my ruined boots in the dim light.

"I bought these at a consignment shop in Boca. Only twenty-nine ninety-five. I'll never be able to replace them." I stuck my finger through the split in the leather near my big toe.

Sammy gave me a bemused look as if he couldn't decide whether he found me irritating or simply too nutty to be taken seriously.

For the rest of the afternoon, the rain drummed on the roof with a deafening roar, while the wind blew as if enraged. The wooden beams and supports shook with each blast. If the roof came down, we were sunk. I remembered what Sammy had said about hypothermia. He said spending the night wet even if it wasn't that cold could bring it on. This wasn't the way I'd imagined leaving this earth, shivering to death. I wasn't ready for that. I had too many things yet to do: dispose of Winston's money, save his stepdaughter from the Russians, buy Grandy a new rain slicker, find Madeleine a boyfriend who wasn't afraid of a gal with coordination issues. If God was in a bargaining mood, I could argue my way out of this one by pointing out the many good deeds I had planned but not yet executed.

Another powerful wind blast shook the rafters, loosening dirt and debris. It fell on our heads, followed by something heavier and … alive. A small mouse dropped onto my shoulder, jumped to the table next to me, then plunged to the floor and scooted away into the shadows. I managed to contain a shriek of panic.

When I got my voice under control and spoke, I sounded calm and sane. "Will this shelter hold?"

"It's been through more storms than you can imagine." Sammy reached over and gave my shoulder a reassuring pat.

"How do you know that?"

He opened his mouth as if to answer, then clamped his lips shut.

"Sammy, you're not being honest with me. You've been here before, haven't you?"

He hesitated a moment, then leaned towards me. "I don't know for certain. There are a lot of shacks like this in the swamp. This one looks familiar. I think Grandfather might have brought me here when I was a kid. I can't be sure, but even if I've been here before, it doesn't mean I know the way out. Not after all these years."

"I was kind of hoping a map of the swamp was in your DNA."

"Don't worry, Eve. I'll take care of you."

But I was worried. Taking care of me might mean we'd set up housekeeping here and live off the land until someone chanced upon us. Some day. That possibility sounded no better than death. I didn't know if I could survive a life where I'd never see a pair of Ferragamos again.

I wiggled my toes in my ruined boots and sighed. "So what do we do then? Wait here until we die?"

"We won't die."

Maybe not, but as the sun began to go down and the wind seemed to shake the small shack until I was certain the rafters would collapse around our heads, my thoughts took a darker turn. I sniffed and wiped my nose on my sleeve.

"You're not going to cry, are you?"

"I never cry." I gave that announcement some consideration. It was true I wasn't a crier, but then I'd never been lost in a swamp while hurricane force winds threw walls of rain at me. To keep myself from becoming a blubbering idiot and succumbing to hysteria, I looked around the shack and thought about Sammy coming here with his grandfather when he was little. There it was, I thought. A way out.

"Your grandfather brought you here? Then he knows how to get back. Does he come often? Would he look for you here? Would he? Would he?" I had grabbed Sammy shirt and was tugging at it like a toddler throwing a tantrum over ice cream. Okay, so I wasn't in control.

"For God's sake, Eve. Let go. You'll strip me naked."

Our eyes met at the same moment. Naked? In the middle of a storm? I had stepped off the edge of rational thought to be considering a tryst under these circumstances. The expression in his eyes told me the same thought had crossed his mind. He took my closed fist in his hand and held it with gentle pressure. We both spoke at the same moment. "Sorry."

After a few minutes, Sammy moved a small distance away from me and looked into my eyes. "Grandfather almost never goes into the swamp anymore. He won't be coming here to find us. I'm sorry, Eve, but we'll make the best of this. I think the wind is dying down now, and soon it will blow itself out. When it does, we'll get some sleep."

Sleep? Here? In a swamp? "Don't you think we should take turns staying awake? Someone needs to guard the place."

I couldn't see Sammy's face, but his voice with its attendant snicker of laughter said he thought my idea absurd. "Guard it from what exactly?"

"Uh, bugs and stuff. Alligators, maybe?"

He sighed, and I felt him move closer to me. "You can go first then. Keep the gators out of here while I get some shut eye."

"Now you're just playing with me."

"Go to sleep, Eve. You're going to need rest to get through tomorrow."

"What are we going to do in the morning?"

"Find something to eat."

"Like what?"

"A Big Mac."

He was playing with me. Soon I heard his breathing slow and soft snores erupt from his mouth. The wind continued to moan overhead, punctuated by other sounds—a screeching of some swamp bird, followed by croaks, roars, then a crack, as if some large beast had slapped its tail on the water. I knew I wasn't going to sleep.

"WAKE UP. I thought you were supposed to be on watch." A hand shook me into a state of consciousness.

The sun hit me in the face and a bug landed on my forehead. I swatted it away.

"It was too dark last night for there to be anything to watch." I tried to move into a sitting position, but my limbs felt weighted down and achy.

I watched Sammy step outside our ramshackle refuge. He stretched his long body and groaned, then bent over and picked up the pot he had wedged between the porch boards. I managed to get up and join him.

"Have a drink. It's not morning coffee, but it's clean and fresh." He handed me the pot and I took a sip. It was the sweetest water I'd ever drunk. I wondered why they didn't sell it in the stores. Someone could make a fortune off this.

The world outside the deserted cabin sparkled in the morning light, raindrops on the leaves catching the sun and reflecting a rainbow of colors.

"It's beautiful." I handed the water back to him.

"Few people see the swamps like this. It is beautiful. I'm glad you think so too."

Sammy took a long drink and placed the container back in the cabin.

"Now what?"

"I'm going to climb that tree." Sammy pointed to a palm that rose above the other scrubbier trees around the cabin.

"Right. You did promise me food last night. Coconuts?"

"This is not a coconut palm." He began to inch up the trunk.

"So get down from there. This is no time to be showing off."

He continued up and once at the top, he moved the fronds to one side with his body and leaned there.

"What the hell are you doing?" My stomach grumbled. Maybe he was getting us some palm fronds to eat. I'd never heard of that but who knew what one ate in the swamps. Folks around here talked about swamp cabbage, something I wasn't familiar with. Maybe that was it. My stomach rumbled again.

Sammy dropped to the ground beside me. "Let's go."

"Go? Where?"

Without another word, he grabbed my hand, and we set off

for the unknown, heading away from the waterway the Hardys had used to bring us here.

"You're going the wrong way." I tugged on his shirt sleeve to slow him down.

He turned to me with laughter on his face. "Oh, so now you're the swamp explorer? Which direction did you want to go? We can separate and see who gets home first. How about that?"

"But we came in here there." I pointed back toward the cabin and beyond.

"And this is the way the black smoke is coming from."

"What smoke?"

"Don't you smell it?"

I stopped and sniffed. I did smell it. Something was burning. "You saw that when you were up the tree."

"Yep. Let's go." We set off again, following our noses and the clouds of smoke now billowing in the sky ahead of us.

Several hours passed. Keeping the burn ahead of us made charting our path through the swamp slow going. We trudged through small ponds and channels of water, but skirted others that were deeper, the ones Sammy said were likely gator holes. I shuddered at the thought of encountering a hungry or angry reptile. We crawled over downed logs green with moss. Sometimes we got lucky and found a game trail to use, but then it would meander in the wrong direction, and we were back to bushwhacking through the undergrowth. The day grew hotter. For water, we licked the droplets of rain off broad-leaved plants.

"What do you think is on fire? A cane field?" I was sitting on a downed limb taking a breather. Sammy stood leaning against a nearby sabal palm.

"Too much smoke and too black. Cane burns smell sweet. This one doesn't. It's a structure fire."

"As in a building of some kind. Maybe a building with people nearby?"

"Exactly. Let's hurry before it goes out and leaves us with nothing to follow."

The acrid smell of the burn got stronger.

"Listen." Sammy put up his hand and stopped me. "An airboat."

"Signal it." I rushed in front of him, running toward the sound of the whirring engine.

Sammy grabbed me, pushed me to the ground, and fell on top of me. "It could be the Hardy brothers."

"I don't care. We gotta get out of this swamp."

"We already are." Sammy pushed aside the grasses. In front of us we could see the broad rim canal. "Look there." Sammy pointed toward the east, down the canal. Smoke continued to pour from a building as fire fighters doused the flames with water.

"It's the Hardys' produce stand and their airboat operation that's burning."

"I wonder if they were inside," I said.

"They tried to kill us and you're concerned about them?"

"I'm not worried about those boys. I was talking about the baby gators they kept in the building."

Out on the canal, the airboat we'd heard sped by, but I couldn't tell who was in it because Sammy and I ducked our heads down.

"This way." Sammy signaled me to follow him in the opposite direction from the airboat landing.

"I want to see what's going on."

"Not now. We need food and water first. Then we can find out what happened to our boys and their business. If they're not dead, I don't want them to know we aren't."

"We're going to your place?"

He nodded and headed back into the swamp.

"We could just hit the road and follow it home."

"Like I said, let's keep our heads down for now. I don't want anyone to see us. Yet."

The steel in Sammy's voice told me he had something special planned for the Hardy brothers if they were still alive. I thought it might be better for them if they were dead.

Another several hours of tramping around in the swamps until we arrived at Sammy's house left me thirsty enough to drink swamp water and hungry enough to consider eating a salad of water lettuce dressed with pond scum. Instead we had tea and biscuits with homemade jam served by Sammy's grandfather.

I was too exhausted to talk much, so Sammy explained what had happened. Grandfather Egret didn't seem too upset by what Sammy had to say. He puffed on his pipe and sipped his tea, finally pausing long enough to say, "I thought maybe I'd have to come looking for you."

"How would you know where to look? Sammy said you never go out in the swamps anymore, and besides, you didn't know the Hardy brothers had taken us out there." I stopped talking for a second. "Did you?"

"I had a visitor right before the storm hit." He set the pipe on the table. "Just a bit of a thing, but a good friend of yours."

"Madeleine was here? But how did she figure out where we were? I didn't even tell her Sammy and I were going to the Hardy's place to snoop."

Grandfather chuckled. "She's got you down good. She knew you couldn't stay away from there. She thought you might have hired Sammy to help you. I told her we couldn't look until the storm was over. I told her things in the swamp—"

"Get lost and then turn up again. You told me that once too."

CHAPTER 10

─────

SAMMY AND I hopped into his truck to head back to my place. He'd insisted on driving me home because he thought I was too tired to be behind the wheel. He was probably right. It was all I could do to keep my eyes open. I propped my elbow against the window and leaned my head on my hand. I was just drifting off when Sammy made a hard turn right that startled me awake.

"Are we home already?" I looked around me. We were at the Hardy's burned-out place of business.

"There's nothing here but charred timbers. Why are we stopping?"

"Go back to sleep. I'm going to take a look around. I'm hoping I can find my airboat here someplace. It looks as if the Hardys or whoever burned the place took theirs. Maybe they didn't sink mine or set it adrift and I can locate it."

As we pulled into the parking area, a police officer signaled us not to go any farther in. "Off limits."

We could see yellow tape strung around the place. This place was certainly getting its share of attention from the authorities. A crime scene twice over.

Frida's police cruiser pulled up behind us.

"There you are. Madeleine called to tell me she heard from you. When were you going to pay me a visit? I understand the Hardy boys took you for a ride in the swamps. And you didn't think I'd be interested?" Frida stood, hands on her hips and anger on her face.

"I'm sorry, but all I can think of is sleep. I'm exhausted, and I have to go shopping for new boots." I opened the door and stuck out my foot, showing her my ruined boot.

She let out a guffaw of a laugh. "Only you would follow up near death with a shopping expedition. So I gather you're okay?"

I nodded. "Sammy and I took his airboat here to, uh, take a look at the place. The Hardys found us and decided we were getting too snoopy for them. Sammy's looking for his boat."

"If he stays out of the taped in area, he's free to search." Frida signaled the officer to let Sammy proceed toward the canal. "Snoopy. Huh? You? I can't believe that."

"Don't get all snarky on me."

"While Sammy searches for his boat, you might as well tell me everything that happened in the swamp." Frida took out her notebook and pencil and leaned against the truck.

I had to tell her everything? Well, I told her most of it. I left out the part about the lustful thoughts I'd had about Sammy.

SAMMY WAS IN luck. He located his boat adrift several hundred yards down the canal.

"It was as if she were heading home to me," he said.

We both chuckled at the thought, although I wondered if Grandfather Egret had been using some kind of mojo to signal it back.

"Look what I brought you from the airboat," Sammy said, holding up my purse.

I quickly went through the contents. Everything was still there, including my cellphone.

Madeleine, probably because Frida had called her and told her we were on our way, waited for me in the driveway of my house. Sammy's recuperative powers were better than mine. He jumped out of his truck and came around to help me out, chattering away about the night in the swamp. Finding the boat had made him positively perky. I was now so tired I welcomed Madeleine's help into my bedroom. Sammy waited in the living room while she ran me a bath.

"Okey dokey, Eve. The bubbles await."

I muttered something like appreciation and stepped into the water.

"Take off your clothes first."

"Why? They're dirty too."

Madeleine shrugged and closed the bathroom door. "Don't drown in there."

The water revived me enough to allow me to pull off my sopping wet clothes and toss them toward the sink. I missed. I took a deep breath and submerged myself. When I came up Sammy stood over the bath.

"What are you doing here?"

"Madeleine left for the store to get some tea. You're all out. Your phone rang, and I answered it."

A red flush worked its way up his neck and onto his cheeks. Why, the guy was blushing. He held the phone in his hand, which trembled a bit. Shy fellow.

"Here. Give me that before you drop it into the tub." I grabbed the phone. Sammy beat feet back into the living room.

The voice on the other end of the line spoke for a time while I listened, thinking that what I was hearing had to be a prank.

"Let me call you back." I checked the numbers on my phone and connected to the lawyer in West Palm. I received the same message as he had delivered just minutes before.

I disconnected and reached for my towel. I heard Madeleine's voice.

I wrapped the towel around me and strode into the living room. Sammy blushed again.

"Look who I found while shopping."

Jerry stood behind her, as if her tiny frame might hide his presence.

The doorbell rang. Jerry opened the door, and Alex entered. When he saw my choice of clothes for entertaining visitors and the identities of my guests, he too turned red. With anger.

"Just get over yourselves. This is serious. Someone emptied all my uncle's accounts. There's not one cent left."

Everyone was silent for a moment.

Madeleine set her bag of groceries on the sofa and sank down beside it. "Well, now you don't have to worry about what to do with mob money."

"I was going to give it to some Russian thugs to rescue Sophia and Boris' sister. Now what are they going to do?" I hugged my towel around me and looked down at my feet. Then I burst into tears.

"We'll think of some way to get her back." Madeleine rushed over and threw her arms around me.

I stopped blubbering for a minute. "I know that. But look." I pointed to my boots still on my feet. "I forgot to take them off. Now they're really ruined."

I wiped my nose with a corner of my towel. "I need, I need …."

Alex was at my side in one bound. He wrapped his big arms around me. Then Jerry joined Alex and Madeleine, getting in on the group hug. Across the room, Sammy continued to blush.

"Hey. I can't breathe here. Get off me. That's not what I need. I need, I need …."

My groupies looked across the room at Sammy.

"Hiiiim?" Alex stammered the word out.

I shook my head. "Nappi. Get him on the phone for me, Jerry. I need money."

"I knew those boots were expensive, Eve, but I can loan you enough to buy a new pair." Alex seemed relieved at my request for money.

I stamped my soggy Ferragamo boot. My towel slipped a touch. Madeleine grabbed a corner and pulled it tighter around me.

"I need half a million dollars to rescue the girl. It's what Winston tried to do, and it's for me to finish. Family was important to him, and it is to me, too."

"But she's not part of your family, Eve," Madeleine said.

"Yes, she is. She's Winston's stepdaughter. He cared about her. Winston told me the day he was killed that family came first. How can I turn my back on that?"

THAT NIGHT, AFTER I'd gotten a few hours' sleep—right after Madeleine had cleared my house of extraneous men, actually, all the men—Nappi arrived with a bouquet of red roses and a look of concern on his face.

"Are you sure you want to do this?" Nappi asked.

"Did you find out anything about Sophia and Boris' sister or the Russian mob, anything that says I shouldn't rescue this woman?"

"You're talking to the wrong person here. The Russian mob is something we in the 'family' try not to get involved with unless it threatens our business. It's something I prefer to stay out of. On general principle, I recommend you do the same."

I took "general principle" to mean family principles, excluding foreigners who didn't speak Italian and not to include anything like "it's against the law" principles.

"I can't leave her to be sold into slavery."

"If their story is true."

"Winston thought it was. His effort might have gotten him killed."

"My point exactly," Nappi said.

"Why would they lie?"

"Half a million dollars is a lot of money. They weren't in his will, so they knew he wasn't going to give it to them upon his death. It was supposed to be taken care of."

"But that's just it. They didn't know they weren't in his will. They and Darlene were shocked to find out I was his heir."

Nappi got up from the couch and walked to the window. The night sky twinkled with stars, a light show following the storm. "I don't like this, especially because it's too connected with your uncle's murder. It might be better to go to the police."

Nappi was suggesting police involvement? I couldn't believe it. "Look, Mr. Napolitani, if you don't want to loan me the money, I certainly understand. I'm willing to put up my share of the business for collateral, although I know it's not worth that much. I'll throw in the house too. The lawyer is trying to track down who emptied the accounts. Once he finds the money, I can pay you back."

Nappi came over to me and took my hand. "My dear, anything you want, I'd be happy to grant. It's not the money, never the money. I'm worried about you. You just said it a moment ago. The last time anyone tried to pay the ransom, he got killed."

"I know, but I'm not the one at risk. The girl is, and maybe Boris and Sophia."

"It appears danger is cutting a wide swath. First, your uncle's death. Then the ransom money disappears, you are run off the road and threatened, the Hardys search your uncle's condo, and you and your Indian friend spend time in the swamps."

"But most of that was the Hardys' doing. Frida's searching for them now."

Nappi chuckled. "I hardly think they burned their own business, especially because it was doing so well."

"It was?"

He nodded and appeared to want to say more about the Hardys, but then he stopped and changed the subject. "You're making light of murder, theft, and kidnapping. Those weren't the Hardys' doing. They were the work of a person or people not yet identified, but probably more dangerous than two good old boys running an airboat operation." When he said "airboat operation," his tone of voice indicated he thought the Hardys had something going other than a simple "buy some veggies and fruit and take a ride" business.

"What do you know about them that you're not telling me?" I asked.

"It's not important now. Once we've taken care of this kidnapping thing, we'll talk further."

"Fine. I'm determined to carry out what my uncle started. You of all people should understand family obligations."

"The money is yours, dear Eve. Now, how about dinner? I like that Burnt Biscuit place. I'm getting quite addicted to ribs."

ALEX WAS IN town and not about to let me get away without some time together. I'd promised to have dinner with him, but didn't feel I could say no to Nappi. After all, the guy had just floated me a loan with no collateral required and no papers signed. When I told him about my previous engagement, he did the gentlemanly thing and tried to bow out, but I said no, insisting that Alex would be thrilled to see him. That was a lie, and Nappi knew it, but having a great sense of humor, he couldn't resist tagging along to see how Alex would handle the threesome.

Alex handled it as I had expected—with a grumpy smile and some mutterings about always having to share me with "my men." He wasn't far from right. When we arrived at the Biscuit, Jay Cassidy, his right hand man, Antoine, and several other cowboys from Jay's ranch came over to say hi to the three of us. Nappi told them to pull up a chair, which they all did. Alex rolled his eyes and ordered a Scotch, neat, double, followed by another one a few minutes later.

"Careful, sweetie. Remember what happened the last time you got drunk in this bar?"

"I ended up in your bed, didn't I?"

"Yes, but you were alone and quite hung over. Unless you want a repeat of that sad experience, you'd better hold onto sober for the evening."

"Does that mean …?"

"I'm not promising anything. I'm just saying I don't share my bed with boozers."

We shoved two tables together, ordered ribs, and soon I was dancing up a storm with all the guys including, to my surprise, Nappi, who preferred the slow tunes.

It was Karaoke night, so in case the participants sang like screaming tomcats, we'd chosen a table in the dining room, right outside the bar area where the singing occurred. As I was picking my last rib clean of sauce and meat, I heard the announcer say "And now, our own singing Miccosukee, Sammy Egret."

I jumped out of my seat and ran into the bar. Sure enough, there stood Sammy, crooning one of my favorite country tunes. His dark hair was slicked back under a cowboy hat with a silver band and he wore tight black jeans and a knitted, long-sleeved shirt that hugged his biceps. Like all the ballads, this one was about lying, crying, and dying. Sammy did it well. And looked so good doing it.

Antoine, an accomplished country artist in his own right, stood beside me. "He's great, isn't he?"

"Yep. And he's also good at swamp survival."

"So I heard."

I looked at him in surprise. "You did?"

"It's all over town how you and he spent the night in the swamps together. I thought Alex was the one."

"I thought I was too." Alex stood beside me, and it was obvious he had heard what Antoine said.

I could almost feel the angry fire coming off him.

"Don't you get all furious with me. You knew Sammy and I were left in the swamp together and that he took care of me, probably saved my life. Back off the jealously act, dearie."

For a moment I thought he was going to walk off, but the anger faded, replaced by a smile. "Eve, you are one sassy gal. You always tell it like it is."

Sure I did, except for leaving out one detail about that night in the swamp—that fluttery feeling in my stomach when Sammy looked at me. And I certainly wasn't going to divulge my hunch that Sammy felt pretty fluttery, too.

CHAPTER 11

―

ALEX DROVE ME home, and I invited him to spend the night. We flung open the French doors that led from my bedroom onto the back deck. I loved to sit here at night, listening to the coyotes call when the train came through. We slipped into the chairs and held hands. The moon was brilliant, making sharp the shadows of the palms and live oaks in the far field.

"Care for a nightcap? I've got Courvoisier," I said.

"I think all I need tonight is an evening with you. Alone." Alex got up from his chair and stood in front of me, holding out his hands. "Let's leave the doors open and let the night air into the bedroom." He grabbed both my hands, and pulling me up into his embrace, he pressed his lips against mine. Lovely. The man could kiss, yes he could.

We parted and headed toward the bed. I lay back on the pillows and patted the space next to me. "It's been so long since we had time together. I'm sorry for all the interruptions."

"Me too. It's not only you and your, er, unusual life. It's also my job. I hate being out of the area for so long." He rolled toward me and began another kiss, this one more passionate than the first. I was crazy about this guy. That's why I wish I hadn't fallen asleep before it ended, but damn, I was tired. Camping in the swamp does that to a gal.

COFFEE AWAITED ME when I awoke. There was a note from Alex beside the pot: "Don't beat yourself up about last night. I know you were exhausted. I didn't even mind your snoring."

I took a sip of java and peeked at my watch. I had arranged to meet Nappi at my bank at ten this morning. It was almost that now. I grabbed a tee shirt and jeans out of my bureau and then spent some time scrambling around on the floor of my closet, looking for another pair of boots to wear. Another run-in with my furry slippers, which I flung over my shoulder and onto the bedroom floor. More time on my hands and knees searching in the dark, but no boots. I really needed to replace that burned out bulb. I grabbed a pair of sandals with open backs and three inch heels in coral leather. Damn. I looked at my tee and realized the fuchsia color did not go with the shoes. Should I check the closet floor once more or change the shirt? I changed the shirt to one in turquoise. I looked a little like a poster for the Florida Department of Tourism, but what the heck.

Someone knocked on the front door.

"Just a minute." I gelled my hair, swiped mascara over my lashes, and looked in the mirror. The mascara was only one shade blacker than the dark circles under my eyes.

"Where have you been?" Sophia said.

"In the swamps, getting killed."

She looked puzzled for a moment, but then recovered enough to push me back into the house and slam the door behind us.

"I need the money. Now. We're being threatened."

"There have been some complications. There's no money in Winston's accounts."

"What? Where is it then?"

"I don't know."

"You don't want to give it to us. You don't care about my sister. Winston cared, but you don't." She turned to go.

"Wait. I want to talk to you." I tried to grab her arm and explain, but Sophia interrupted.

"There's no waiting. No waiting at all. We are dead people. My sister is dead. And you want me to wait." She stalked to the door, and before leaving, she turned and fixed me with her cold eyes. "I will get you for this, Eve. I will."

She slammed the door.

Her threat sent shudders through my body and almost toppled me from my fancy footwear. I tried to run after her, but she was already in the car. She gave me one last hard look then gripped the wheel and squealed off.

Oh crap. Now what could I do? I'd just have to meet Nappi, get the money and drop it off in West Palm. Maybe Nappi was right. Maybe I should forget about going through with paying the ransom. Could I trust Sophia? She sure did not want to listen to anything I had to say. And where had all my uncle's money gone? That was a question I'd have to pursue with the lawyer and perhaps a good private detective. I was a lucky girl. I knew a great PI.

I was still standing on the porch watching Sophia's car in the distance when Frida pulled up. Now what? I'd have to hustle her out of here if I wanted to be on time for my date with Nappi.

She got out of the police cruiser with all the enthusiasm of someone on her way to get a root canal.

"I was just leaving. What's up?"

"You're not going to be happy with me, but I thought I owed it to you to tell you."

Oh, oh. I hated it when people said they needed to tell me something. That usually meant bad news.

"I just arrested your friend, Nappi Napolitani, at the bank."

"Was he robbing it?"

She gave me a look of disgust. "I'm doing you a favor here

and you have to get smart with me?"

"Sorry. Let me do this again. Why in the world would you arrest Mr. Napolitani?" I wanted to remain calm, but my voice rose to a high-pitched squeal, a sound of distress Frida couldn't help but detect, being a detective and all.

"Calm down. Let me explain."

"I'm calm, but you? You are out of your mind."

"He's connected to the mob."

"I know that, but so what? You have to have a reason to arrest him, more than just his family connections."

"I arrested him for murder. Your uncle's murder. With the placement of the bullet and all, it sure looked like a mob hit and we're pretty certain Nappi took the contract."

Did he? Was Nappi involved in the hit on Winston? Not impossible, but improbable.

"What are you thinking, Eve? I can tell you've got something on your mind. I can almost smell the smoke from the gears grinding."

"When can I visit him?"

"He'll be arraigned tomorrow. I assume his lawyer will get him out soon after. Look, I've got to run. Detective Tooney and I are letting him sweat a bit; then we'll question him. Unless he lawyers up. I told Tooney I'd go out for pastries before we started."

"I don't think Nappi likes pastries much. He's more of a bagels man, I'd guess."

"The pastries aren't for him. They're for us." Frida shook her head, got back into her car and drove off.

I knew Nappi could take care of himself. I was certain he'd been "sweated" many times and in places more sophisticated in police interrogation than our little jail. But I was in a real pickle. I needed to get the money to Sophia, but someone had taken all of the inheritance Winston left me. Who? I shoved that concern to the back of my thoughts. I couldn't deliver the money to Sophia and Boris, not Winston's money, not money from Nappi. I knew Nappi was good for the loan, but right now, he was tied up with two pastry wielding detectives. Maybe Sabal Bay was small potatoes in the police department, but until he got out on bail—*if* he got out on bail—I was empty handed. All Sophia had to do was to make the Russians believe her. All I had to do was make her believe me.

I called Winston's condo and there was no answer. I really didn't expect one, because Darlene said she had moved out of it and was sharing digs with Sophia and Boris. I had no number for them. Perhaps Winston's lawyer did. He was in court when I called, but his secretary said she'd check my uncle's files.

"There's no phone number listed for them, or for Darlene. But I do have a street address in West Palm."

I jotted it down and tapped my fingernail on my phone case. God, I needed a manicure. And a pedicure. And new boots. And half a million dollars. And a shoulder to cry on. I called Alex and got voicemail. Sammy and his grandfather didn't answer either their home phone or the one at the airboat business, and neither place had an answering machine. I tried Madeleine, followed by Grandy, then Jay and Antoine. I ran out of names. I considered calling Jerry but thought better of it. I rescued Jerry, not the other way around. All my contacts seemed to have something better to do than listen to my troubles. I again scrolled through my phone contacts and considered calling Lord and Taylor's. *Really, Eve?*

I grabbed my purse. Off to West Palm to track down the kids and Darlene. If Sophia had been angry with me this morning, she'd pop a rivet when she heard how my loan fell through.

THE ADDRESS WAS east of City Place, somewhere off Okeechobee Boulevard. When I located it I was surprised. It was a bit seedy, a two story condominium built in the early seventies and in need of renovation. Well, I never did ask Darlene and Sophia and Boris what they did for work or even if they worked. Winston seemed to be crazy about Darlene when they were at my place. And if he was willing to put up half a million dollars to rescue the sister of Sophia and Boris, he must have also felt something for them. None of this made sense.

I pulled over to the curb and punched the lawyer's number into my phone. This time I caught him on his way back from court but with a client sitting in his office.

"This will only take a minute. I want to know who owns Winston's condo now."

"Winston didn't own the condo. He rented it."

"Any leads on those accounts?"

"I'm working on it," he said.

After thanking him, I ended the call. So it wasn't because she couldn't handle the sad memories evoked by being in the condo. Darlene had probably moved her things out of there because she didn't have the money to pay the rent. Hmm. What else had she lied about? I mentally chided myself for my suspicions about Darlene. Maybe she was just too embarrassed about her financial situation to tell the truth about living off the kids.

The plantings around the aging buildings were mature and lent a softening effect to the drabness of the stucco gray walls. I pulled into a slot marked for visitors and followed a broken concrete path to the back of Building #1 to the door marked 1G. I knocked and waited, then knocked again. The third time I banged on the door, I heard a voice from inside. "All right, all right. I'm coming. Don't get your Spanks twisted."

Someone released the safety latch and opened the door. It was Darlene, clad in a ratty flowered bathrobe, a towel around her head. Red dye dripped from beneath the towel and ran down her face. Without her makeup she looked ten years older, not at all like the glamorous, mature beauty I had grown to know and dislike.

"You have the money? C'mon in. I was just doing my hair. Have a seat. I'll be back in a jiffy. Got to rinse this out." She fled toward the back of the condo. She seemed happy to see me.

I looked around the room. This place was sad. It wasn't dirty or messy, but it was certainly not what Darlene was used to with Winston. The décor was in keeping with Florida—coral and turquoise, white rattan furniture—but the pieces were worn, one sofa arm split along the upholstery seam. It looked as if the place contained the furniture selected when it was built fifty years ago. The laminate countertop on the pass-through to the kitchen was chipped in several places.

"It ain't The Ritz, is it?" Darlene had reentered the room, using the towel to dry her bright red hair. She had applied coral lipstick and a swipe of mascara when she was in the bathroom.

"No." I felt guilty. Darlene had been Winston's partner for over a year, and he had married Boris and Sophia's mother, but he left the three of them almost nothing. Yet he was willing to pay the ransom. What did he mean when he talked to me about family coming first? I thought he meant his stepchildren and Darlene. Did he remove the money from his accounts? What had he been thinking?

Darlene gestured to the couch. "Have a seat." She fell into a matching chair and sighed.

"I don't understand all of this." I gestured with my hand to take in the room and its contents.

"I don't either, honey."

"Why would Winston not leave you and the kids his estate?"

She shrugged. "I understand from Sophia that you were going to come through with the money and then you backed out. I guess if I were in your shoes I might do the same. I mean, you don't know their sister. Or them, for that matter. And that's a lot of money."

"Sophia did not let me explain what happened. All of Winston's accounts have been emptied. There's nothing left."

I don't know how I expected her to react, but her fit of laughter took me by surprise.

"That's rich, it is. So you've got nothing to give us." She was laughing so hard that tears streamed down her face. She wiped it with the end of her towel.

"I don't have Winston's money, but I have other money."

"You? And just where would you get ready cash? You've got that little consignment shop and your house. You get some kind of divorce settlement from your ex-husband?"

Now it was my turn to laugh. "You've got to be kidding. The divorce settlement left both of us nothing." I decided not to share with her that I got a house through Nappi and Jerry got a job with him.

"So?" She leaned back into the chair and crossed her arms over her chest.

"So I've got a source, but I need a few days to get the cash together. Where are Sophia and Boris? Can they figure out a way to put off the Russians for a few more days?"

Darlene stared at me squinty-eyed, as if trying to peer into my truth center to see if I was putting one over on her. I guess she decided I was honorable.

"I'll let them know you were here and what you said. Sophia's pretty hot over this. I think she went off for a while to think things through. She's unpredictable sometimes."

"Do you have a number here? I can call when everything is arranged and we can meet."

Darlene shook her head. "She's got a cellphone, but I don't know the number. I had to discontinue my service. Too expensive. You know, when we rescue that little gal I'm going to get out of here. All this sun is too much for a redhead's delicate skin. I'm going back up north. I got friends there who'll be glad to help me out."

"You certainly should be commended for your support of Sophia and Boris. And they of you, letting you stay with them and all."

She smiled. "It's what Winston would have wanted."

"When do you expect Sophia back? Is Boris with her?"

"I think she may be working some kind of deal to get the

money from other sources, since she indicated she couldn't count on you."

I wondered what her other sources might be, but since Darlene had avoided answering my questions about the siblings' whereabouts and when they would return, I surmised her earlier positive assessment of me was only temporary.

"Or she may be off diving," Darlene added.

Now that answer took me by surprise. "What do you mean 'diving'?"

She tucked her legs under her and leaned back into the couch. "When she gets stressed out, she goes diving."

"But her sister's life is in danger. Don't you think that's kind of odd?"

"Sophia is Russian. She does all kinds of odd things. I don't pretend to understand her, but she and Boris are very athletic people. They jog every morning, work out in a nearby fitness center, and they dive. I think she also told me they've done Ironman Triathlons in places like Hawaii."

"Do they have jobs? Where do they get the money for all this? Renting scuba gear. Not to mention paying for airline tickets and hotels."

"Aren't you the nosey one? Why all the questions?"

"I intend to give them a lot of money, as soon as I contact my, er, supplier. I am just trying to figure this all out. Sophia is a mystery to me, as is this kidnapping. She's—"

"Abrupt? Unpleasant? Sharp? Yeah, I know. That's why I gave up asking them questions. Besides, if I get too pushy, I'll lose the roof over my head." She rolled her eyes ceiling-ward. "Such as it is."

I gave up trying to pry information out of Darlene about the siblings. What she knew about them, she seemed unwilling to share with me, but I had the feeling she didn't know very much. Her relationship with them seemed unusual, inexplicable, opaque. The whole situation seemed a bit fishy to me.

It was early afternoon when I returned from the coast. I assessed what the trip had netted me: aside from money for gas, not much.

I was fortunate to have Madeleine as a partner. I knew I hadn't been holding up my half of the business. When we set up our shop, we decided not to hire clerks. We'd cover the hours ourselves. In the last week, Madeleine had been responsible for opening the store and holding down the fort while I was wandering around in the swamps. Good old Madeleine. I'd stop by the store and tell her to take the rest of the day off.

When I pulled into the parking lot in front of our shop, I noticed the lights were not on inside, and the sign in the window read "closed." What was going on? There was an envelope taped to the door with my name on it. Oh no. Maybe there was an emergency in her family. But then why wouldn't she call me on my cell?

I unlocked the store, entered and ripped open the envelope. The note inside was worse than anything I could have imagined.

CHAPTER 12

———

THE NOTE READ: "Missing something? Missing someone? We've got her. To get her back in one piece, we will need money from you. We'll call to make arrangements. Please don't make any trouble for us, like contacting the authorities."

Despite its cavalier tone, the note was deadly serious. So was this what Sophia meant by the *other* sources she mentioned to Darlene? I slipped the note back in the envelope with my pointer and middle finger. There might be fingerprints on it that Frida could use, but for now, I had no intention of contacting the police. I called Madeleine's cell, then her home phone. Both went to voicemail.

If this was Sophia and Boris, they would not get away with it. I'd track her down and then I'd … I had a plan, but I wasn't going to be foolish enough to confront them by myself. I needed backup, serious muscular help for what I had in mind. And I needed it now. With Nappi in jail and Alex off on a case in the Panhandle, I had no choice but to jump in my car and head for my swamping partner, Sammy.

He was heading back up the path to his chickee with a load of tourists following him. Others milled around the chickee.

With the Hardy brothers out of business, Sammy's trade was as brisk as that tea. I was happy for him, but right now I was desperate. I pulled him aside.

"I hate to do this to you, but I need a favor. A really big one." I explained about the loss of my uncle's money, Sophia's threat and the note, then told him my most excellent plan.

"Don't you think you should step back and reconsider? The cops are pretty good at handling this kind of thing."

"Sophia is crazy right now. I'm not letting the police negotiate the release of my best friend."

"But you're better at dealing with her, right?"

"Look, I can get the money needed to rescue Sophia and Boris' sister. I understand she's a little stressed out right now with her sister in Russian mob hands."

"I thought you said she was crazy, not merely under a strain."

"She is, but it's understandable, given her circumstances."

"So this woman, maybe crazed, maybe just having a bad day, is doing the same thing to you that is being done to her, and you think that's reasonable?"

"Yes."

Sammy thought for a minute. "Why me?"

"Because you're a big guy."

"You're expecting trouble, physical confrontation."

"Maybe."

Sammy gestured to the people still milling around the chickee. "Look, I've got business here for the first time in years, well, since the Hardy's came to town. I need the money."

"I do too. Who knows how much she'll ask, but she needs half a million to rescue her sister so I expect it to be that and maybe more for aggravation."

I leaned forward and touched Sammy's chest with my hand, looked up into his face and said. "Please." I fluttered my eyelids at him.

Despicable behavior on my part, I knew, leading him to believe there was more to my reliance on him than just accompanying me on a crazy caper, but my friend's life was at stake. I'd do anything to save her, even lie to a great looking guy who probably was responsible for saving my life.

He placed his two hands on my shoulders and looked me in the eye. "Okay. I guess I can get Grandfather and my cousin to run the show here. Give me a minute to arrange things."

He informed his customers there would be a short delay before the next ride, then turned and ran up the path to the house. In less than five minutes he was back with Grandfather Egret and another Indian, younger than Sammy but similar in build and features. He introduced me to Willy Turtle. We shook hands.

Grandfather gave me a warm embrace, whispering in my ear a warning I knew I should heed. "Slow down and let your anger go before you take on this woman and her brother."

I knew he was right, but I also knew my anger was what was propelling me into action, and I didn't want to lose time while Madeleine suffered who knows what at her captors' hands.

I still didn't have my damaged Mustang back and was driving a small compact rental that wheezed when I pushed it over seventy. And I intended to push it today. Sammy slid into the passenger's seat, and I took the wheel, spinning my tires as we left the parking area.

"I brought this just in case." Sammy held up a huge machete, which in my eagerness to get going, I hadn't noticed when he got into the car.

"Whoa."

"And of course, this." He pulled a Bowie knife out of a scabbard. The blade shone gleaming silver in the afternoon sunlight.

Double whoa.

"So she likes to dive? But what makes you think she went to Key Largo? Wouldn't she hole up somewhere with Madeleine until she contacted you?"

"Darlene says she likes to dive to release tension. She's

stressed right now. A prisoner can only add to that. I'll bet she needs something to bring her down, the way I fancy a Cosmo after a bad day at the shop."

"Cold."

"Shaken with ice."

Sammy glanced at me. "What?"

"The drink."

"No, I meant the woman must have ice water running through her veins to be diving while her sister's being held captive and she herself is holding another woman for ransom."

"Not ice water. More like ice cold vodka."

"I don't see how you're going to find her. There must be over twenty dive boats there. Then there's the possibility she'd rent a private boat."

"I'll have help on this one. I called Grandy. She and Max know everyone on the water down there. They'll call around with the description. If Sophia and Boris are on a dive boat this afternoon, I'll be there to greet them when they get off." I pushed on the accelerator and the little car gave a gasp, balked, then jumped forward.

SLOWING DOWN TO 55mph on the strip connecting the mainland with Key Largo made me grind my teeth in frustration. I tailgated the car ahead of me until I got to the first passing lane, then flew by at around seventy. So did the cars following me.

"Why do they post speed limits if no one obeys them?" Sammy gripped the door rest on his side so hard his knuckles were white. I thought it might crumble in his hand, and I'd be paying damages at the end of my rental contract. I didn't care. I'd pay for the whole damn car to be replaced if I could just see Madeleine trip or stumble her way back to us.

The next passing lane came up and the car behind me and I jockeyed for position. I won.

Worse yet, the speed limit when we entered Kay Largo was

45, and I knew the local cops watched for out-of-area licenses to give visitors a "welcome to the Keys here's your speeding ticket" greeting. I nosed in behind a truck going over 50, hoping the cops would choose him and ignore me. We made it to the marina, and I squealed into the parking area and chose a site a few cars down from Grandy and Max's dockage. Grandy met us at the dock.

"She and her brother are on the Sea Raiders dive boat, due back in here in a few minutes." Grandy pointed toward an empty slip.

I heard the afternoon horn of the dive boat from Penny Camp State Park as she entered the turn marked "Dangerous Curve," right before the entrance to the state dock. I checked my watch. I must have set some kind of record for getting from my place to Key Largo. And no ticket. Another dive boat was traversing the waterway toward us. As she turned to enter her slip, I read the name on the side.

"Okay. She's here." I ran down the dock with Sammy close behind me. The passengers from the afternoon dive began to leave the boat. It was a small operation, taking no more than ten people aboard for a trip. Sophia and Boris weren't among the divers leaving.

I rushed past the divers and grabbed the crew member tying the lines. "I need to talk with the captain. It's an emergency."

He pointed toward the stern of the boat. I jumped on board, ran over to him, and breathless, described the two siblings. "I was told they were on this trip, but they never debarked. Where are they?"

He laughed. "Now there was a pair of kooks. They arranged for this afternoon's dive trip, but made an odd request. We have a sister boat that goes out an hour later than we do. They arranged to go out with us, but come back on the other boat so they could dive longer. They seemed to know a lot about diving. I thought what the heck and charged them double. The other boat was diving a mile away from us, and I told them I couldn't ferry them over, but they insisted they wanted to swim anyway. You can be sure I had them sign some waiver papers. I don't need to be sued. I watched them as they swam for the other boat. They seemed to be having no problems. Hold it a minute, would you? I'm getting a message on my radio."

The captain listened to the message, shaking his head all the while. He finally signed off and came back to me. "I was right when I called them kooks. They wouldn't get back on board for the return trip. The boat is looking for them right now, but they went back down for a final dive, and now there's no sign of them. We've called the authorities."

I grabbed him by his shirt. "We've got to find them. They're holding my friend for ransom. If they drown, we'll never find her."

The captain gave me a look that suggested I was as kooky as they were.

Sammy pulled me off the captain, apologized, then took me back to Grandy and Max's boat.

"I guess you could use that Cosmo right now." Sammy had his arm around me as we sat together on the banquet bench in the galley.

"What?"

"To calm you, you know. Because you're stressed."

"Oh she's more than stressed. She needs serious medication to get through this one." Grandy rummaged around below the sink and pulled out a bottle of Scotch. She poured us all generous shots. Sammy, whom I've never seen drink, took his and held the glass awkwardly.

I tossed my shot down, then reached for Sammy's glass and did the same with his.

"Don't you think now is the time to call in the authorities on this kidnapping?" Sammy asked.

Grandy, as if reading Sammy's mind, opened the fridge and withdrew a bottle of beer, handed it to him and nodded. He saluted her with the bottle and took a swallow.

"No, no, no. No authorities. What can they do? It's up to the Coast Guard now."

"If they can be found, the Coast Guard will find them." Max gave my shoulder a comforting pat. "We just have to wait."

Outside we could hear the sounds of late dive boats tying up and off-loading gear and passengers. As the wet, happy and exhausted divers made their way past our boat, I caught snippets of their conversations—comments about the weather, raves about what they'd seen on their dives, and their plans for the evening. All happy people, pleased to be in a warm tropical climate, enjoying what it offered. I envied them those feelings as I struggled to hang on to my reason. Anxiety for my friend threatened to overwhelm me. French, German, and Canadian accents mingled with American, but one stood out from the rest. It was Russian, and the voice belonged to Sophia. I jumped up from my seat, banging my knee on the table, and limped up the stairs, across the boat and onto the dock. She didn't see me coming. She was past the boat, so when I grabbed her arm she spun around, surprised.

"You. What are you doing here? Trying to ruin my vacation time?"

"Vacation? How can you call it vacation when you're holding Madeleine for ransom and your sister is being held hostage for money? What kind of woman are you? You're doing to me what the Russian mob is doing to you."

By now Max, Grandy, and Sammy stood by my side. Boris had gone ahead, then turned when he heard my voice and returned, taking up a fighting stance by his sister's side.

"No. It is my sister who is being held. You are some crazy woman. First you promise money, then you take it back. Now you accuse us of holding your friend. You are, how do you Americans say, you are 'certifiable.' " Boris took a step forward, and so did Sammy, dwarfing the stocky Russian by at least three inches. And one machete and Bowie knife.

"Where is she? Did you smuggle her down here? Why here?

Except you needed some recreational diving. You're a horror." I was working myself up into a stroke.

Sammy placed his hand on my arm. "Let's all just calm down. Are you saying you don't know anything about Madeleine's whereabouts?"

"Why would we? Your friend doesn't have the money, does she?" Sophia asked.

"No, of course Madeleine doesn't have the money. I have it." I bristled at the absurdity of Sophia's assumption.

"Good. It's about time. Let's go get it, and we can pay to get my sister back. The Russians are getting anxious, and they may decide to back out of the deal. If they do, it will be your fault."

"Just a minute, Sophia. I'm still not certain what's going on here. You threatened me, and then I got a kidnapping note. It has to have come from you."

Sophia and Boris exchanged looks filled with disbelief and suspicion.

"I don't understand. You say someone took your friend and they want money for her? Who would do that?" Sophia hesitated a moment. "Unless …."

I grabbed Sophia's arm. "What are you thinking? Tell me."

"Maybe the Russians decided to put pressure on you by taking your friend, huh?" Sophia looked pleased with herself for figuring that one out. And she could be right.

I was so overwhelmed by all this, I struggled to stay upright on my Jimmy Choos. I stepped back and reached out for one of the pilings to hold onto. "I never thought of that." I began to cry. Everything was so confusing, and I was no closer to finding out where Madeleine was. Max handed me one of his handkerchiefs, red and blue and about the size of a table cloth.

Sophia pulled me toward her and began walking. "Hey. No time for crying. We need to get the money."

"Are those the two?" A man's voice came from behind me. I shook off Sophia, wiped my nose and saw the captain of the dive boat accompanied by someone dressed in a Coast Guard uniform.

The captain nodded. "They're the ones."

The uniformed man strode up to Sophia and Boris. "You two will have to come with us." He gestured to other Coast Guard personnel who surrounded the pair.

"Why?" Boris resumed his pugilistic stance.

"Come now or we'll handcuff you. We have a few questions to ask you, like why you left the second dive boat and how you got back here."

"We got a ride from him." Boris pointed to a man who had just finished tying up his boat.

"We didn't like the second dive boat. Too old. It didn't look safe, so we swam toward shore, and he came along." Sophia seemed matter-of-fact about the incident.

"You can't just swim off. There are rules, you know." The Coast Guard official appeared shocked at her utter disregard for dive regulations.

"We can. We swim very well, and we could have made it here without any boat. Who says we can't swim here?" Sophia stood toe to toe with the Coast Guard officer.

"I think both of you and your ride need to come with me."

"Me? I didn't do anything but offer them transportation to shore." The man who had given them a ride appeared to be reconsidering his generosity.

"Not until we find Madeleine." I pushed between the Coast Guard men and the siblings.

"You mean someone else is lost?" The Coast Guard captain looked about to take action to retrieve whoever had been left out on the water.

"Yes. Her name is Madeleine and I'm certain these two took her or they know who did."

"She's still at sea?"

"Yes. I mean, I don't know where she is."

By the time we sorted it all out in the harbormaster's office, the sun was going down and I pined for another few fingers of Scotch. Sophia and Boris played the "I don't speak much English so I didn't understand the rules" card. The Coast Guard bought it. I let it go because I didn't want them taken away. I reneged on my contention that Madeleine was also lost. I lied and said the worry over my Russian friends being lost at sea had confused me. There was no way I was going to let the Coast Guard take Boris and Sophia into custody. I needed to talk with them.

Max, Grandy, and Sammy seemed to think Sophia and Boris were telling the truth. I was not convinced, but I'd go along with it if I could get some information out of them. It was just possible, as Sophia had said, that the Russians took Madeleine thinking they could get their money from me. What bothered me most was that I hadn't heard from the kidnappers. Their note indicated they'd be in touch, but there were no messages on my cell, which seemed the likely place for them to make contact. Could they have put another note on the shop door? Kind of a stupid way to make a ransom demand.

As we left the harbormaster's office, I again checked my cell. No voicemail, no texts. What was going on? As if my touch had somehow activated it, it rang. I was so shocked, I dropped the phone. Sammy picked it up and handed it to me.

"Hello?"

It was Madeleine.

"Okay, here's the deal. This guy says he's working for the mob and they want half a million in cash for my safe return." Her voice sounded fine, calm, almost normal.

"Are you all right?" I asked.

"I'm fine, but I think this guy wants to get rid of me."

I turned to Sammy. "She says she thinks the guy wants to kill her."

"No, I did not say that. I said I think he wants to get rid of me, as in unload me into your hands. Or someone's. He says I'm too much trouble. I don't think he's ever done this kidnapping thing before. He's not real good at it."

"What did you do to him, Madeleine?"

"Oh, so now it's my fault I got kidnapped?" Her tone was snappish.

"Of course not, but you must have done something for him to want to get rid of you."

"I sort of hit him in the eye when he tried to grab me. It was an accident. My elbow got in the way of his head somehow and …. Well, he's going to have a real shiner, I'll bet. I can't really tell because he's got a mask over his face. Then when he pushed me into the car, I stepped back on his foot. He was wearing flip flops. I'm certain I broke one of his toes. It's terribly swollen now." She paused for breath.

"There's more?"

"I bit him."

"That's it?"

"I didn't mean to bite him. I kind of turned fast and our faces made contact, his ear in my mouth, so I pulled away and took off part of his ear."

"Don't lie to me. You meant to bite him."

There were some rustling noises on the phone and another voice came on.

"Please pay up. I can't stand one more hour with this woman. Every time I get near her, something happens. To me." The man sounded distraught.

"I've got bad news for you," I said.

"No money?" he asked.

"No you'll get your money, but it will take a day or so." I thought I heard crying on the line.

"Madeleine, are you crying?"

"Not me. Just get the money, would you? And get me out of here. He keeps licking his lips and muttering to himself. I think he's thinking of biting me back. I could contract rabies."

CHAPTER 13

"So. You found your little friend. Yes?" Sophia didn't seem as happy to hear the kidnappers had made contact as I thought she might.

"Yes. And she confirmed the guy who has her is working for the mob. They want half a million to free her."

"Did your friend say anything about my sister?'

I shook my head. "Something wrong?"

"Yes. They are cutting us out of the deal. Now they are making contact with you and not me as they did before. I wondered why we had not heard from them in over twenty-four hours."

Boris poked his head right in my face, so close I could smell garlic and something else on his breath. Fish, maybe? "These guys are smart. We told them they had to wait for the money and explained you were willing to borrow it, but they figured you needed more reason to deliver the money. So they took your friend. Our sister is irrelevant now. She is lost to us."

He wrapped his arms around his sister, and the two of them clung to each other. I thought I saw Boris' eyes fill with tears, but maybe it was only the wind making them water. It was hard to tell with these two. They were so stoic. Yet I couldn't help but feel for their plight. What Boris said about the focus of the ransom was possible.

"We'll stay in touch and see how this plays out. They may still want the money for your sister. These are ruthless and greedy people. I'll bet they will make contact with you soon," I said.

"And then what can we do? How much money can you get your hands on? Not a million dollars," Boris said.

Boris was right. Nappi was generous to loan me half that, but would he be willing to go another half simply because I felt obligated to ransom Winston's stepdaughter?

Sophia continued to bury her head in Boris' shoulder, but when she pulled back, his shirt was dry, as were her eyes.

"We've got to get back to Sabal Bay right away. I have until tomorrow evening to get the money together," I said.

I punched Frida's number into my cell and was surprised when she answered.

"I thought I might hear from you. The answer is no. Your mob pal is not out of jail yet. His arraignment isn't until tomorrow morning. And no. I'm not telling you what we've got on him." She paused. "Something puzzles me about Winston. We were hoping to pick up numbers off his cell that we could trace to known mobsters like your friend Nappi, but there's nothing there. How did he do business if not with his cell? I find that odd, don't you?"

"Hey, you're the crime expert here."

"Right. I'm glad you know that so you won't be trying to do my job for me like you did the last time you were in the proximity of a murderer."

I understood what she was saying: stay out of police business.

"Something else puzzles me about this," she said.

Oh, oh. I held my breath.

"Eve, why do you care so much about someone who's likely your uncle's killer?"

Why indeed? How could I tell her he was supplying the money for a kidnapping that my uncle was to have paid the ransom for and that there were actually two kidnappings that I hadn't let her in on? Did friends keep secrets from each other? Yes, if the friend was a cop and the other friend was doing something a tad illegal. My relationships with friends sure were complicated.

I didn't answer her question, but I did ask one of my own. "Any chance I can see Nappi before the arraignment, like later tonight?" And then I told a lie. I didn't mean to, but it slipped out. "Maybe I can get something out of him you could use."

She bit. "Okay. Where are you now?"

"I'm in Key Largo visiting Grandy. But I'm leaving in a few minutes. I should be back there around nine."

"I'll leave word at the county jail that you're allowed to visit. Call me after the two of you have talked."

"Right."

"Don't forget. I don't care what he says to you. I want to hear it all," Frida said.

I crossed my fingers. "Sure. You'll hear it all."

"Before you go, Eve. Several of the women I know said your shop was closed today. Don't you and Madeleine cover for each other? Is there something going on I should know about?"

"What do you mean? Nothing's going on." I thought I sounded defensive, but I plunged ahead with my story. "Madeleine was tied up with another matter today, and I'd already arranged to see Grandy. We didn't think one day would be a problem."

"The shop must be doing well. Most businesses around here need their doors open on a regular basis."

"Ours are open. Usually. Why are you hassling me?"

"Why are you getting so upset?"

"Sorry. I've got a lot on my mind. I suppose you've heard all about Winston's estate."

"No, but … hold on a minute."

I heard her talking to someone; then she got back on the line with me. "We've got a call. Gotta run. We'll talk later. Bye. Call me at home if you want."

I heaved a sigh of relief. Our conversation kept turning in directions that left me no choice but to make up stuff. I was becoming a great little storyteller.

SOPHIA AND BORIS were as eager as I to settle the money problem, so they checked out of their motel while Sammy and I waited in my car. I mostly believed their story about having nothing to do with Madeleine's kidnapping, but a tiny bubble of doubt told me I should not let them out of my sight. They seemed as anxious as I to stay in contact. I followed them off the Keys, up the turnpike, and on to their condo.

With both parties satisfied that we knew each other's whereabouts, Sammy and I sped back home. I dropped him at his place and headed for the county jail. All the way home I kept glancing at my phone, willing it to ring with the news that the kidnapping was a fantasy and Madeleine was safe in her bed.

Nappi was being held in a large cell with several others. They were engaged in a lively conversation about gambling when I arrived.

"Sorry I can't give you more privacy." The guard at the jail was the husband of one of my best customers at the shop. His apology sounded sincere.

Nappi got up off the metal bench at the back of the cell, giving his fellow prisoners a congenial goodbye and telling them he'd be back soon. They seemed to understand what he meant and moved farther down the bench, increasing the distance between them and us.

"I see you've made friends here," I said.

"Ah, Eve, you sound upset with me."

"Do I? I don't mean to, but it has been a very long day." I filled him in on Madeleine's kidnapping and my trip to the Keys.

"Little Madeleine? We must do something."

I liked that he said "we."

"You think the Russians have given up on Sophia and Boris' sister and instead have taken your friend?"

"I don't know. Sophia awaits another call from them, but she admits it's not very likely, now that they have me on the hook. On the other hand, maybe they think they can collect on both women." I held my breath to see what Nappi would say about that.

"The money is Madeleine's lifeline, and you're responsible for throwing it to her. This is more than living up to a promise. This is your best friend who is in danger. We'll focus on that for the time being. Rescuing the Russian girl is not my priority right now."

"Time is running out. On the phone Madeleine confirmed that the guy who is holding her was hired by the mob, and they want their money by tomorrow evening."

"I'll be out of here by then, but like you, I'm concerned about arranging the money transfer and obtaining the funds so quickly. You won't mind if I ask you to do me a favor?"

"Of course not. You're doing me a big one. Name it. Anything."

"Could you call Jerry and have him work out this money thing? He can serve as my liaison."

Oh crap. Jerry again.

"Sure. Great."

Nappi laughed. "You can't fool me. I know how you feel about him, but he's reliable."

Reliable? Well, then it was a trait he recently developed, but I said nothing.

"I feel funny asking you this, but Frida won't say anything about you. Uh …."

"What evidence do they have on me?"

"Yes."

"I hope you have no doubts about my innocence. You know how much I admire you and your Grandy. You are two of my favorite people."

"Yes, but we're talking about my uncle here. He delivered money for a family, one probably a rival of yours."

"Your uncle came to me several months ago wanting to retire from the family work. It was a courageous move on his part. He heard I could be reasoned with and that I might intercede for him with his family. And then, when we found out we had you in common, well, it cemented my determination to help him out of the life. Through her connections up north, Frida found out we had been in touch. She thinks I set him up to get killed. It's all circumstantial, and she knows it, but I think her boss wants results and fast. Don't be angry with her. She's a good cop doing what the job dictates."

"Frida said something odd to me on the phone today. She said Winston's cell contained no numbers that were mob connected. She wondered how he did business."

Nappi laughed. "Oh, I can tell her how. He used a burner phone, a discard, one that's thrown away often and replaced by another. He must have tossed his shortly before he was killed."

"Did he contact you by phone?"

"We met in person to make the arrangements for his retirement."

"Too bad we can't find that burner phone. Your number wouldn't have been on there, but others would be. It might tell us something about his murder."

"That phone is long gone by now."

My shoulders slumped. The people I cared about were in trouble, and I felt helpless.

Nappi must have noticed my sense of defeat. "Don't worry. I called a lawyer in West Palm, one I've used before. I'll be out of here and cleared by the end of the week."

I gave him a hard look. "How many people will you have to bribe to accomplish that?"

He smiled. "My lawyer will see to it that I am cleared. That's his job and not your worry. Now get in touch with Jerry, go home, and crawl into bed. You look exhausted."

I knew I did. Nappi, on the other hand, looked fresh and tidy, as if he'd just stepped out of the shower. How did he manage that in jail? Practice probably helped.

As always, when I talked with Nappi I felt he was holding back something. I knew better than to ask any more questions. Much of his life was private, and it was a part I didn't want to know about. I left the jail convinced he would come through for me, yet I had to acknowledge that this was a man I trusted where others would not. I wondered if I was being foolish.

I had Jerry's cell number, so I called him on my way home. He wanted to meet me there to work out details, and I agreed. I must have been so tired I'd lost my sense of reason. Another evening of Jerry.

He waited for me on my front doorstep.

When I walked past his car, parked on the near side of my driveway, I felt the hood. It was cool.

"How long have you been hanging out here? Don't you know the neighbors might call the cops and have you arrested? And it makes me look bad to have you camped on my doorstep."

"Grandy got in touch with me and told me everything. She thought you might need my help."

If Grandy reached out to Jerry, she must have been frantic about me. He was not one of her favorite people, but she felt he still had a thing for me. She probably thought he'd do anything to help me out.

"Come on in. Let's make this short," I said.

I threw my purse on the couch, and my body followed. Jerry headed for the other end of the sofa. I stretched out the length of it and pointed him to the chair across the room. "There."

"I'll bet you're tense."

"Of course I'm tense. My best friend is being held for half a million in ransom by a mob flunky. Why wouldn't I be tense?"

He waggled his eyebrows at me. "So how about …."

"No. No drink. No comforting hugs. No massage."

He waggled them again.

"And no sex."

"Aw."

"You can leave right now."

"Bad idea. I think the two of us should stick together. I'm your money man, and you're the contact. They'll be calling you with the details for the exchange. I've got to go to West Palm tomorrow to arrange a money transfer with Nappi's bank there. You come with me, and we'll both know when the call comes through."

Jerry had a point, and I knew it. "What do you mean, exactly, by 'stick together'?"

"I stay here tonight. If they've got the house under surveillance, they'll think I'm just a friend holding your hand."

"Fine. You sleep on the couch."

"C'mon. You've got a perfectly good guest bedroom."

I conceded. I was being mean not to let him used the extra bed.

"You can use the bathroom first."

"Great. I'll hop out to my car and get my duffel."

"You packed your overnight bag? So you expected I'd agree to your staying here?"

"Sure, Eve. You're a smart gal. It was the best plan." He waggled his eyebrows at me and headed out the door.

"Stop that thing with your eyebrows. It's creepy."

That's the last thing I remember that night. When I awoke on the couch the next morning, someone had placed a blanket over me. I sat up, checked to make certain I was fully clothed, and noticed the only item missing from my body were my boots, which lay on the floor beside the couch. I smelled coffee.

"Rise and shine, morning glory. Here's your java. Take a sip and hop into the shower. Your limo leaves for West Palm in fifteen minutes." Jerry handed me a cup.

"What time is it?"

"Around eight."

"If I don't get some decent sleep in a bed following a normal day, I'm going to age a year in a week."

"Nah. You look great."

I could tell he was lying, but I took a few gulps of coffee and dragged myself to the bathroom. A shower could only help.

The water woke me up enough to make me realize that I had to do something about our consignment shop before I left for the coast. There was no one I trusted to take over the shop, unless ....

"YOU WANT TO stop by where?" Jerry's face registered shock and disbelief. He almost drove off the road.

"Sammy's airboat business. Watch where you're going. Should I drive?"

Jerry made a sound in his throat that sounded like a growl.

"What's wrong with a stop at Sammy's?"

"It's damn hard keeping up with you and all your men. You have half the cowboys in this county at your beck and call and now you're moving in on the Miccosukee tribe. I thought Alex was the one, but this Sammy guy keeps popping up lately."

"It's not Sammy I'm after today."

"No?"

"I need to talk with Grandfather Egret."

"He know something about the kidnapping?"

"He might, but what he knows he won't share, at least not yet. Not until he thinks it around some."

"You're beginning to talk funny. Like you're going native. I think you could use a visit back to Connecticut when this is all over. The fumes from the traffic in Hartford will clear your head and a brief trip to Neimen Marcus should reestablish the core of your life."

"What's my core?"

"Shopping."

I thought about Jerry's assessment. Maybe that was true of me a year or so ago, but I felt different now. I never shopped in fancy department stores anymore. I rarely went to a city or a mall. My life was here. I'd landed in an odd place for a city gal, but I realized I thought of it now as my home.

"You are so wrong about me, Jerry. Here's the drive. Pull in."

The chickee was abandoned, but I knew just where to find Sammy and his grandfather. I jumped out of the car, telling Jerry to wait, and ran down the path to their house. Sammy stood on the porch.

"Heard the car, did you?"

"No. Grandfather said about a half hour ago that he was expecting you."

I laughed. "Good. Then I won't have to twist his arm. You're back in the airboat business, and your grandfather will be learning a new trade today."

Sammy looked puzzled, but his grandfather came out onto the porch wearing a colorful shirt and jeans that looked so new I wanted to check to make certain the price tag had been pulled off. He clapped his cowboy hat on his head and smiled at me. "I'm ready."

"Wait. Where are you two off to? You're not going to put my grandfather in danger, are you?"

"Some danger, being surrounded by women shoppers. When they see a bargain, you better get out of the way or you could get trampled." I wiggled my fingers in a goodbye wave.

Grandfather headed down the path toward the parking area, a jaunty lilt to his walk.

He carried a woven bag slung over his shoulder.

"What's that?" I pointed to the bag.

"My lunch and some of my wood carvings. If we're doing what I think we are, I thought I might entertain the ladies with my skills."

"You can sell them if you like."

"No. I'll give them away."

"This will be an interesting place for you today. I'll bet you've never done anything like it before."

"No, but I'm thinking it will be a good spot to meet women."

Grandfather greeted Jerry, who still looked puzzled at my behavior, though now there was an added element of annoyance in his expression.

Grandfather introduced himself as Sammy's grandfather and shook Jerry's hand. He looked at me, then leaned over and whispered, "Hands are as soft as a girl's. Doesn't this man work?"

"You know how we white folks are. We prefer to work with our heads."

"You pay big for it too. That always puzzled me."

Grandfather got into the back seat, Jerry and I the front, and we drove off.

"What's he doing here, Eve?" Jerry asked.

"Frida pointed out to me that most folks around here open their shops on a regular schedule. We missed yesterday because someone nabbed Madeleine. To protect our business, I'm having Mr. Egret tend the store today. Right, Mr. Egret?"

He nodded. "I'm looking forward to it."

"He's an Indian, an old Indian."

"Yup, he is, and that's why I wanted him. Of all my friends here, I'll bet he's the smartest one, so I knew he could handle the shop with no problem."

We pulled up in front of the consignment shop.

"Here are the keys." I handed them to Grandfather.

"Aren't you going to go in with him and tell him what to do?" Jerry seemed both amazed and exasperated.

"He knows what to do, dummy. He's there to sell stuff."

"And meet the ladies." Grandfather waved and entered the store.

CHAPTER 14

─────

WE DIDN'T TALK much as Jerry drove down the Beeline Highway for West Palm. Jerry sat hunched over the wheel, grinding his teeth as if he had eaten something for breakfast that required extensive chewing. I leaned into the seatback and checked the side view mirror every now and then, keeping an eye on the black SUV that followed us. Maybe Jerry had become more reliable and arranged for protection.

I let my mind wander while we cruised by fields of cattle and a citrus plant north of Indiantown. I could smell the sweetness of the fruit being pasteurized. It smelled as if someone was baking lemon poppy-seed muffins, an aroma I liked, but then I didn't have to sniff it day after day.

It felt like weeks had passed since my uncle's death, yet little more than a week had gone by. In that time, my life had experienced ups and downs: the agony of his death, being run off the road and threatened, inheriting his estate, losing it, and now Madeleine's kidnapping. I also realized I didn't care anymore if this money freed the sister of Sophia and Boris. My concern was Madeleine and only Madeleine. As if thinking about my recently acquired Russian relatives set up a disturbance in the cosmos, my cell rang. I looked at the ID, hoping it was the kidnapper making contact. But no. It had to be Sophia. And why was I not surprised at her first question?

"Do you have the money yet?"

I sighed and tried to control my temper.

"I'm working on it, Sophia. We're on our way to the bank in West Palm. I'm doing my best. You'll have to forgive my terseness, but this is my friend we're talking about and I am worried. Your sister is being held hostage and my best friend who is like a sister to me is also being held hostage." There was silence on the line.

"Are you still there?" I asked.

"They haven't called, not last night or this morning." There was a small catch in her voice.

"I'm sorry. I'll be in touch." I ended the call. The cell rang again, but I ignored it.

"Good for you. She's putting far too much pressure on you," Jerry said.

"Do you use a burner phone?"

"Why would you want to know that?"

"Nappi said the family uses them to do their business."

"They do. So?"

"No one found a burner phone on my uncle."

"He got rid of it then. That's protocol."

"There's protocol in mob business? It sounds like the state department."

"There are ways we do things, yes."

"You don't think Nappi had anything to do with my uncle's death, do you? I mean, this money he's giving me, it's not out of guilt?"

Jerry slowed for the PGA Boulevard stoplight and looked over at me.

"You're so suspicious. You know that was what ended our marriage, don't you?"

"What? No, you dunce. What ended our marriage was your

philandering and getting Nappi's daughter pregnant."

"But she wasn't pregnant."

"That's not the point. You thought she was. So did Nappi, so did I. Only she knew the truth. If you thought she was, then you were messing around while we were still married." I stopped talking. It was no use explaining this to Jerry. Sometimes his version of logic left me breathless. "Leave it. You'll never understand."

He stepped on the gas, and we drove in silence until we got to the Turnpike, took it south, and exited at Okeechobee Boulevard. We drove several miles to City Place, parked the car in the parking area, and walked to the bank, arriving just as the doors were opened. Jerry headed right to the Vice President's office. We were expected, and after we'd signed numerous documents, the VP handed Jerry a briefcase that held the money.

Jerry hefted the heavy case. "It's not marked, is it?"

"What do you think?" The VP looked at Jerry as if he thought he was the class dunce.

As we walked through the bank, I grabbed Jerry's arm and stopped him on the sidewalk. "Is it marked? They'd know, wouldn't they? That's not smart."

"I'm not having this conversation with you in the middle of the street, holding half a million bucks."

"You're right. Where's the security?"

"What security?"

"You know. The guys who were following us all the way from Sabal Bay. In the black SUV."

He looked confused.

"Jerry? You did arrange for security, didn't you?"

"Sure." He patted his pocket.

"You're packing. You. You've got a gun. Give me that. You'll hurt yourself." I grabbed for his pocket.

He swatted away my hand, and we continued into the parking complex to the car. Just as Jerry unlocked the doors, two individuals dressed all in black like ninjas confronted us. Their faces were covered, making it impossible to see any distinguishing feature other than the cold gray of their eyes.

Without a word, the shorter one performed a karate chop on Jerry's hand, forcing him to drop the briefcase. The taller of the two patted down Jerry, extracted the pistol from his pocket and hit him across the face with it. Jerry slammed into the car and slid down the passenger's side onto the cement. I rushed at the one holding the briefcase, grabbing for the money, but the other ninja stepped between us. I grabbed his arm as he raised it to hit me and held on. He stepped back and my hand slid down his arm. I fumbled with his fingers, thinking I could at least break his thumb before he turned the gun on me. My hand slipped free, and I came away with his black glove. As suddenly as they had appeared, the two ran down a line of parked cars. I watched them toss the gun away before they disappeared at the far end of the garage. Soon I heard an engine start and the squeal of tires as a black SUV careened down the parking ramp. I couldn't get the license number or see the occupants because the windows were so dark.

Oh crap. I was cursed. I couldn't hang onto an inheritance, and now I couldn't hang onto a loan.

My cell rang. Sophia again. "Do you have …?"

"Yes. I'll get back to you later."

"Well, you don't have to yell." This time I could hear traffic noises in the background.

"What's that noise? Are you in the car?"

"No we're sitting out in front of the apartment having coffee. I thought you would keep in closer touch."

"This is not a good time." I ended the call.

Right now I had to call for help and then concoct a story about the money that would make sense to the cops. As I'd acknowledged to myself earlier, I was becoming a great storyteller. Little did I know it was a skill I'd need over and over again.

When the police and an ambulance arrived to cart Jerry off to the hospital, I was weaving my tale for the police. "It was money from my uncle's estate. He was recently, uh, I mean he recently died and left me some funds. We just retrieved them from the Palmetto First State National Bank. You can ask the VP there."

When the cops asked me how much was in the briefcase and I gave the amount, the two officers exchanged glances. I crossed my fingers that the bank's VP would cover my story.

"Half a million bucks?" The older officer jotted something in his notebook.

"Yup."

"Your uncle must have been a rich guy. What kind of work did he do?"

"He was a mediator of sorts. He did business with large families and connected them with other big businesses."

I was sweating so hard that, had it not been waterproof, my mascara would be running down my cheeks. I worried my antiperspirant was failing, and I would ruin my Ralph Lauren shirt—thirty bucks at that consignment shop in Port St. Lucie. I'd never be able to find one like it at that price. I kept spinning my tale, however, all the while wanting to scream that my friend was going to die at the hands of some Russian thugs.

Finally the police let me go, making me promise I would come down to the station and sign a statement after I visited Jerry in the hospital.

I sped off to the emergency room and told the nurse there that I was Jerry's wife. She allowed me to enter the cubicle where they were treating him.

"He's suffered a concussion and contusions to his head. He should stay here for observation." The doctor sounded upbeat about his recovery.

"Am I dying?" Jerry asked.

I leaned over and patted his cheek. "No, you'll be fine, but you've got to stay here overnight."

"Who will take care of you, Evie?"

I let the "Evie" go for once and gave his cheek a pinch. "I'll take care of me for now, and Nappi will be out of jail today."

I left the hospital with a promise to Jerry I'd be in touch. I had no intention of retrieving him tomorrow. I'd let one of Nappi's men do that. Right now Jerry's expertise as my bodyguard had proved to be no better than that of any amateur. I wondered if his gun was loaded or if he had a carry permit. Well, that was Jerry's problem. I was sure the police would be in contact with him tonight.

At the police station I again told my fancy tale of being an heiress picking up her loot, signed the statement about the robbery and then sped off toward Sabal Bay in Jerry's rental. He wouldn't be needing it today.

I SAT IN the car, waiting for Nappi and his lawyer to emerge from the arraignment. When they exited the building, I got out and waved. Nappi took one look at me and knew something was wrong.

"I lost your money."

He signaled to his lawyer to give us some privacy, and the man moved off to talk with several others, big guys in black suits who obviously didn't belong here. I did note that the lawyer wore cowboy boots with his expensive suit. Nice touch. Nappi certainly knew how to pick 'em.

I worried Nappi would give me one of his mobster looks and offer me to the goons speaking with the lawyer. I should have known better.

"Where did you lose it?"

"Some ninja types took it from us in the parking garage near the bank. They hit Jerry, and he's in the hospital. The money's gone."

"Do you know who took it?"

"It could have been anybody. It was pretty obvious that there was something important in the briefcase. Anyone watching us leave the bank could figure that one out, but given their outfits I think they were waiting for us." People in Florida can be pretty flamboyant in their dress, but even here, no one would run around town dressed like something out of a bad dojan.

"What about the security detail with you?"

"You might want to rethink your use of Jerry as your go-to guy, the same way I rethought him as my husband."

Nappi sighed and looked toward the fields of grass and palms trees in the distance. "No security. The boy never learns."

"Nope, but he had a gun. They hit him with it."

"I need a drink. Do you mind? Is the Biscuit open this early?"

"It's almost three, but you'll get better service and better booze for a lower price at my place."

I drove him in Jerry's rental, tailed by two SUVs, which Nappi assured me were filled with his guys.

OVER TWO SCOTCHES, neat, I let Nappi know I hadn't heard from the kidnappers yet.

"I hope they're not doing to me what they did to Sophia and Boris. Silence. That feels worse than hearing their demands. At least I'll know she's alive."

"These kidnappers are strange. Not the way I'd do it at all."

"They're Russian. Maybe they do things differently there. They said they'd be in touch, and we'd do the exchange sometime this evening. But we've got no money."

Nappi leaned back into the couch and twisted his diamond pinky ring on his finger. "They don't know that, do they?"

"We can't show up with no money."

"No, but perhaps we can delay them. I can get the money by tomorrow."

"You'd do that? You'd give me another half million?"

"Well, I know you didn't take my money. You're too honest and too concerned about Madeleine. As for Jerry, he's not clever enough to work out a robbery, especially if it meant he'd have to get hurt. And he'd never intentionally cross me. Never."

"You're going to get your money back, aren't you?"

"I am. I'm getting every red cent of it back. Even the money Winston dropped. Someone took the ransom money and someone took the drop money he was carrying for the mob. Neither of his duffel bags reached their intended parties. I don't know if the Russians are behind all of that, but I intend to find out. I owe him. I owe you."

"You feel responsible for Winston's murder, don't you?"

Nappi set his glass on the coffee table and leaned forward. "I thought I had it all worked out. Winston would do this last drop for the mob, and they would let him go. His boss gave me his word. Now, the boss won't talk to me. Thinks I took the money. I am insulted. This is a slur on my good name."

"The mob didn't kill him, did they?"

"I don't know who did it, but if I find out it was the family who employed Winston or another family, I will have my revenge." He picked his glass off the table, took a sip, and then slammed it back down with such fury I thought the glass would shatter. "This cannot go unpunished. Promises were made. Winston should have been safe. My family reputation is at stake here."

In the ensuing silence Nappi and I looked at each other, and I knew I had seen the mob boss persona for the first time. It was not the face of my friend. I wanted all this to be over, and I never wanted to see that face again. I wanted the Nappi I trusted and liked back.

My cell rang, and I jumped and grabbed for it. It was Madeleine's kidnapper.

"Okay, lady, here's how it's gonna go down."

"Wait a minute. Something's come up. We're missing some of the money. We can get it tomorrow morning, but I need more time."

"No way. Now. How much you got?"

"Uh, we're missing about a hundred grand." One of my tiny lies again.

"Well, you just find it. You've got an hour, then we meet at the closed restaurant at Deer Mound Lock. You got small bills, right?"

"Fifties, hundreds, a few thousands—"

"Come alone. No cops. I want to get this filly off my hands as soon as possible."

"Wait. I want to talk to her."

There was the sound of raised voices, then Madeleine came on the line.

"Hi, Eve. He's been feeding me nothing but peanut butter sandwiches. Could you bring my toothbrush when you come?"

"He hasn't done anything to you, has he?"

"Nope. Aside from keeping me tied up, he leaves me alone in some kind of room. I can smell the swamps nearby. I think he's afraid I'll bite him again if he gets too close."

"I'll be there soon. Just hang on."

Again, it sounded like Madeleine and her captor were arguing.

"Why should *she* hang on? It's me who's been suffering here. I think three of my toes are broken and my ear's infected. Five o'clock. Don't be late. I can't wait." I heard a chuckle and then a disconnect.

"I think Madeleine is driving him insane," I said.

"I can't believe this is the work of the Russian mob. It sounds more like the guys from the Feed and Seed Store. These aren't professionals."

Nappi would know a professional from a rube.

"So who are they?"

"I think someone hired this guy. He's obviously a local, and he probably won't be able to tell us much about the person who's giving the orders, but I'd like to question him anyway. Before he takes the money back to his bosses and they kill him."

"And the money?"

Instead of answering, Nappi pulled out his cell and made a

call. Several minutes later I heard a knock at the door. The man who stood there was the size of a Mountain Gorilla but better dressed.

Nappi gestured him into the house. "Ah, Sid. What did you get?"

"Between the six of us, we got seventy five hundred dollars. Sorry boss, but we went out to dinner last night, then to the gambling casino."

"Run to the bank and use your debit cards. See how much you can add to this. We just need enough layers of money to dazzle a country boy."

By the time Sid returned and Nappi and I had made our own run to the automatic tellers, we had collected almost twenty-five thousand dollars. Not close to half a million, but enough, as Nappi suggested, to make a country boy stop and think before he turned it over to the mob.

"We'll give him a choice. All this money now, or a chance on more later. I'll convince him later will be too late. He'll be dead." Nappi looked pleased with himself.

I held up the Scotch bottle. "One for the road?"

He nodded. "Ransoming is thirsty work."

CHAPTER 15

———

THE LOCKS FROM the Rim Canal to the lake always gave me the shivers. From the other side of the canal, they looked tall and cold, imposing, and taking a boat through them and onto the lake was a claustrophobic experience. I'd only done it once in a friend's craft, and I never wanted to repeat the event. First you drove your boat to the gate, grabbed the signal button hanging there, and waited until the gate keeper opened them. The concrete gray locks loomed over you as your tiny vessel rode up and down on the waves. If there were boats in the lock waiting to enter the canal for the lake, you stayed out of their way and then took your turn. Then you proceeded forward until you nosed the gate at the end. The gate closed behind you and the water began to drop to the level of the lake water. To me it felt like descending into the depths of hell. After too long a time, the gate in front opened, releasing you into the lake.

I remembered the experience as if it had only been days ago, and I shook as the memory flowed through me. This evening I only had to meet the kidnapper, give him the money, and get Madeleine back. Thank goodness I'd be on dry land tonight and not in the middle of some boat bouncing around on the water, waiting for the gates to close in on me.

Traffic at the Deer Mound lock was brisk at this time of the evening. Boats were coming off the lake. Few were entering it. Fishing was over for the day. When the restaurant was in operation, five o'clock was the hour when the guys who had been on the lake since early morning tied their boats up at the dock and kicked back on the wooden deck overlooking the canal, ordering the place's famous bucket of beer and pound of shrimp. The stories began, becoming more exaggerated as buckets were emptied of bottles and refilled again. With the establishment closed now, the boats cruised past and headed for a fish camp some fifteen miles south on the canal. No shrimp there, but I'd gobbled down boiled peanuts, their specialty—one most northerners considered an acquired taste. I loved the Cajun ones.

I pulled into the parking area behind the restaurant. There were no other cars. Nappi and his men had left their vehicles on the road and walked down the winding sandy lane, taking cover in the vegetation alongside the buildings that stored boats. We expected the exchange to be in one of those buildings or in the closed restaurant, reasoning it was unlikely anyone would be around to interrupt us.

I turned off the engine and waited. My cell rang. The kidnapper guy.

"You know how to drive a boat?"

"I think so." Although I sounded doubtful, the truth was I'd grown up on the sound in Connecticut and had been around boats of all sorts most of my life. I didn't want the kidnapper to think I had any skills that might lead him to believe I was competent. Let him think I was just a silly blonde Yankee gal.

"See that boat approaching the lock?"

"Yes."

"Okay. You can see your friend is aboard, right?"

From this distance and in the light from the setting sun, I

could just make out someone with red hair. Madeleine. It had to be.

"If you walk around the restaurant to the canal side, you'll see a boat tied up there. Get in it and start it up. Don't hang up. I'll let you know what to do."

I hurried toward the canal. The craft there was an old pontoon boat, difficult to steer and slow. I got on board, found the key in the ignition, and started the engine. It caught on the third try. I slipped all lines except for the bow line, which I held onto, waiting for instructions. The other boat gathered speed and headed toward the lock.

"We'll make the exchange in the privacy of the lock."

No, no, no. Anything but that damp, cold lock. I couldn't go there again. I just couldn't.

"You toss the money to me once the gate is closed. I count it. Then your friend comes aboard your boat, and we head out onto the lake."

"There's not enough room for both boats in there."

"We'll make room."

I knew several boats could go through the lock at one time, but usually they were the smaller bass boats, not one of those clunky, bulky pontoon boats. It would be a squeeze.

"Stay on your phone. I don't want you getting in touch with anyone and calling for help."

Whoever was piloting the boat Madeleine was on wore a hooded sweatshirt. I couldn't make out his features, but he appeared to be a small man. As he came abreast of the gate, he reached out and grabbed the control that hung there and pushed the button, signaling the gate keeper. The gate began to rise. While his attention was directed toward the control, I heard a thump behind me. I steered away from the restaurant and toward the open waters of the canal. Oh, no. Something was wrong with the boat. But the sound didn't repeat itself, and I sighed in relief. All I needed was for this boat to sink before I could get to Madeleine.

With Nappi and his men stranded on shore, it was up to me to argue the kidnapper into taking the lesser sum of money and answering a few questions. How was I supposed to do that?

The boat ahead nosed the far gate as I idled into the small area. Then the gate behind me started down. My heart began to race as the walls closed in on me. Our two vessels banged against each other and then into the walls.

"Cozy, huh?" The kidnapper turned toward me, his face hidden within the hoodie. All I could see were his teeth when he smiled. They weren't good.

Madeleine's hands were tied behind her, and she sat in the bottom of the boat. She looked scared, but defiant. Good old Madeleine. She was a trooper. I waved at her and smiled in encouragement.

"Get his thing over with, will you? I need a bath," she said.

Yep, she was a trooper, all right, one with attitude.

"Money." The man reached out and wiggled his fingers. "Throw it."

The gate was now all the way down, and without the sun overhead, the lock was dark. I looked up at the mossy, wet walls and the steel doors that towered over me. We began to descend, the water making a low whooshing sound as it sought a lower level. I hesitated.

"I said, throw it!" he said.

I was frozen with fear. My hands and arms were paralyzed. I stood on the rocking deck of the boat like a cement statue.

"Damn it, Eve. Throw the money or I'll take back that silk blouse I bought you for your birthday." Madeleine sounded annoyed.

"You bought me that blouse I wanted?" Tears filled my eyes.

"Yes, but now I think it was a mistake. You can't so much as rescue me from this boat, and you think you deserve a blouse?"

The walls around me faded and visions of a blue and green mottled silk Donna Karan blouse floated before me. I threw the satchel.

The kidnapper grabbed it from the floor where it landed and opened it. He began to rummage through the bills inside, then looked up. "Hey, there's no more than twenty thousand or so in here. The rest is newspaper. No deal. You cheated me."

A hand touched my shoulder. Nappi stood there, a grim look on his face. "Take it. It's all yours. Your bosses will only kill you when you hand the ransom over to them. They'll think you screwed it up, or worse, that you took the rest. You can have all that's there for some information."

The kidnapper looked up in shock. "Where the hell did you come from?"

"I'm a stowaway. That's all you need to know."

The water level in the lock had reached its low point, and the gate began to open toward the lake.

"Your decision. That money now, and I guarantee your safety."

"It's a no brainer, you dolt. Take it. You can eat something fancier than peanut butter every night." Madeleine had gotten to her feet and was moving toward him.

"I like peanut butter," he said.

"I don't." She threw herself at him, stomping her foot on his.

He let out a scream of pain. "That's the foot you broke. Get off me." He pushed her away and she fell into the water, into that black, black water.

I hesitated for only a second, then dove in after her, swallowed up in the inky depths of water so cold I almost gasped it into my lungs. I could see nothing. All I could do was feel around with my hands and plunge deeper into the coldness. My hand touched something. It felt like seaweed. Probably some water plant. Ugh. Or perhaps it was … hair. Madeleine's hair. I grabbed a handful and pulled, rising as I tugged. We broke the surface in time to see the bass boat charging through the gate and heading toward the open waters of the lake.

Madeleine sputtered. "I held my breath. I knew you'd save me. I knew it."

"So do I get the blouse?"

The boat was gone, the kidnapper was gone, and of course, the money was gone. I didn't care. I held my friend in my arms, thankful to have her back. Nappi was relieved to see Madeleine and me alive, yet I knew he was disappointed not to be able to question the man who had kidnapped her.

"Now what?" I sipped a brandy in my living room while Madeleine ate her way through two orders of take-out ribs from the Biscuit.

Nappi scowled his way through another Scotch. "I can't believe the Russians would hire someone so inept to do their work."

"I don't know. I thought that lock exchange bit was kind of clever," I said. Clever, yes, but it almost killed both of us. I shivered, remembering the black water closing in as I searched for Madeleine.

Madeleine wiped sauce from her mouth. "And it worked."

There was a knock at the door. When I opened it, Sophia, Boris, and Darlene stood there. They were all bundled in coats against the cold front that had rolled in during the evening hours.

"You didn't keep in touch." Sophia looked furious. "I tried your cell, and it was busy, then you didn't answer, so we had to come. I see you paid the money and got your little friend back."

"Where does that leave our sister?" Boris looked at Nappi and nodded. "I am Boris Nankovitch and here is my sister and a friend. Our sister is still out there, held by the bad men. They do not get in touch."

Boris and Nappi shook hands. Sophia and Darlene nodded.

"Why don't we all sit down and see what we can do. I'll make coffee." I headed toward the kitchen.

"You don't have vodka?" Sophia slid into the armchair near the sofa. I couldn't tell if her look of dislike was because of her sister's dilemma or because I hadn't offered them vodka.

"No vodka. Only Scotch. Look, let me explain what happened."

"There's no explaining now. We know you do not care about us and our sister," Boris said. He looked as if he might just leave, but then added, "I might try some of the Scotch."

I poured him several fingers in a glass.

"He held it up to the light and examined it, then tossed it down in one gulp. "Good, yes, but not as good as vodka."

Darlene wandered over to the dining table. "We didn't stop for supper on the way here. Those ribs look good."

"I don't have enough to share." Madeleine picked up her plate and went to eat in the kitchen.

Darlene plopped herself down on the couch, giving Nappi a friendly look. "Name's Darlene."

"I know." Nappi gave her his mob look.

She scooted away from him. He ignored her.

"Madeleine has a right to eat her ribs. She's been through hell." I filled everyone in on the stolen money and the rescue operation.

"Since they only got twenty thousand or so, I'm sure they will get in touch with us for money for my sister." Boris seemed certain of this, even though I calculated it had been several days since the Russians had made contact with them. And the Russians had only contacted me through the peanut butter guy.

Nappi had been quiet while I recounted the evening's events. Now he rose from his seat. "When they contact you, you tell them to deal with Nappi Napolitani. I am a family man also, and I've been at it for longer than they have."

Sophia jumped out of her chair. "What do you say? They wish only to deal with us."

"Sometimes they seem to like dealing with me. Although I still don't understand why they sent the guy they did."

I gave a shudder at the thought of Madeleine's having to spend two days with that guy.

Sophia ignored me and locked eyes with Nappi. "You cannot bargain with Russian thugs. They are tough. They will make you pay for such insolence. They will make us pay."

"We Americans use the phrase, 'jerk around.' They've jerked your family and Eve around enough. Eve has gone out of her way to find money for you. I have been generous too. Now this will stop. I will handle this. No arguments." Nappi shook his finger at them. "And now, everyone will leave. Eve and her friend need rest."

Sophia and Darlene buttoned their coats as a cold wind hit them upon stepping out the door. Sophia drew on a pair of black leather gloves. Boris fumbled in his coat pockets for a moment, then withdrew his hands. He saw me watching him.

"I guess I forgot my gloves. I wasn't expecting this cold. We Russians think Florida is always warm."

I smiled. "This has been an odd winter. These cold fronts seem to roll through every month."

I found Boris more approachable than Sophia. I wondered what their sister was like. And I wondered if Boris really forgot his gloves or remembered there was only one of them in his pocket. Had I found him out? Did he know I suspected the glove I grabbed off the ninja who attacked Jerry and me might be one missing from his pocket?

Nappi saw the look on my face when I turned from the door. "What do you know?"

I wanted to let my suspicions about Boris simmer a while, but I did have something else on my mind.

"I'm wondering if I've been taken for a complete idiot. Sophia and Boris have been so in my face with the kidnapping of their sister I forgot about the other bag of money, the one Winston was dropping off for his bosses, his one last job before he retired. I am also wondering who took the money from the bank account. I have been too busy to bug the lawyer."

"I've been wondering about that also. Perhaps Madeleine was not taken by the Russians but by family members."

"You mean family as in 'Family,' right?"

"Yes. They wouldn't send people down here to do their work. As you can tell from my men, we don't fit in well with the cowboys and ranchers of the Okeechobee Basin. We can't pass for bass fishermen or tourists driving through from the coasts. Put a short-sleeved palm tree print shirt on us and the result would scream 'mob guy trying to fit in.' "

I laughed at the image and agreed. "They would use someone already here and in their organization, or they'd hire someone with peanut butter on his breath."

"Any candidates leap to mind?"

"Well, Sammy and I did spend a night in the swamps, courtesy of the Hardy brothers. Then their place burned, and we don't see them anymore. A message, do you think? Aren't they the kind of men the family would hire to do their work down here?"

Nappi looked thoughtful. "Maybe."

I remembered talking to Sammy about the Hardys. He said they transported people into and out of the swamp. Exactly what did he mean by that? I wondered if he would be less cryptic in his explanation of their work if I shared what I was thinking about their associates. He didn't like the brothers before we spent the night in the swamp. I wanted to know if he felt as I did: that the Hardys were around, but hiding out, not only afraid of the law because of what they did to us, but also scared of what would happen to them if they didn't find that money. Why hadn't I talked with him before? *Because you were being whipped right and left by Sophia and her demands, you dummy*, I said to myself.

"I need to pay a visit to someone who did me a favor. I never said thanks because I've been so tied up, but I'm sure he'll understand."

"You'll want to do this alone."

"Yes. Will you stay here and keep an eye on Madeleine?"

"It's late and you're tired. This will keep until tomorrow."

"No it won't. It was a really big favor."

CHAPTER 16

━━━

WHEN I PULLED into the airboat parking lot, I could see a light in Grandfather's house. I moved along the path to his place, certain he would be there waiting for me. And he'd forgive my not checking in with him about the store when he heard of Madeleine's return. Who was I kidding? He probably already knew of Madeleine's rescue and of my role in it.

I smelled the tobacco from his pipe. As I got closer I could make out his figure in the old rocker on the porch. Its creak, creak on the floorboards was the only sound in the cold night.

"Grandfather. Isn't it a little chilly to be sitting out here?"

"It clears my head from my work in your shop."

"I'm sorry. Too much inside work for your taste?"

"No. Too many women."

"I thought you liked that about this job."

"I like the women, but I can't stand the scent of them. Too much phony fragrance. My nose got tired. I could hardly wait until I left and came home to light up my pipe and smell the good clean aroma of tobacco."

"I thought you might appreciate these." I handed him a box.

He opened it and sniffed at the contents. "Oh. Chocolates.

My favorites, dark with coconut." He selected one and offered me the box.

"No. They're for you. Don't let Sammy eat too many. I'd pay you for your hours at the store, but I know you wouldn't take it. You've been truly kind."

He smacked on his candy with gusto, took another and popped it into his mouth. When he finished with it, he closed the box and set it on the floor within reach.

"I knew something was happening, and that it was important. Why wouldn't I help?" He paused, and I could just make out the whites of his eyes as they fixed on me. "I understand Madeleine is safe."

"Yes, she is."

"Did I hear someone mention my name?" Sammy stepped out onto the porch, his tall angular frame backlit by the kerosene lantern on the kitchen table when he opened the door.

Grandfather scooted the chocolate box under his chair with his foot. "Eve came for a visit and to thank me for helping all those ladies find the best clothes for themselves."

"She also brought you chocolates. I can smell them. Don't worry. I won't take them."

I smiled to myself. Sammy was like his grandfather in so many ways. Nothing got by him.

"I need to talk with you, Sammy."

Grandfather got up from his chair, picked up the chocolates and headed into the house. "I'll leave you two to plot whatever it is Eve now wants to plot."

I heard a chuckle as he closed the door behind him.

"The cold has chased the mosquitoes away. Like to take a walk down by the canal?"

I nodded and took his arm. He seemed to accept my touch as the friendly gesture I intended.

I got right to it. "No one has seen the Hardy brothers around since the fire, and Frida tells me it was arson. I've been so wrapped up in my own troubles with money and with Madeleine's kidnapping, I haven't thought much about them, but I imagine they're still on your mind."

We stopped by the chickee and he pulled two stools out from under the counter.

"Sit. I wish I had something warm to offer you."

"No, that's fine. You can offer me your opinion on a number of things. That will keep me warm."

"Sure." He settled onto the stool.

"You told me the Hardy brothers were into transporting people in and out of the swamps. What do you make of that?"

"I can't prove anything, but I think they were picking up illegal aliens at a drop-off spot in the swamp and taking them up the river to another location where the 'cargo' was transferred and carried north by truck."

"This was their operation?"

He laughed. "You give them too much credit. They were working for someone, someone big, someone not from around here."

I nodded. "Maybe, just maybe they were given a second job for the same folks."

"Go ahead."

"My uncle was carrying drop-off money for the family that employed him, really the one that owned him. Winston came to my friend Nappi because he wanted to retire. He was tired of the life. He had his own family, children in trouble that he needed to see to, and a woman he cared about. Nappi arranged with Winston's mob bosses to do a final big money drop, here in the swamps. I'll bet it was to the Hardy brothers."

"Okay, but why did your uncle dump it in the swamp? Why not just hand it off in some inconspicuous way to the Hardys?"

"He didn't drop the Hardy's money in the swamp. He had that money in another duffel, which he placed at his feet. He dropped a ransom payment, his own money to pay the kidnappers, in the swamp. Someone took it before the kidnappers could pick it up."

"He was carrying a considerable sum of money then?"

"A total of one million, all in cash, in two separate duffel bags, half a million of the mob's money for the Hardys' and half a million of his own money for the kidnappers. And like the one dropped in the swamp, the bag for the Hardys never made it into their hands. At least that's what I think."

"So, they couldn't come up with the money they were supposed to take care of. Ah, now I get it. The people they worked for were furious, wanted the money and threatened them."

"Yeah, but the money was gone. What could the Hardys do?"

"Not much."

"They didn't see it that way. I think they were the ones who ran me off the road and threatened me. Then they tried to find the money at my uncle's condo. That's why they were at the funeral and the get-together after. I found them rummaging through the bedrooms. They did nothing for a while, something their bosses didn't think well of. The bosses wanted action, so they decided to light a fire under the brothers, to remind them of the kind of people they worked for. They burned the airboat and produce stand operation to make their point."

"So you're suggesting the reason we haven't seen them around is that they're dead?"

"Nope. As Nappi has pointed out many times. The mob does not kill you when you owe them. They do things to make you wish you were dead. And you find the money. Somehow."

"Madeleine."

I nodded. Then whispered, "The bastards."

Sammy reached out and took my hand. His was big and warm and totally enveloped mine, a comforting feeling, a feeling of safeness.

"Thank you."

He looked puzzled. "What did I do?"

"I know you're not real crazy about white folks, yet you helped me when I needed you. You gave me the information I needed tonight and listened to my suspicions and you didn't laugh at me."

"I didn't give you much information, only what I knew about the brothers."

"Yes, but because you listened without a word of doubt when I connected all of what I suspected, it confirmed I was on the right track."

Sammy shrugged. "I can't prove any of what I said. I was lucky to spy them doing one drop-off. I couldn't go to the authorities and say they seemed to have a lot of people on their boat at night and were transporting them up river. What does that prove?"

I looked at Sammy and wondered how honest I could be with him. "Of course there was your inherent distrust of the authorities …. Didn't that also keep you from reporting them?"

At first I thought I'd made a mistake. He drew back from me, got off the stool, and took a few steps toward the canal. He stood there a moment, hands in his pockets, looking out over the water. Then he returned to his seat.

"Grandfather and I have discussed in detail what I saw, what all of us in the tribe have seen and think about the Hardys. They seem to us to be the worst of the white people around here. I think a sense of despair settled over me and I felt as if no one other than my family would care what they did in the swamps. The people in Florida—the politicians, ranchers, farmers, and developers—only think about the swamp when it creates problems for them. They'd like all of it to disappear."

I agreed with what he was saying. I'd seen the bulldozers and earth moving equipment churning through the watery expanses of land alongside the highway as I drove between Sabal Bay and the coast one morning last month. By the time I headed back in the afternoon, piles of trees, brush, and other vegetation stood in mountainous heaps and the land was stripped down to bare earth. I could only imagine what this rape did to the wildlife that depended upon the swamp to breed, nest, and eat.

He continued. "What good is swampland unless you can drain it and build condos or plant sugar on it? Look what they've done to the Everglades and the Big Lake? Confined the lake with feeder canals, levees, and locks and almost succeeded in draining the Everglades. Most people consider it a big dump, like folks out west see the deserts—land where trash can be tossed. Why should I want to step in?" His voice was filled with anger, disdain, and fear.

Then his face brightened for a moment. "Grandfather says we have to trust some of the white people or we will lose everything. Maybe he's right."

"I think we can begin by taking down these two brothers."

"Their bosses will only send others."

"Maybe, but it's better to take a stand against two brothers instead of waiting until many more like them cruise the swamps with boats full of desperate people. I've got a way to confirm part of what I suspect. It's a beginning."

Sammy wrapped his arm around my shoulders. "And I'll bet you're going to bait them out of hiding. Right? Offer them something so enticing they can't resist. I want to be in on it."

"Sure."

NAPPI AND I had split up the responsibility for bringing Madeleine's kidnapper and Winston's killer to justice. He would deal with the Russians, and I would handle the Hardys. With a little help from my friends, of course.

One friend I hadn't counted on was Alex, who rolled in that night from Pensacola, announcing he had finished his case and was free to hang around. He was promising to wine and dine me. How could I tell him I was hot on the heels of a kidnapper, that a romantic interlude didn't fit my schedule right now? Oh, that would change, I was certain, but at this moment I didn't have time for the two step, tango, candlelit dinners, and hot kisses, even if they were great hot kisses. I couldn't tell him that. He'd be hurt. And he'd be furious that I'd plunged my acrylic nails into another bowl of murder.

I thought I should ease him into what I was up to. Of course, I had no intention of telling him every little detail of what I was doing, but I'd practice a bit of easing and see how it went. I couldn't lie to him forever.

THE NIGHT AFTER I enlisted Nappi and Sammy as co-conspirators in my plans to find the Russians and the Hardys, Alex took me to the coast. We sat overlooking the St. Lucie River, sipping a bottle of very nicely chilled Pinot Grigio, my very favorite wine. Asparagus with hollandaise sauce topped with crab meat was the appetizer, followed by blackened mahi and a side of polenta. Yummy.

Things were going so well. I was about to start my easing into the truth approach when Madeleine walked in with a date. Uh-oh. There was one little detail I'd forgotten about. I hadn't told Alex that Madeleine had been nabbed. Well, give me a break. I was busy trying to figure out how to rescue her. Over the phone he kept saying I should tell the authorities about the ransom demand for Sophia and Boris' sister, which I took to mean I should report any ransom demand. I'd again indicated I wouldn't go to the police, so while Madeleine was being held by the peanut butter guy, the calls between Alex and me were short. I was in no mood to reveal what I was doing, so why would I tell him I was trying to borrow money from Nappi to rescue Madeleine? Why would I tell him she needed rescuing? He didn't need to know that I was ignoring his advice … as usual. Or that I was into something not quite legal … again.

I'd neglected to tell him about losing Nappi's money, Jerry's stint in the hospital, or Madeleine's diet of peanut butter followed by our swim in the canal lock. So I guess he didn't know much of what had transpired in the past few days. The truth? He didn't know anything about what I'd done.

All of this raced through my head as Madeleine came over to our table and gave Alex a hug. "I'm so glad you're back. You can't imagine what it was like all that time …."

I tried to stop her from saying more, but I knew this was a train wreck I couldn't stop. Alex turned accusing eyes on me and indicated how much he'd like to hear more. He invited them to join us just to ensure he didn't miss a detail. I was screwed.

They had a great evening while I lost my appetite for my dinner. Why hadn't I phoned Madeleine and told her to hush up about her kidnapping and the mugging until I filled Alex in on the story? Again, I said to myself, it's because I'm involved in yet another scheme that's taking up my psychic energy and chasing other items out of my brain. Like who knows what and who shouldn't know anything.

We were in the ladies room repairing our lipstick when she gave it to me. I knew it was coming, so I'd steeled myself with a brandy after dinner.

"Alex is your boyfriend. How can you not tell him what happened to me, to you, to Jerry? Besides, it's over now. How mad can he be?"

I looked at her reflection in the mirror and gave her a nervous smile.

"*Now* what are you up to, Eve?" Madeleine said.

THE RIDE BACK to the coast was accompanied by loud silence.

"Want to come in for a nightcap?" If I sounded less than eager to spend any more alone time with Alex, it was only because my plan to tell him slowly about my adventures of the last few days needed serious revision. I had such a headache from the tension over dinner that I couldn't think well enough to construct another approach.

"Do you want me to? I mean, because you seem to be so preoccupied with your other men: Nappi, Jerry, that Russian guy, the Russian mob, the missing Hardys, Madeleine's kidnapper .... Have I left anyone out?" He snapped his fingers. "Oh yeah, Sammy Indian and his grandfather. Am I right?"

"Don't be mean, Alex. I'm sorry."

"You're always sorry after you get caught. How about your vow not to get involved in this business? Tell Frida everything and let it go."

"I can't. I made promises. I have to keep them."

"You made promises to your uncle's stepchildren, which was fine until you found out you didn't have his money to pay the ransom. It's not your problem, Eve. The police need to be in on this one. Now."

"It's not as simple as that."

"How not simple is it?"

"Come in and I'll tell you everything. Then maybe you'll understand." I had my fingers crossed behind my back. How could I tell him everything without lengthening the distance between us?

He nodded, and I unlocked the door.

"Have a seat. I'll get us coffee."

He sat on the couch, but got up again. "Something's poking me in the butt."

He flipped aside the cushions and extracted a small plastic object, a cellphone.

"You left your phone here, and you also forgot to charge it. It's dead."

"What?" I left off brewing the coffee and came to see what he was talking about.

"See. It won't even turn on." He handed the phone to me.

"It's not my phone."

"It must belong to one of your many men."

"Don't start that again, Alex."

But I figured he was right. It did belong to one of my "men." I was sure it was Uncle Winston's discarded burner phone.

CHAPTER 17

—

I HELD THE phone in my hand and knew I'd confronted one thing I ought not to keep to myself.

"You know what you have to do, don't you?" Alex's voice was calm and steady, the kind of lifeline I needed with all the craziness happening around me.

Maybe he was right. I was trying to take on too much. I'd start here. Whatever was on this phone couldn't hurt Winston now, but it might just reveal who had killed him.

"Unless you're afraid there's an incriminating message on there from one of your mob friends." Alex searched my face for a reaction.

Nappi? No, I knew there was nothing, not even Nappi's phone number, that could connect him and Winston. He'd told me they only met in person. Unless he lied to me and thought I'd never find out because the burner was destroyed.

"I'll have to take that chance, won't I?" I said.

I reached for my own cell, but before I could call Frida, it rang in my hand.

"Eve? It's Darlene. I need to talk to you."

"If it's about the ransom money, Mr. Napolitani is handling that now."

There was a moment's hesitation on the line.

"Oh, he is. That's … good, right? I'm not calling about the money. Well, not really. I just have to talk to you. You're the only one I can trust. I think someone is trying to kill me." She began to sob.

"Take it easy. Can we meet tomorrow?"

As quickly as she had lost control, she regained it. "Yes. Meet me at Macy's in City Place at noon."

"I'm not driving down there. I've got a business to run, and it's not had much of my attention lately. You can drive up here and come to the shop."

"I'll have to rent a car then."

"Borrow Sophia and Boris' car. Tell them you need to go shopping for something."

"Sophia would want to come with me. She watches me like a hawk. I don't think she trusts me. Sometimes I get the impression she thinks I'm responsible for the money disappearing."

"Are you?"

"What? Like I'd be crawling around in a swamp absconding with that."

"You're still living with them?"

"Where else can I stay? I've got no money."

"Winston left you something in his will."

"I already spent that."

"On what?" I was about at my wit's end with her and the siblings. I felt as if I was the parent of clinging, needy children.

"I had some debts."

"Tomorrow. At the store."

"Can we go to lunch?" she asked.

"Lunch. I thought you were afraid someone was after you, but you can think about food?"

"Why should I die on an empty stomach?"

Why indeed?

I ended the call.

Alex frowned. "Don't tell me. This had something to do with the alleged kidnapping?"

"Only indirectly." I told him what Darlene wanted.

"I swear you're like a social worker with too many cases. You can't rescue every Russian girl who comes to you for help."

"Arguing about it won't get us anywhere."

"You're right. I'll keep my mouth shut. For now. Call Frida."

I did. She wasn't on duty, so I tried her home phone. She didn't sound happy to hear from me.

"You said I could call you here, you know."

"It's after midnight. This better be important."

"A burner phone?"

"You found it?"

"Yup. In my couch. If you're too tired, we can talk about this tomorrow, although I've got a pretty full schedule. Some cop told me I'd be better respected in the business community if I opened my store on a regular basis. I'll try to fit you in between customers."

"Don't get uppity on me. I'll be right over."

Alex and I were only on our second make-up kiss when she pounded on my door.

"Hi Alex. Long time, no see. I'm glad you're back here. Maybe you can keep a rein on our gal here."

I batted my lashes in a feigned look of total innocence. "Whatever do you mean?"

"When I don't hear from you in a while, I know you're up to something. I heard a rumor that you and Madeleine took a dip in the lock at Deer Mound the other night. Any truth to that?"

"We'd have to be out of our minds to swim in alligator infested waters."

"My very point. Hand it over." She held out her hand for the phone.

"Don't I get to know what's on it?"

"It's evidence in a murder case. You'll find out when I decide to tell you." Her expression softened. "Look, I know you want to find out who killed your uncle as much as I want to arrest the bastard, but it is evidence, and I'm glad you turned it in. Thanks. You did the right thing."

"He helped me do it." I leaned back into Alex, and he put his arms around me.

"She would have called you without my advice." A few kisses and Alex had good things to say about me.

"Yeah, but she would have done it next week." Frida took the phone, winked at me to let me know she was kidding, and left.

"Where were we?" Alex turned me around in his arms so that we were facing each other.

"I think we were about to make up."

There was a knock on the door.

"Tell them to go away." Alex always had great ideas.

"Go away."

"It's Jerry. I need to talk to you."

"Go away." Alex and I spoke in unison.

"I thought you'd like to know they released me from the hospital. I wanted to thank you."

"At this hour?"

"Hospital? Jerry was in the hospital? What happened?" Alex threw open the door. "Jerry, old man, are you okay?"

"Eve didn't tell you?" Jerry's face was black and blue and his mouth puffy.

I groaned. This was not going to be a night of fun.

MADELEINE AND I arrived at the shop the next morning within minutes of each other.

"Are you sure you don't want to take off a few days? Take some down time and recover from that awful experience. I can cover for you." I hugged her and unlocked the door.

She shook her head.

As we readied the shop for opening, we talked about her

kidnapping and the events leading up to it.

"I think I blew it with Alex last night, but I was certain you would keep him abreast of what was going on. You didn't tell him a thing, did you?" she said.

"No. I always want to, but he gets so mad when I insert myself into anything he thinks will be dangerous. It's not as if I look for trouble, you know."

"Don't you? Sometimes I wonder, when you have an appetite for adventure, if you're bored with the life you have here. In business. With me."

"No. Don't say that. I love working here with you. You know how I feel about fashion and a bargain."

"How does it compare to murder?"

Opting not to answer that, I changed the subject. "Guess what I found in my couch?"

I told her about the burner phone and what it was used for among mob folks.

"A clue?" Madeleine's eyes danced with delight.

"Maybe. Or there could be nothing on it."

"Did you and Alex make up last night?"

"Kind of, at least we were trying until Jerry showed up. Again he hadn't arranged for a motel room and there's that mud bog racing thing in town. Alex took him home with him to his apartment."

"You and Alex get all the breaks."

"And how did your date turn out? He sure is a hunk of a man—tall, muscular, dresses well, too. You met him on that Internet dating site, right? He's handsome and he seemed nice when we met at the restaurant."

Madeleine's eye started to twitch, and she turned her attention to one of the skirt rounds. "We should put some of these items on sale this weekend, don't you think?"

"Okay, honey. What happened?"

"Oh, Eve. What's wrong with me? We were having such a great time! Then he asked me to dance. We were doing a slow dance, and he looked down at me as if he was going to kiss me. I panicked."

"Panicked? How?"

"I thought to myself, this is just silly. We'll date for a while, get attached to each other, and then I'll do something to hurt him somehow. I pulled away and told him I didn't want to see him again."

"Madeleine Boudreaux, how could you? Letting something that hasn't happened stand in the way of something that might be good."

"I'm jinxed. You know that."

Well, yes. I knew she was jinxed, but things could change. At least I hoped they could. I told her so, and she seemed to perk right up.

"Maybe I should call him tonight and talk," she said.

"Good idea."

We gabbed though the morning, reestablishing our old camaraderie. Nothing could come between us—not a murder, not a kidnapping, not her clumsiness or my lack of social sensitivity. We loved each other like sisters. For the first time since my uncle died I felt as if everything would turn out just fine.

Then Darlene showed up.

At first I didn't recognize her, which I guess was the point of her costume. She wore a brown, long-sleeved sweater, slacks in another shade of brown, brown shoes, and a brown wig made of polyester hair.

"It's me."

"What is this? You've come out of mourning and wearing black and now you're in your brown period?" I asked.

"What do you mean?"

"You know, kind of like Picasso's blue period. Oh, never mind."

I'd alerted Madeleine earlier to Darlene's impending visit. She'd declined my offer to accompany us to lunch.

"Someone needs to tend the store. You two girls have fun." Madeleine stood in the shop door and waved us goodbye. When I turned at my car to look back at her, she rolled her eyes and put her finger down her throat in a gagging gesture. Still didn't like Darlene, I guess.

We settled into a back booth at the Burnt Biscuit and each ordered a chef salad.

"I know it's too early to think about dating again, but I want to keep my figure." Darlene ordered her thousand island dressing on the side, poured all of it onto her salad and ordered two more portions of the dressing.

"Now what's all this about someone trying to kill you?" I wanted to get right to it. I wasn't going to spend one more minute with this woman than was necessary. I knew my uncle was fond of her, but I didn't have to be.

She looked around the restaurant, then leaned forward and whispered across the table to me. "I've been seeing a black SUV roll by the apartment several times a day. Someone's watching me."

I shrugged. "SUVs are pretty common."

"I've been getting hang-ups on Winston's cell. You know Frida returned it to me the other day. Nice of her, don't you think?"

A number of possibilities about the hang-up calls ran through my head: police surveillance courtesy of Frida, Nappi's brand of psychological warfare, Winston's mob family, the Russians .... Any of these.

"Good afternoon, ladies." The voice drew me out of my musings.

"Mr. Napolitani." I started to get out of my chair.

"Don't get up, my dear." He reached for my hand and kissed it. My gallant mob guy.

He turned his attention to Darlene. "Ms. Banks, I believe."

Darlene looked as terrified as a preteen watching *Halloween 25: Jason Returns from the Dead.*

"Oh, my. I have another appointment. I must leave." She grabbed her purse, but before she could get up, Nappi placed a hand on her shoulder.

"But you're just the woman I wanted to talk to. Isn't it fortunate you're here?" Nappi smiled, a toothy, malicious grin.

She shot me a look of anger.

"I didn't tell on you. I'm as surprised to see him as you are." That was the truth, but I knew Nappi's appearance was more than happenstance on his part. He had something planned for Darlene.

"I thought we could talk about that day—the day of Winston's death. You know I went out of my way to make things right with his family?" Nappi said.

She gulped and nodded.

"So whoever took the money that was meant for the mob really did a disservice to me as well as to Winston. And to his family."

"Yes." She squeaked out this single word.

"I know you've gone over and over this with the police, but now I'm asking personal-like. What do you think happened to that money?"

She shook her head. "I don't know."

"Do the children?"

"No."

"Here's the problem for all of us. I'm mad, yes. So is Eve here. So are the police. But his family? Those mob folks? You know about mob families, don't you, Darlene?"

She nodded and grabbed her glass of water, took a gulp.

"They can be patient, but they'll find out who took it. You know that, don't you?"

"Yes."

He continued to look at her with his black eyes, then leaned back in his chair and put his hands in his lap. "You said something about an appointment?"

She jumped up from her chair and ran out of the restaurant.

"Madeleine's right about that woman. Darlene is a real pain in the you-know-what," I said.

Nappi tilted his chair forward. "I think she may be a killer."

"Likely. And now she's a frightened killer, the worst kind. She may decide she needs to cover her tracks."

"That's fine with me."

"Have you been watching her apartment? Or calling and hanging up?"

"Not me." His smile was all innocence, which meant it could have been him.

"But someone wants to make her bolt."

"Care for dessert, my dear?"

CHAPTER 18

———

I PASSED ON dessert, as did Nappi, since the restaurant was all out of Florida Sunshine Cake—the orange-flavored, five layer cake with the orange zest butter cream frosting. Nothing compared, not even double whammy chocolate brownies with chocolate chips and dark chocolate ganache. As we finished our coffees, I told Nappi my plans for tracking down Madeleine's kidnapper.

"I'll sneak that in early because Alex and I need some together time. I've been neglecting him."

Nappi nodded. "He's a fine man, but a bit insecure when it comes to you and other men. Even me." He looked across the table.

"I know."

"I also have a full evening."

"Do you?" I waited, hoping he would reveal his plans, but he seemed reluctant.

"I'll keep Jerry busy tonight." He winked at me.

Nice of him.

THERE ARE ONLY two chain markets and the large supercenter

in Sabal Bay. The center carried most items at lower prices than the other two stores, and guessing that the person I was searching for was probably frugal out of need, I headed to the cheapest place. The town had the largest population in the county, yet it seemed small to me because I was acquainted with so many people, if not by name, then by sight from my store or the cowboy bars Madeleine and I frequented to get our fix of country bands. Those I hadn't met knew me as that "Yankee with the spiky hair whose car blew up in front of the Mexican restaurant last year."

The assistant manager of the supercenter was on duty and had a minute to talk, so I told her about the person I was searching for.

"Oh, yeah. That guy comes in here at least once a week. He buys the largest jar we have. He's got a real craving for it."

"Any particular days he comes in?"

"No schedule that I know about, but he hangs out at the Busted Boot, you know, that biker's bar out near Deer Mound."

On my way out of the store I called Madeleine.

"Here's a perfect opportunity for you to make up with that guy you dumped. How do you feel about a little two-step tonight?"

"Dancing? I'd probably trounce all over his feet."

"Maybe not. Give it a try."

We agreed to meet at the Busted Boot at nine. Whether Alex wanted to or not, our evening together would include Madeleine and Dan Hostel, the fellow she'd rejected last night. He was more than eager to try again with her. If we got lucky, we'd be dancing to the band called the Alone Rangers, one of my favorite groups. They played a lot of slow tunes, guaranteed to make Alex happy, at least on the dance floor.

I reconsidered. I'd better not get pushy with him. I'd let him choose what we did tonight.

At the door when he arrived, I put my arms around him, slipped my hands down to his tushy and gave it a squeeze.

"How about some sexy music and a little bump and grind?"

He stepped back from my embrace and looked me in the eye.

"What are you up to now?"

Why didn't anyone trust me?

But he agreed, thinking I was trying to help out Madeleine with her boyfriend issues. His choice.

The assistant manager at the supercenter didn't have a name for the guy I was trying to track down, Madeleine's kidnapper, but she had a description. He was shorter than I, had shoulder-length, greasy hair, eyes that sat close together, and a low forehead. Oh, and bad breath.

When Alex and I entered the bar, half of the patrons there fit that description. All of them stopped what they were doing and stared at us. I always seem to look out of place.

"I'm trying to find someone." I thought I should forewarn Alex.

"You've got someone," he said.

"I mean, someone else."

"Eve."

"Don't worry. This is harmless." That was one of my versions of the truth—not the whole truth or even half of it.

I walked up to all the short, greasy-haired, gorilla-browed men, smiled and said hello. I did this about twelve inches from their faces, watching for an expression of both recognition and fear. No one appeared to have played bumper boats with me, but I inhaled enough beer breath for a contact high.

Some of them thought I was coming onto them, others thought I wanted to fight. I dragged Alex with me, but kept between him and the fellas to make certain no one assumed they could throw a punch his way. It was his choice to come here, but I felt responsible for his safety somehow.

I was about to give up for the evening when I spotted a skinny guy leaning against the pool table. He fit the description and was sporting a bruised face. Hmmm.

"How about a game?" I put two quarters on the table.

He looked shocked. Not a telling enough reaction to convince me he recognized me and had reason to be suspicious, but he acted surprised all the same. He could as well have been stunned that a woman wanted to play him. There was nothing about him that signaled "I'm a babe magnet" and he knew it.

I broke and sunk two stripes, but missed my next shot. When I moved around the table to get close to him, he scooted away.

"I cain't shoot with you hanging over me." He took aim and missed; it was evident he couldn't shoot regardless of whether anyone was near him.

This game of keep-away continued for several minutes, neither of us doing well at our shots, although I was better than he was by a slim margin. He finally had a straight line at the pocket, but as he set up to sink it, I could see he wasn't going to use enough backspin, meaning that the cue ball would follow into the pocket.

He was as bad a pool player as he was a thug, and this was taking far too long. I moved up behind him and leaned into him. "Here. This is the way it's done." I touched his hands as if to guide him. He turned his face to me in surprise. Bingo! He exhaled beer and ....

Two strong hands pulled me off him.

"What are you doing, Eve?" Alex did not seem pleased.

At that moment, I spied Madeleine, entering the bar with Dan. I waved her over while my pool buddy continued lining up the ball and ... missed.

"What did you say your name was?" I smiled at him as he backpedaled down the length of the table. By now he knew something was up other than chasing balls around on a felt surface with some crazy broad.

"Bradley." He laid his pool stick on the table. "Uh, I got somewhere else to be."

"Bradley, you just settle down. I want you to meet a friend

of mine." I pulled Madeleine over and nudged her toward him.

Alex seemed to sense something was up. He stepped behind Bradley blocking his path to the exit and preventing him from putting any distance between himself and Madeleine.

Good. Alex had the way out covered.

"Go on, Madeleine. Shake hands with Bradley." I pushed her forward.

Trapped between Alex and Madeleine, Bradley began to sweat, nervous sweat that did nothing to improve his aroma.

She moved within two feet of him and stopped. "It's him."

Yup, the old beer and peanut butter lie detector works every time.

We walked him out to the parking lot to continue the discussion.

"This your truck, Barkley?" It was locked. I held out my hand. "Key, please."

"It's Bradley."

"Sure." I wiggled my fingers at him.

He looked at Alex, then at me and decided the two of us, given our heights, were not to be messed with.

I unlocked the door and got in. The entire truck smelled as if Smuckers, Jiff and Teddy's were holding a peanut butter convention. It didn't take me long to locate what I was looking for tucked into the space behind the seat. I moved several empty jars out of the way and extracted the bag.

"What's this?" I held up the satchel Nappi and I had stuffed the twenty-five thousand dollars into for the Madeleine's ransom. I unzipped it. Empty.

"You've got no right to search my truck or that. You need a warrant." Bradley crossed his arms and looked triumphant.

"That's for cops. But we're not cops," Alex said. Nice touch, I thought.

"We just have a few questions, and then we'll consider what we're going to do with you." *What could we do with him?* I wondered. We hadn't informed the authorities of a kidnapping, so technically no crime had been committed. But Bradley didn't know that, did he?

He hung his head. "Okay."

"We know you didn't set up the kidnapping. You're working for someone," I said.

"I never seen their faces. Never."

"But you talked with them on the phone, right?"

He nodded.

"So what did they sound like?"

"Huh?"

"Their voices. Did they have a foreign accent?"

"What do you mean by that?"

"Do you think I have a foreign accent?"

"Sure. You talk like all those other snowbirds."

I was tired of dancing around with this cretin. I grabbed him by his collar. "What did they sound like?"

"They sounded kinda like snowbirds speak when they want to make us believe they're just good old folks like us."

"So they were Yankees gone native?"

"That's it." He smiled. "Didn't fool me for a second. We say 'yawl' and Yankees say 'you all.' They was 'you all' guys."

"You're scum." Alex looked as if he wanted to punch him.

"They made me do it. I didn't want to, but I was out of money, and I needed supplies."

Alex looked at me. "So he's a drug addict as well as a kidnapper."

Madeleine stepped forward. "Of sorts. What he means by supplies is peanut butter. He's totally addicted."

"We're not finished here yet, Bradley. A few more questions and you're free to go." I couldn't stand his smell one more minute.

"Don't make me say anything else. Those guys are real mean. See my face?"

I nodded.

"They did that."

"Then you did meet with them."

"They had their faces covered. I had to give them the ransom, didn't I? They sure weren't happy it wasn't all there, and they accused me of taking it. So they beat me around a bit. I guess I convinced them I didn't do nothing. They told me they'd call if they needed me. They grabbed the money and took off."

"You're lucky to be alive. These men don't fool around." Alex sounded eager to scare him into saying more. It was great to have him in my corner.

"Distinguishing marks, tattoos, scars on their hands?" Alex was asking the right questions. We just weren't getting much in the way of useful information.

"Nope."

Alex grabbed his shirt and shook him. "You've got to give us something. It's for your own good. They might decide to come back and do more than beat you."

Bradley's face turned white. "Well, I can tell you this. One was a big guy and the other, shorter and smaller."

"Both were guys?" Call me suspicious, but I wasn't convinced Sophia and Boris weren't in on this somehow, especially after I saw Boris look for that missing glove, the one I'd pulled off the hand of one of the ninjas who attacked Jerry and me and stole the money.

"I don't know. I didn't hear the small one's voice."

Damn. We were no closer to finding out the identity of these guys than before the kidnapping, yet Nappi was convinced that all of these events were related. So was I but I couldn't see how.

I gave Bradley a few bucks for more peanut butter so he wouldn't starve before we got back to him or take another kidnapping job, and we told him to make himself available for when the cops decided to talk with him. I assured him I'd help him out by telling the authorities how he'd cooperated. Madeleine said she wanted him hanged for feeding her peanut butter for two days straight.

Madeleine and Dan returned to the bar to continue getting

acquainted on the dance floor. Since I didn't hear from her the rest of the night, I assumed she hadn't hurt him. Alex and I went back to my place, talked for a while, then turned our attentions toward one another. It was his cell that rang when our lips made first contact. I leaned in to hear the caller.

"Hey, buddy. It's me, Jerry. Eve seems to have turned off both her phones for the night, so I told Nappi I'd call you, that you wouldn't mind."

"I do mind."

"But this is important, too important to wait until tomorrow. Tell Eve that the kidnappers called Sophia and Boris."

"I don't want to."

"Listen, buddy. I'm not trying to one up you, but let me tell you from my experience being married to the gal, she doesn't take kindly to being left out of stuff, especially stuff she thinks is her stuff."

Alex gave me a funny look and then sighed. "Fine." He handed the phone over to me.

Nappi came on the line. "The kidnappers contacted the siblings with their final demand of half a million dollars. I was there when the call came in. I insisted they put me on the line. It was a woman with an accent, sounded Russian to me, although she disguised her voice by holding something over the receiver. Boris said it was the same person who got in touch before."

"Now we have confirmation of the kidnapping not filtered through Sophia and Boris. What did you think?" I asked.

"I think she's serious. She refused to let me talk with the sister. I think they're getting anxious, worried the sister is too much of a liability. They might just kill her."

"Did you do what you said you would if you made contact?"

"I offered the woman half that sum. She thought I was kidding, but I assured her I was not. I told her to take it or leave it, that I had the money, not Sophia and Boris, and that was all I'd offer them. I think the woman understood I was now in charge."

"And?"

"She said she'd get back to me. I don't think she's running the show. I think she's checking with someone."

"Sophia and Boris must be horrified. They didn't know you would do that, did they?"

"No, they did not. Now we just sit and wait."

"How did Darlene react?"

"I thought she'd swallow her cannoli whole. That woman sure can eat, can't she?"

"Are we any closer to solving this thing?"

"Maybe."

I told him about my evening at the Busted Boot.

"We'll have to decide which of these two we tackle first. Tomorrow at the Biscuit?"

"Nappi, aren't you tired of the food there?"

"Okay. How about the Mexican restaurant?"

"I'm getting my car back tomorrow," I said. "I don't want to take the chance someone will decide to blow up this one too. I think I'm burrito phobic."

"Your place then?"

"Take out?"

"I'll cook." He hung up.

Alex sat on the couch with one of those looks on his face. "What now?"

I had no choice but to tell him. Some of it, not everything.

"So you're still dancing with the Russian mob." He crossed his arms and shook his head.

"No. I'm not the one. Nappi is."

"Right. And he's such an ethical character, trustworthy, law abiding. It's pretty clear to me that I'd have a better chance spending time with you if I killed someone, kidnapped someone, or blew up your car."

"I would never forgive you for doing that to my car. It would not win my heart."

"What would?"

"One of your kisses would go a long way toward making me reconsider if I like you better than I like chasing criminals."

He reached for me. The phone didn't ring, the doorbell didn't ring. No one fell through my roof. But he didn't kiss me.

"I've been withholding from you too," he said.

"What?"

"I've got to get back on the road tonight. I'm due in court in Pensacola early tomorrow morning to testify in this case I've been working on."

Alex and I couldn't catch a break. Alex's testifying against criminals and my snooping into murder and kidnapping seemed to always get in the way of a night of uninterrupted romance. I hoped Madeleine and Dan were faring better in the romance department than I. I wished them no serious injuries and a few passionate embraces. Someone should get lucky tonight.

CHAPTER 19

A FTER ALEX LEFT, I couldn't sleep, so I got out of bed and went to the kitchen for a glass of water. Since my brain wouldn't turn off, I made a list of who the kidnappers might be, assuming that whoever did the kidnappings could also be my uncle's killer. The list included almost everyone I knew except for those I loved: Grandy, Max. Madeleine, and Alex. I knew Madeleine might like Darlene to be first on the suspects' list, but she was with us when my uncle was killed, and she had no reason to kill him, or at least I couldn't think of one. Darlene believed Sophia and Boris' story about the Russian mob and so did Winston. From what Nappi discovered tonight, I concluded the kidnapping was real. Madeleine's certainly was.

Sophia and Boris weren't on the airboat ride, so they might be the killers. They were Russians. Maybe they were in cahoots with the kidnappers. How that could be, I didn't know.

Given what the peanut butter man told us about his bosses, I was almost certain it had to be the Hardy brothers who were responsible for Madeleine's kidnapping. They might well be working for the mob Winston was delivering the money for. If they'd lost it, then they'd have plenty of incentive to obtain it from somewhere. Hiring a good ol' boy like Bradley to do the dirty work was just their style.

Either the Hardy brothers or Sophia and Boris might be the ninja couple who robbed Jerry of the money Nappi loaned me, although I couldn't see either of the brothers as light enough on their feet or heavy enough in the brains department to make the hit on Jerry. I still liked Boris for the one-gloved ninja.

Finally, there was the unknown factor: the Russian mob. Until Nappi spoke with one of them on the phone, no one except for Sophia and Boris had been in touch with them. Now I could almost feel their malevolence in the orchestration of the kidnapping, and I felt genuine concern for Sophia and Boris' sister. How awful it must be for them. I knew how I'd felt when Madeleine went missing. I hoped Nappi knew what he was doing taking over as point man for them.

My head hurt from trying to untangle suspects and motives, kidnappings from murder.

I had to include some other people I wanted to trust, but knew better than to exclude from my suspect list. Otherwise I couldn't see the whole picture. I hated to write down their names but the Egrets, grandfather and grandson, knew the swamps better than anyone. They had reason to hate the Hardys, and they were capable of finding and hiding the money.

I looked at the names remaining on the list: Nappi and Jerry, unlikely suspects. They both cared for me in their own ways, and they certainly wouldn't harm my uncle. Nappi was a made man and Jerry his lackey. My pen remained posed over their names, then I scratched through them. I went back over the list, my sleep-deprived brain wandering in circles. Just before I fell asleep I'd almost convinced myself that none of it mattered. Madeleine was safe, and Nappi was working to rescue the sister. Of course he would succeed. If I shared with Frida my suspicions about the Hardy brothers being behind Madeleine's kidnapping and why, she might arrest them, or they might suffer some horrible fate at the hands of Winston's mob connections. The money Winston carried appeared to be lost forever, but it was mob money, both satchels of it. That left my uncle still dead, the murder unsolved. Did it matter? It did to me.

The next morning, while I was rereading my list of suspects, someone knocked on the door. I'd fallen asleep at the kitchen table. I unfolded my achy body from the chair and hobbled to the front door. As I passed the mirror in the entryway, I caught a glimpse of myself. The pen imprint on my cheek told me I'd fallen asleep on it.

"Who's there?"

"Sammy."

I swung open the door. He looked at me with his eyebrows raised in disbelief.

"I know I look bad, but that bad?

"What's that line on your face?"

"I slept on a pencil."

"Rough night, huh?"

"I'll make coffee."

He stepped into the room, but seemed antsy, as if he wanted to turn around and dash out the door.

"I can't stay. I've got to get back to the business. Grandfather sent me. We have something we want to give you."

I hadn't noticed the duffel in his hand until now. It looked familiar, despite the mud on it and a few rips and tears in the side. One of the carry straps was gone too.

He dropped it on the floor and looked at me with trepidation in his eyes.

I met his look with a stern face. "Is all the money in it?"

"I guess."

"Where?"

"It washed ashore near my uncle's old fishing shack where the river takes a turn eastward."

I reconsidered my earlier impulse to remove the Egrets from my list of suspects.

"Like Grandfather told you. The swamp takes things, then gives them back."

"Don't hand me that line of Indian mumbo jumbo. Why did you take this? You created nothing but trouble for a lot of people."

"Okay, okay. The swamp didn't take it. The explanation is pretty simple. Some kids in the tribe saw your uncle dump it off. They got excited and took it, even more excited when they found the money in it, then terrified because they knew it wasn't theirs. They didn't know what to do, so they hid it for a while, then finally told their parents. The parents came to us for help, and Grandfather said we would take care of it."

"You should have taken it to the cops and spun this story for them to laugh at." I knew I was being mean to him. I could see the truth in his face, but I was crazy with lack of sleep and with how losing this money had probably resulted in Madeleine's kidnapping and worse. It had to be connected to my uncle's murder somehow. I dropped my gaze to the floor and refused to meet his eyes. I wanted to believe him, but could I?

"I'm going. Believe what you want to believe." He shoved the duffel toward me with the toe of his shoe as if it was contaminated with some disgusting virus. He slammed the door, leaving me with half a million soggy dollars at my feet. Well, wasn't this a fine mess?

I determined not to make a move until I talked with Nappi tonight, but for now, I had a business to run. I shoved the duffel into the back of my bedroom closet, took a quick shower and headed for the shop.

WHEN I ARRIVED at the shop Madeleine had already opened the doors. And we had another visitor. Frida.

"Okay, Eve. Let's talk. Actually, I mean you talk and I'll listen. I'm sure you have a lot to tell me."

Oops. From the expression of complete certainty on her face, it was clear Frida had done her homework on my uncle. I had no idea how much she knew so I couldn't decide what to tell her and what to keep to myself. Anything to do with ransom money was off the table for discussion with the cops, and Frida was a cop. The rest of the story I would be safe spilling.

Frida leaned against the counter in the back room. "Just to get you in the mood for chatting, I can tell you this. Winston's phone, a 'burner' I believe it's called, was meant to be destroyed, but instead found its way into your couch, probably fell out of Winston's pocket the morning of the airboat ride. It had some interesting numbers on it. Contacts for his business. All mob related. Nothing from his personal life. Nappi's number was there. Did you know they were doing business together?"

I know I looked shocked, but not for the reason Frida suspected. Nappi had lied to me. He said they never used the phone, that they only met in person.

"So here's where I'm at in this investigation. The only contact in that phone who has direct ties to this area of the country is your Mr. Napolitani. Aside from him, a known family man, the other possibilities for Winston's killer or killers have to be the Hardys. We know they were working for someone, and we're certain their airboat business was only a front for drugs, money transport or other illegal activities. Now they're in the wind. We'd like to have a chat with them, like the one we had with your friend, Nappi. Can you help us with that?"

I shook my head.

"Okay, then is there anything you can fill us in on that we don't know?"

"There was money involved." I thought about the bag filled with cash that I'd moved into the back of my closet. *Not that money.*

I swallowed. "Here's all I know. Winston made a deal with his bosses to do a final job for them before he retired."

Frida let out a snort of a laugh. "No one retires from the mob."

"They do if they can get someone in the mob to broker the deal."

"Nappi. So you're saying that's why his number was on Winston's burner?"

Well, no, I was not saying that, but it was fine with me if Frida thought so. I'd deal with Nappi later. Tonight, over pasta and clam sauce.

"Winston was to deliver a large sum of money for his bosses to someone here. I think it was the Hardys." There, I said it.

Frida smiled. "Bingo. He left the money in the swamp, and it got taken or lost or misplaced or something. The mob got mad and killed him." She paused, giving me time to collect the pieces of a story I could tell her.

"Nappi told you as he did me that the mob never kills someone because that person takes their money. They get it back first; then they may kill the individual. Or worse. I don't think the mob did in my uncle."

"Just testing out a theory, but I know you're right. The bullet that killed him according to ballistics probably came from a rifle, maybe a Kalashnikov. Not the way the mob does hits."

Well, not the American mob but Russian mob, maybe.

"Okay, Eve, you tell me. Who do you think killed him?"

"I don't know."

"I don't either, but I'm going to keep the pressure on to find the Hardys, and I'll be talking on and off with Mr. Napolitani. They're my best leads."

"So you don't think Nappi did it?"

"He produced an alibi for the time. Of course, he could have had your uncle killed."

I shook my head.

"You still trust that guy? You are one naïve woman. We had to drop the charges because of the alibi, but he's still on my radar."

Mine, too. Why had he lied to me and told me he and Winston never made phone contact? He seemed so certain his number wouldn't turn up on my uncle's burner phone.

Frida left, cautioning me again about continuing my friendship with Nappi. If only she knew he was cooking me dinner at my place tonight. I contemplated telling her, but thought better of it.

THE STORE WAS busy, giving Madeleine and me little time to talk about Frida's visit. The last time I promised to drop by our clients in West Palm I'd reneged and came back with nothing to add to our stock. After all the sales today, our store looked as if we had just had an "everything must go" event and were about to close up shop forever.

"It's a poor showing for two gals who pride themselves on their fashion sense," I said. "One of us is going to have to nag the matrons on the coast for items. Just because the stock market has bounced back doesn't mean they won't need a bit of cash to use at the casinos."

I combined two racks of dresses into one, making it look full, but tricks like that wouldn't put more inventory in our store.

"I'll pay them a visit tomorrow," Madeleine said as she pushed the empty rack into the back of the store. "They'll come through with something. What other consignment shop comes to your house to pick up items?"

The bell dinged, signaling a customer had entered.

"Go ahead and take off, Madeleine. You've been doing more than your share here, and you'll need to get up early to drive to the coast tomorrow."

Madeleine stared at the customer. "It's just as well. She's not someone I want to deal with anyway."

I was surprised at her comment until I realized the person was Darlene. Madeleine gave her a curt nod of the head and left.

"I'm getting ready to close." I wasn't keen on dealing with Darlene, either.

"That's why I'm here. I've got something important to talk about. She reached back and flipped the sign in the window to closed. "I don't want anybody to see me."

I wasn't quite comfortable being alone in the store with her. I was taller than she was, sure, and younger too, but there was something edgy about the woman that set me on guard. Usually. Today, however, all I picked up from her was raw terror.

"Let's go back here. I've got a pot of coffee on."

"No booze?" She followed me into the back room.

"It's a consignment shop, not a bar."

She unwound the scarf she was wearing around her neck and over her hair. I noticed she'd been neglecting her roots, which were stark white against the bottle red.

"I'll just come right out with it. I took the money. Here." She plopped her huge purse on the counter, and with shaking hands, extracted the other satchel Winston had carried the day of his death. "You take it. I know someone is tailing me, watching me. I don't want it. It's too much trouble."

I tried not to look surprised, but I was in a state of shock. Two missing bags of money appearing in one day. And dropped into my hands. I did not want the responsibility for either of them.

"It's not my money, Darlene. It belongs to the mob."

"Right. So you can return it to the mob."

"Why me?"

"Cuz you've got mob contacts."

"So do you."

"Mine don't like me or trust me much, and I feel the same about them. Your contact is your buddy, friend, the big Kahuna. He can get it to the right people." She cleared her throat and looked around the room as if expecting someone to jump out from under the dress racks. "I gotta run."

I reached out and grabbed her arm. "Whoa. You're not leaving until you answer a few of my questions. Sit." I pushed her into a chair.

"First, why did you take it? You knew it would cause trouble for Winston."

"I don't know. I sort of panicked. It was sitting there on the floor of the boat, and Winston was babbling on and on about the ride with you. It just seemed so easy. I reached down and dropped the duffel into my purse. Once I'd done it, it was as if the money didn't exist anymore. It was gone. It was mine then."

"You did this just before he was shot?"

"Right after the driver of the boat did that wheelie thing, before we pulled up to the dock. Don't you see? There was all this money and it was going into the hands of the wrong people. I've never had much of anything and—"

"And he'd just dropped the ransom for the Russians in the swamp. He'd gotten directions to do that from the kidnappers, right? He was killing two birds with one stone: money dropped in the swamp for the Russian mob and money in the remaining duffel the delivery for the American mob, his bosses."

"Yes. I knew about the Russians taking Sophia and Boris' sister. And he told me this was his last job for his bosses."

"You're not making any sense. It was so stupid taking the money. You'd have been found out sooner or later."

"I know, I know. I wasn't thinking …. Then Winston was shot and I was …." Darlene teared up.

"You were home free. And wasn't that a lucky break for you? I thought you loved my uncle. You had us running around in circles trying to figure out what happened. But eventually someone would suspect you."

"I know that now. So I returned it."

"Did Sophia and Boris know you took it?"

"No."

"Do you think they suspect you took it?"

"Maybe."

"You can't make this all go away by giving me the money."

"I guess being around so much money that day made me kind of crazy for a while. But now I know better." She jumped up from the chair and ran for the door. She was faster than I expected for a woman of her age and girth. Before I could stop her she ran out into the parking area. I caught her just as she unlocked her rental.

"I'm going to talk to Mr. Napolitani. I'll tell him what you said and about the money. We'll see what we can do. Where will you be tonight?"

She turned to me, a black look on her face. "You are a foolish woman. Don't you understand that he would only support his mob associates? I'm as good as dead if that man or Winston's bosses get a hold of me."

"I have a place for you to hide," I said. It was a stupid gesture on my part, but it meant I could keep track of where she was.

MADELEINE'S SMILE AT seeing me on her doorstep faded quickly when she heard what I had to say. She was almost too enraged to speak. "Are you out of your mind? Absolutely not. First, I can't stand the woman. Second, she's a criminal. Who knows what else she will do? I don't want it done in my house."

Madeleine had a right to be angry with me. Everything she said about Darlene was true, but I didn't know where else to stash the woman. It had to be a place where I could keep an eye on her and where no one she knew would look for her. Since everyone was aware of the enmity between her and Madeleine, it seemed like a perfect solution. Except Madeleine didn't like it, and it was her house. She stamped her foot and stood unmoving in her front doorway. There was no way of getting beyond her without the help of an army of invading Visigoths.

Darlene sat slunk down in my car, my wonderful Mustang that I'd just gotten back from the repair shop. I'd followed her to the local rental place to drop off hers. I knew it wasn't an ideal solution if anyone wanted to track the car. They'd find it here and soon figure out she was no longer on the coast but in Sabal Bay. Still, it was the best I could do. I was running low on schemes.

Madeleine slammed the door as I walked back to my car, my shoulders slumped in defeat. I'd used up any reserve good will she might feel toward me by asking her to hide Darlene. I'd be lucky if Madeleine spoke to me again this month.

"She hates me." Darlene slid farther down in the passenger's seat.

"Not enough to kill you but enough that she won't have you staying with her." I started the engine and stared ahead into the gathering twilight. The streetlight overhead came on like a light bulb in my head. I pulled away from the curb.

"Where to now, jail?" Darlene's voice dripped with sarcasm.

Why was I trying to help this woman? I asked myself again for about the tenth time.

"To a friend's house. He's gone for a few days."

I'd tell Alex I stopped by to water his plants. And left Darlene.

CHAPTER 20

———

"YOU LEFT HER where?" Nappi was clad in my apron and stirred a pot of bubbling sauce at the stove.

"She was terrified. I had to do something. I was afraid she'd bolt, and we'd never find her again."

"I can find anybody." He held the spoon out to me. "Taste."

"You're quite a crook, I mean cook."

He gave me a grim look, then burst into laughter. I joined him. When we recovered, the two bags of money sitting on my living room floor captured our attention.

"What do we do about those?"

"It's impossible to make a sound decision on an empty stomach. We eat first, have a little vino, an espresso and a cannoli. Then we plot our next move."

The food sounded delicious, and I favored the idea of plotting rather than merely reacting. Before I twisted linguini onto my fork, I knew there was something I had to clear up with Nappi.

"Why did you lie to me about how you contacted my uncle? Frida said the burner phone I found in my couch had contact numbers on it for you."

He picked up his fork and directed his attention to the pasta. He took a bite and nodded as if in approval. "I assumed the burner phone had been disposed of in the manner intended, so why should I worry you? You'd only do something foolish if you found it, like dispose of it. As it was, you took it to Frida."

I thought about his answer. So cavalier, but so in keeping with what I knew about Nappi. Yeah, that sounded about right.

We finished out meal, cleared the table and put the dishes into the dishwasher, then took more comfortable seats in my living room.

"What did the Russians think of your offer of half the amount?"

Nappi's look of contentment changed and his eyes clouded over. "They turned me down."

"Maybe I was mistaken about that glove thing. Maybe Boris really did lose his glove and it wasn't the one I grabbed off the ninja couple who robbed Jerry and me. If Sophia and Boris were the guilty parties, you'd think another quarter of a million would satisfy them and give us some evidence they were the kidnappers."

"Not so. Who was the couple then?" Nappi took a sip of his espresso.

"I guess I just don't like the siblings and want to believe the worst of them. I was certain they were the ninja robbers and the original ransom demand was just a ruse to get money. Now that we know it was real, we don't have a clue who the robbers were, and the Russians still want half a million dollars."

We both leaned forward and our gazes landed on the duffels.

"We have the money, and I have the drop-off instructions." There was determination in his voice.

"Is this the end game? We give it up, and that's all? We never find out who killed my uncle or why?" I put my head in my hands.

Nappi got up from his chair and came over to wrap his arms around me. "We're not through with this yet. We have until late tomorrow night to find out more. Then we'll give them this money." He pointed toward the beaten-up duffel.

"Because it was what Winston wanted."

As for the money in the other duffel, the one Darlene had taken, I knew it would have to go back to Winston's bosses. Nappi would take care of that in time.

Neither of us was happy with this outcome, but unless tomorrow produced some detail we didn't already know, we were stuck. Our only hope was to foil the drop-off, get the sister back and hope the pieces of this puzzle would realign themselves to reveal my uncle's killer.

It was a lousy plan.

I AWOKE IN the middle of the night and knew it was simple. The kidnappers insisted that the authorities not be contacted, and that was Kidnapping 101. The parties involved—my uncle who was a mob lackey, Darlene with her mob connections and the Russian siblings whose experience in their home country made them suspicious of the police—would never want the authorities in on this. That made sense to me. Frida didn't know a thing about the kidnapping of Winston's stepdaughter. Our only source of information was another mob member, Mr. Napolitani, but he didn't have any "ins" with the Russian mob.

The background information that the Feds and other police organizations might examine in a kidnapping wasn't in play, and when I thought about not having it, that bothered me. A lot. I knew nothing about my uncle's Russian family: where they came from, who they were, any details about their personal histories or their present status. What a dope I'd been, letting myself be run back and forth, panicked by threats about the kidnapped sister and then Madeleine. It kept my adrenaline pumping and sidelined my thought centers. I should have done this before. I needed the services of a good PI. I knew one. I called, even though it was two in the morning.

"Hi, Alex? Look, I know it's late but this is important. You have contacts. Could you help me out?"

There was a lot of grumbling at the other end of the line, but when I assured him I only needed information, that I wasn't planning anything illegal, he said he'd work on it. I told him he had until tomorrow afternoon.

"What happens then?"

"Nothing."

"Eve."

"Really. Nothing. Not until later." I told him about the ransom drop-off.

"The authorities still aren't in on this?"

"No. No one wants to play around with the Russians. They're too unpredictable. But Nappi's going to spearhead the drop-off." Once the words slipped out of my mouth, I regretted them.

"Oh, well, then things should be great." Alex was wide awake now. I could tell, because his words were dripping with sarcastic dislike of Nappi.

"Call me. And thanks, honey. Oh, and before you hang up, I thought I'd let you know I watered your plants."

"I don't have any plants."

"That's just my way of saying I dropped by your place. I should buy you one. Maybe a cactus."

"For getting you this information? I was expecting something a little more personal."

"No, the thank you is for putting up a person I know."

"Eve?"

I hung up and made a note to buy Alex a thank you philodendron. He'd overwater a cactus.

I got out of bed and fired up my computer. By five in the morning, I had information on my uncle's Russian family. I couldn't track their background in Russia, but I was certain Alex would ferret that out for me. I had another source I hadn't mined yet, but I intended to do some excavating there later. I signed off and slid back into bed, setting my alarm for seven—time enough to pick up breakfast for two, then go to the shop.

I fell asleep at once and dreamed of sailing with my parents on the sound. When I awoke, I felt refreshed, as if I'd slept for days. I made a pot of coffee and called Grandy to share my pleasant dream.

"You sound better than I've heard you in days. Getting restful sleep is good for you," she said.

"Yep and so is using my head a little."

"You've always used your head, dear. Sometimes you're a little impulsive."

"I know, but I've stepped back and looked at this kidnapping thing and I think I've figured something out."

"What is that?"

"Did Winston contact you over the years, I mean, since I last saw him when I was a teen?"

"Yes, he did. He called many times, always asked about what you were doing. I felt a little guilty not letting you know but he thought you'd find his business connections unpleasant. I encouraged him in that, I know, but I wasn't keen on ruining your childhood memories. It was bad enough you lost your parents when you were so young. I wanted you to have good memories of Winston. He was so proud of you, although not really crazy about your choice of Jerry as a husband."

"Did he know about my friendship with Nappi and that Jerry was working for him?"

"No. I don't think he would have liked it, wouldn't have understood."

"Well he found out right before his death. I think he did understand. He trusted Nappi, and since I did also, it might have been what influenced him to retire."

"Do you think that's somehow related to his murder?"

"Only indirectly." I paused. "Hey, I've got to run. I just called to say I love you and Max."

"Wait. You said you figured out something about the kidnapping. What was it?"

"I always thought to be connected to another human being

was more important than anything, but not everyone can feel that way."

"That's it?"

"Oh Grandy, that's everything."

"UP AND AT 'em. Open up. It's room service." I had to bang on the door and yell twice before I heard footsteps inside.

Darlene opened the door an inch and peered out at me. "Oh, it's you. What time is it anyway? The sun's barely up. I need sleep. I've been under a lot of stress lately."

"Yeah, I can relate. I have to open the store today, so I thought I'd bring you a little breakfast. I don't suppose Alex has anything in the house. He hasn't been home much of late."

She opened the door wide enough for me to squeeze in, poked her head out and looked up and down the street, then slammed it shut and turned the lock and the deadbolt.

"I am hungry, now that you mention it." She grabbed the coffee I'd set on the table, ripped open one of the breakfast sandwiches and took a huge bite. "Aren't you having anything?"

"I thought I'd eat the other sandwich."

"These are so small, only a few bites." She grabbed the other one and held it to her chest. "You can get another on the way to the shop."

I brought her the food to make nice, get her to trust and like me, but now I thought I should turn her into the cops and tell them what she said about taking the money. Frida would believe me. I resisted the impulse. I wanted to pick her brain, and she might be more agreeable to spilling information if she was well fed and caffeinated.

"No sign of anyone? No SUVs driving past?" I hoped I sounded concerned for her safety.

"I didn't see any. What do you know?"

"Nothing. I think you're perfectly safe here." I pulled out a kitchen chair and gestured to it. She plopped into it, shoving the last bite of her first sandwich into her mouth at the same time she unwrapped the second one.

"I feel pretty safe. The bed is comfortable and I took a long shower last night. Sophia and Boris are so mean about the hot water. They say it costs too much for me to have a hot shower whenever I want."

"Are they mean about everything like that?"

"I thought they'd be nicer to me after Winston was killed, but they seem to resent my presence in the apartment. The worst is Sophia. No one likes her. Boris can be nice if he wants to."

I pulled out the chair across from her and sat.

"I find Sophia pretty unpleasant myself. Boris is an enigma. He rarely says anything. What did the two of them do when they were in Russia, I mean what kind of work?"

"They were in the army. She was a slupner."

I couldn't make out the last word because she was talking with a mouthful of egg and muffin.

"What?"

"She was a sniper."

Interesting.

"Was Boris, too?"

"No, he had some kind of desk job. But then the family immigrated here. The Russian army was behind in paying their personnel anyway. I'm not certain what they did once they got here. Winston seemed to always be giving them money."

"He was a generous man. What about the other sister? She was younger?"

Darlene put down the last of her sandwich and gave me a suspicious look. "Are you pumping me for information? What's that all about?"

"I was just curious, that's all. Don't forget that I was being tapped for ransom money also. I thought if I knew more about them I might find out something to lead us to the Russians holding the sister. If the authorities had been pulled in on this, they would have examined the family's background in depth. Yours, too."

She coughed on her muffin and took a gulp of her coffee. "Dry. Must have been made really early this morning."

"I don't recall the sister's name."

"Me, either." She spread out the muffin wrapper and picked crumbs and melted cheese off it. It seemed all her willingness to talk about the family evaporated as the food disappeared down her throat, and I had no more time left before I opened shop to purchase her more.

"There is one thing I remember about the sister."

I turned at the door and looked back at her. "Yes?"

"Sophia really did not like her sister. Sophia hated her, actually."

"How do you know this?"

"Boris told me. I think Sophia would have been happy to let the sister remain in the Russians' hands."

I found that fascinating, given Sophia's insistence on getting the money out of me. What an actress she was.

"Stay put. Nappi's going to make the ransom drop tonight. Everything will be over by then."

"Nappi. Phew. That man gives me the jitters."

Nappi had that effect on some people—the ones with something to hide.

MADELEINE RETURNED FROM the coast with her arms full of dresses, skirts, blouses, and shoes, thanks to our patrons there. All the garments were name-brand merchandise so gently used that occasionally the tags had been left on them. I knew that those had been worn with the tags tucked inside, in case their purchasers decided to return the merchandise. Even the wealthy can be frugal or cheap, to be honest. I guess Madeleine nagged them enough that they gave her even those items they intended to return along with used articles they wanted money for. It was easier because we picked up.

They loved us because we made them money, but they didn't want our van camped on their doorsteps. We tried to be discreet and decided against having our name on the side of the van, only the logo of a woman dressed in evening wear. Classy, very classy. "Oh, that van? It was the dry cleaners," I heard them say to friends, the very friends who also used our services. "Admit nothing, ask no questions, provide no answers" must have been the catch phrase of West Palm matrons.

We sorted through what Madeleine had obtained and were about to begin tagging the items when my cell rang. It was Alex, not happy that he had Darlene bivouacked in his apartment, but thrilled to have reached me, which meant I wasn't in jail or being held at gunpoint. The information he obtained, along with what I'd learned earlier in my computer search, gave me a more textured picture of Sophia and Boris. It was the sister I needed to know more about. Alex found out she lived in Pahokee, only thirty short miles from here, not up north as Sophia had led me to believe. The sister had changed her name several years ago, perhaps an indication she wanted to put as much distance as possible between her and her siblings, probably Sophia. She was now known as Mary Ford, a nice, American-sounding name. She was in the phone book. I punched in her number, expecting it to be disconnected. If I was lucky enough to get an answering machine, I thought I might leave a message. "Sorry to hear about your kidnapping. Hang in there. You'll be rescued tonight." I knew she'd not get it before the ransom drop, but it might be a nice sentiment to come home to. If she made it home.

A woman answered on the third ring. "Hello."

I almost dropped the phone. I recovered as fast as I could. "Is this Ms. Mary Ford?

"Yes. Who is this?"

The accent sounded Russian.

"This is the catalogue department at JCPenny. Your order is in."

"I didn't order anything. Goodbye." She hung up.

I couldn't tell from our short conversation if she was stressed or not. The kidnappers could be holding her at her own house. What better place, but in plain sight?

I connected again.

"This is JCPenny again. You don't want your order?"

"You stupid American. I didn't order anything. Leave me alone." She hung up again.

She certainly didn't sound stressed. Perturbed, yes. Angry, put out, annoyed enough to want to jump through the phone and grab me by my Vera Wang shirt? Absolutely. This was no kidnapping victim. This was a Sophia clone. The attitude must have been in the genes.

I tried again. This time I had something I thought she'd want to hear.

"I tell you, don't call me. I hang up again."

"No, don't do that. Now that we know you haven't been kidnapped, here's a message from Mr. Napolitani you can deliver to Sophia and Boris. There's been a change in plans. If they want any money, tell them to meet at the original drop-off site in the swamp. Tonight at eight. We'll exchange money for the identity of my uncle's killer. If they try to get in touch with Mr. Napolitani, then they get no money at all, and we'll turn this all over to the cops."

I ended the call, my heart pounding.

What if she knew nothing about the kidnapping? No problem. She'd either call Sophia and Boris and deliver my message anyway or forget about the call. I was certain now there was no kidnapping, so no one was in danger. No one except perhaps for me. What the hell was I doing? It sounded a bit risky even to my ears, but I'd just call Nappi and tell him what I had arranged. He'd be happy to provide back-up. I'd be quite safe. Quite safe. Sure.

I then wondered who Sophia and Boris would put up for my uncle's killer. I bet it would be Darlene. I was curious to hear how they'd work that one out. They'd want to get rid of her so she couldn't defend herself, but I was convinced I'd hidden her well. I'd let her be for now, safe and snug in Alex's apartment, raiding his refrigerator, swearing when she found nothing.

"Who were you talking to on the phone just now?" Madeleine's voice brought me back to the present.

"That was Alex. He was doing a job for me."

"A job? You hired him?"

"Kind of. I promised him compensation in the form of nights spent together without interruption."

"Maybe you can tell me all about it when you get the chance. I have a feeling I'm not going to like what you're up to."

"I'm not up to anything."

"You're breathing hard. You only do that when you are hot over some guy, hate someone, or have some crazy plan in mind, usually one that threatens someone's life, often yours."

"Okay. Listen to this. I called the sister of Sophia and Boris. She answered. Can you believe that? She certainly didn't sound like she was under duress. In fact, I think she's a co-kidnapper, if there is such a thing. It was all a hoax, set up by Sophia and Boris, and it got my uncle killed."

I hit the contact number for Jerry. It rang and rang, but didn't go to voicemail. The service came on, saying the individual was away from the phone. Damn. Jerry was my only contact with Nappi, and I needed them both tonight. Alex was out of town, and I didn't have enough information to go to Frida. I was screwed. No I wasn't.

"Madeleine, could you close up for me? Sorry to ask, but I have an errand to run."

She shook her head and gave me a pitying look. "Eve, Eve, Eve. You are so bad. You're going to get yourself killed one of these days."

"Don't worry. I have a plan."

"You always say you have a plan when what you really mean is that you have an impulse to meddle."

I love Madeleine to pieces, but she's always so negative, especially when it comes to murder.

Chapter 21

—

"He's off fishing tonight." Grandfather sat on his porch, puffing on his pipe. He leaned forward to give my request additional consideration. "But I guess I could help you."

"I don't want to put you to any trouble."

"No trouble. Besides, I want to be in on this. You're going to find your uncle's killer, aren't you?"

"Yes, but—"

"It's more exciting than selling clothes to ladies. You and Sammy have all the fun."

"I'll come here at seven, and we can get to the site early."

"Maybe the real cops would like to be in on the action."

"I'd tell my friend Frida, but she doesn't know about the kidnapping and it would take too long to explain and she wouldn't believe me anyway and then she'd yell at me." I stopped long enough to catch my breath. "I don't think it would work out well."

"Okay, I get it, but I think we should do this sooner."

"Why?"

He pointed toward the western sky, where black clouds were thickening. "Big storm coming in."

"We'll be quick about this."

He smiled. "What's the plan?"

Plan? I didn't have one. Except maybe to bluff my way through this.

Maybe I should rethink this meeting. I tried Jerry's phone again. Same message. With my luck, he'd left his phone in a motel room with some bimbo he met. I'd framed the message I gave to the sister in such a way that Sophia and Boris would expect me and Nappi. Where there was a Nappi, there would be weapons and men who could shoot them. It was certain Sophia and Boris would arm themselves with as much firepower as they could carry. Grandfather and I would have a shotgun and two sharp things that required us to be in stabbing distance of the enemy. And Sophia was a sniper. Yeah, that sounded like a fair fight. Maybe I could just stay home and watch television.

Madeleine was right. My plans were always the product of impulse rather than strategy.

Grandfather Egret could see I was struggling. "How do you feel about snakes?"

"Ugh. I hate them." I shivered just thinking about them.

"Most people do. Did you know there's a bounty on Burmese pythons?"

"Grandfather, I hate to interrupt you, but I think I've made a mistake. These people will have weapons. What do we have? Nothing."

He chuckled. "We've got snakes."

His plan was simple, but clever. I hoped he was right about most people hating snakes. Ugh. I couldn't stop shivering at the thought of the creepy creatures.

The wind picked up as we loaded our gear into the airboat. It reminded me of the time, not so long ago, that Sammy and I spent time in the swamps.

In his usual way, Grandfather seemed to read my mind. He

tossed the duffel of money into the boat, then set down his burlap bag. "This storm will be bigger than the one you and Sammy weathered, close to hurricane strength winds. We'd best hurry. I want to get back and make myself a hot toddy. My sinuses are bothering me. They always do when the air pressure slides."

On the way out to the site, Grandfather pointed out the inherent flaw in my information for money exchange: if Sophia and Boris were the ones who killed my uncle, why would my offer of money make them confess to being the killers? He slowed to idle so we could hear each other.

"They'll tell me because they intend to kill me anyway."

"That won't do you any good."

"You'll be listening."

"That won't do you any good."

"I know. You're right. Turn the boat around and let's go back home."

"We can do this. We just have to out-think them and be quicker than they are. And surprise them."

"Are you sure?"

"Nope." Yet the grin on his face said this was something he fully intended to enjoy.

"Do you have some kind of a death wish?"

"Do you?"

"No."

He chuckled. "Me either."

He kicked it up, and we flew over the water toward our rendezvous.

WE WERE A good hour and a half early and there was no sign of Sophia and Boris. I trusted they would come alone. They'd be well-armed, so why would they need back-up?

I untied the small rowboat with its tiny motor from the back of the airboat and left it pulled up to the shore. Grandfather drove the airboat down the shore and hid it in the reeds there.

I stepped into the clearing with care, making sure that the mama alligator was nowhere around.

"Don't worry about her. She's in her hidey hole, waiting out the storm."

"Who?"

He smiled at me. "You know, the big gal you're worried about."

Damn. His ability to read my mind made me feel weird.

"Let's get these weapons up there." He pointed up at the top of one of the palms in the small clearing where my uncle had left the money.

Grandfather tossed a rope up, and it caught in one of the palm fronds. When he tugged on it, it came down. Time seemed to rush by, and we were not yet set up to receive our guests. He tossed the rope again, and it flew over the fronds and dangled on the other side, just out of reach.

"I'll go on up there and get it."

I watched in awe as he shimmied up the tree, using only his hands and feet to grip it until he could reach the end of the rope.

"Here." He pulled the rope down and threw it to me. "Now tie the end around that sack."

I shook my head.

"Don't you know how to tie a knot?"

"That's not it. I don't want to get too close. Those things are armed."

"Okay, I'll come on down and do it." He sounded disappointed in me.

"Never mind. I'll do it." I approached the bag and tried to pull it along the ground with two fingers, but the contents were too heavy and I had to grasp it with both hands to meet the end of the rope. I tied a knot as fast as I could, but my fingers were shaking, and I worried it might not hold.

"If that knot doesn't hold, the contents of that bag will be all over the ground." He sounded amused at the possibility.

Again with the mind reading. I examined my knot, adjusted it and signaled him to pull it up. He grabbed the other end of the rope and we watched the bag move heavenward. With all the wind blowing and the sky darkening, I couldn't track it all the way up. I tossed another rope to Grandfather, who tied it around his waist and used it to help him ascend to the top of the tree. He too disappeared from sight, and I felt alone.

"You okay up there?" The wind blew my words back to me. I waited for his response, but heard nothing. Suddenly, I heard something drop at my feet. I jumped, then sighed with relief. It was only the extra rope.

The wind let up for a moment and Grandfather shouted to me. "I'm all set. What time is it?"

I looked at my watch. It was only seven fifteen, but because of the black clouds covering the final rays of the sun, it felt later. I heard the sound of an airboat. Sophia and Boris were arriving early, as I suspected they would. Maybe they were already in place before Grandfather and I got here. I tried to swallow my fear. That was a chance we'd have to take. I carried the duffel nearer the water and stood behind it. If this crazy plan of Grandfather's was to work, we had to time everything with precision and make certain Sophia and Boris were in the right position.

The airboat pulled up beside the motor boat I wanted them to assume I'd driven here.

They stopped the engine and jumped off the vessel. I couldn't see them well. They seemed to fade into the blackness of the impending storm. Then I realized they were both dressed in their ninja attire. All I could discern of their faces was their eyes—cold, colder than arctic winds. I worried about Grandfather in his aerie but I knew I couldn't look up to check if he was safe.

"Open up the bag. Let's see the money." The voice was male, but it was difficult to tell with all the wind noise if it was Boris. I thought I caught the Russian accent.

"Tell me first who killed my uncle."

He laughed and I knew it was Boris "Sure, why not. You don't really think you and that old Indian in the tree are going to get out of here alive, do you? We're not stupid. We watched the two of you arrive and then he went up the tree, but he didn't have a weapon. What's he going to do, throw coconuts down on us?"

I crossed my fingers that the poor visibility had made it impossible for them to see the bag go up the tree.

"He can stay up there if he likes. When I shoot him the drop to the ground will make his death all the more certain." Boris sounded happy at the prospect of Grandfather's death.

"Tell me. If you killed my uncle, why did you do it? He was your stepfather. He was going to rescue your sister."

"We led him to believe my sister had been taken by the Russian Mafia, a story easy for him to buy because of his own mob connections. The money was for us. And why not? We knew he left everything to you. Then someone took our money, and we had to try to persuade you to give us your inheritance. You weren't as easy to convince."

"You mugged Jerry and took that half million in cash. Wasn't that enough for you?"

"It was less than we figured out we could have when Nappi arranged to give us his money. Then you called today and told us you would deliver the money. I liked dealing with you rather than with your mob connection."

"You shot my uncle from across the canal. Your sister is a crack shot."

"Yes, she is." Boris turned to the individual beside him. "She knew just when to shoot, because Darlene removed her scarf as a signal that the money was in place."

Boris took a step forward and held out his hand. "I see from the expression on your face that you didn't know Darlene was in on this."

I was shocked. I'd believed that woman, but I could hand out surprises too. "And did you know Darlene took the other duffel with the money Winston was to deliver to the mob?"

"We must pay her a visit then. And talk to her. And get that money also. Tie up loose ends."

I smiled.

"Oh, we know where she is. We followed her when she fled. Very suspicious. She's at your boyfriend's house. We had no intention of sharing the money with her. We were going to kill her anyway, so it's just a small detour for us. Now, I think it's time for the money. That was the deal, wasn't it? You know how and why your uncle was killed, and now we get our money." He gestured with his hand toward the duffel that lay at my feet. "Kick it toward me."

"It's heavy." I bent over and shoved the satchel toward him. The momentum of my push sent it rolling down the incline and toward the water. Boris kept his gun on me and would have shot me then, but the bag slid farther, not stopping at the swamp's edge.

"Go ahead and shoot her," Boris said to his sister.

Sophia raised her rifle as Boris stooped to grab the bag to prevent it from rolling into the water. At that moment something came hurtling down from the palm. It was not coconuts. It was more snakes than I'd ever seen in one place, several three- to five-foot-long Burmese pythons and an abundance of smaller ones, all toppling out of the bag which he'd hauled up there earlier. The snakes were in a bad mood. They'd been bunched up in such a tiny space for so long and now freedom meant being tossed down on the heads of two humans.

Grandfather was right. Most people do not like snakes. They like them even less when the creatures fall from a stormy sky onto their heads. Boris yelled, torn between getting out of the way of the largest snake and making certain the bag with the money didn't slide into the dark waters. It did, and Boris slid with it. I couldn't see well, but there was a lot of thrashing around, yelling in Russian, and then silence.

Sophia dropped her rifle and screamed, a really girlie kind of scream. I was surprised that the ice lady could be so creeped out by a few snakes. I would be—and I was, actually—but I'm not a sniper with nerves of steel and a personality to match. I saw my opportunity and tackled her before she could pull herself together. Once I got her down, I jumped on her chest and pounded my fists into her face. I forgot about the snakes surrounding us. Well, maybe my pummeling her was as much out of fear one would snuggle up to me as my anger at what she did to my uncle. She was strong, but not strong enough to roll me off her. I was taller and heavier, and I'd knocked the breath out of her with my tackle. I took no chances. I continued to whale on her. It felt good.

Two arms pulled me off her. I whirled around, thinking it was Boris. Instead I looked into Grandfather Egret's eyes. "I think you've knocked her around enough. She's in no shape to do anything." Just to be certain, Grandfather held her rifle pointed at her.

I jerked her to her feet and tore off the mask, wanting to see the expression on Sophia's face. Pain, fear, anger, or her usual cold expression? To my shock, it wasn't Sophia hiding behind the mask.

I gasped. "Who are you?"

What she intended as a look of bravado was replaced by a grimace of pain. "You broke my nose."

"Who the hell are you?"

"My name is Mary Ford. We talked on the phone. You must be the JCPenny catalog lady." She tried to spit in my face, but she telegraphed her intention by puckering her lips. I stepped back.

"Settle down. Grandfather, where's Boris?"

"Gone into the swamps with the money."

"Okay, then where are all the snakes?"

"Here and there. Let's tie this one up and look for them." He handed me her rifle and grabbed the rope.

"Are you out of your mind? Let them go."

"Didn't you hear me say there's a bounty for these guys? I stumbled onto a nest of little ones the other day. Where did you think I got them from?"

The wind changed in volume from a rumble to a deafening roar, thrashing the trees and reeds as if it was punishing them.

Grandfather finished tying Mary's wrists and looked up. "Maybe we can look later. I think we need to head home." He grabbed her arm and pulled her toward the hidden airboat.

"I can't breathe well." Mary's voice sounded muffled from the blood still pouring from her nose.

I grabbed her shirt and pulled it up over her face, wiped her nose, then jerked it back down. "That's the best I can do."

"I need medical attention."

"You'll get it. When we get back home." *If we get back home.* Then I added, "And after we visit the police station." It was time to get Frida involved.

Grandfather climbed into the pilot's seat of the boat. "It's past time for Frida to be involved."

Yeah, yeah, yeah. That's just what she would say. And more.

The wind threatened to capsize the boat once we were out on the large open canal, but Grandfather guided the craft through the waves and around pieces of debris now floating on the water. When we glided up to the chickee, I could see a figure waiting for us.

"Where have you been? Who is this?" Sammy tied up the boat and helped me onto the dock. I grabbed the prisoner and pulled her after me.

"This is the woman responsible for killing my uncle."

CHAPTER 22

WE ALL PILED into my Mustang, Sammy in the backseat with Mary, guarding her. I drove with Grandfather riding shotgun, really riding shotgun because he carried the rifle. I wanted this woman off my hands into those of the law as soon as possible. Now that I'd captured her, I found the thought of official custody comforting. We called ahead and found Frida at the station, and although she wanted to come pick up the prisoner, I was determined to deliver her myself.

The drive into town was as dicey as the ride in the airboat. The highway looked like a river. Waves of water flowed from one side of the road to the other, then changed direction and washed towards us. I gritted my teeth, gripped the wheel and listened to Grandfather take up a chant, low and atonal.

"Calling on the storm gods?"

He ignored my question and kept right on with his song. It must have helped, because we made it into town. None of the stoplights were working, and the wind blew them sideways when it hit. It didn't matter because no one else was stupid enough to be on the road. I roared through one intersection and heard a loud ping, followed by the sound of something metal hitting the pavement behind me. I looked in the rearview mirror and saw the traffic signal bounce once onto the roadway, then roll off into the grass.

Mary was quiet for the entire ride and, when she got to the station, she asked for a lawyer.

"I haven't arrested you yet. Or read you your rights. Have a seat." Frida pushed her into a chair in one of the interrogation rooms, shut the door behind her and came out to talk with us.

"Here's the rifle she had in her hand tonight. I'll bet it is the same one that killed my uncle." I handed it to Frida.

"We'll have ballistics check it out." She gestured to several chairs in front of her desk. "Have a seat. You guys look as if you could use something hot."

"I wanted to stay home with a nice hot toddy, but Sammy insisted I come to give my story." Grandfather slid into one of the chairs.

"He was right. Now let's hear the story again. From the beginning. Don't leave anything out." She fixed me with a glare.

"Grandfather and I—"

"No, Eve. The beginning, not the beginning of tonight."

I slumped into the chair. "So can I have some of that awful police station coffee? I'm wet and cold."

"Oops." Grandfather pulled something out of his pocket. It was one of his snakes. This one must have been injured during the fall. It didn't wriggle much.

"Will it die?" Not that I cared. I was just curious. As much as the little bugger had helped us tonight, my sensitivities did not extend to reptiles.

Grandfather laughed. "It's only a rubber snake. I threw it in with the others. Why not? The more, the better."

Frida looked at him in disbelief. "Put it back in your pocket."

It was the beginning of a long night.

"SHE'LL GET HER lawyer." Frida looked exhausted as did we all. Grandfather had put his head into his arms on Frida's desk and appeared to be sleeping. Sammy and I sat on a bench outside Frida's office and leaned into each other.

"Can we leave now?" I unfolded myself from my seat.

"Sure. Listen, I'm about to send two uniforms over to Alex's to pick up Darlene, but here's the bad part. Mary won't talk, we don't have Boris, and I haven't located Sophia. I'd like to be able to put some pressure on Darlene to see what she might be willing to say to save her skin. I know you're exhausted, but you do owe me. How could you not tell me about the kidnapping?"

"There was no kidnapping, remember? It was a hoax to get my uncle's money and then mine." Since she hadn't mentioned Madeleine's kidnapping, I didn't see the need to complicate things further.

"Of course I remember, but you thought it was real and didn't inform the authorities."

"They didn't want the authorities involved. I wanted to do what my uncle would have wanted me to do." I flapped my hand at her. "We've gone around and around on this one tonight. You're right. I owe you."

"I hate to put you in this position, Eve, even though I know how you like to do my job for me, but I could use your help." All the spunk seemed to have gone out of Frida, too, because she could hardly work up one of her crooked, snide smiles.

If there was a chance these creeps could get away with my uncle's murder, I was willing to do anything to prevent that, even tolerate Frida's sarcasm and not reply in kind.

"Can I take Grandfather with me? Make it seem like we just got out of the swamp?" I shared with her what I had in mind, and this time, it was a decent strategy with police backup and everything. Frida approved.

"DARLENE, ARE YOU here?" I used my spare key to Alex's house to let Grandfather and me in.

She wandered out of the living room looking wider awake than I expected.

"What's going on? I couldn't sleep because of this storm. I've been listening to Alex's transistor radio. I guess it missed us, went south of here. I hope Boris and Sophia are okay."

She seemed too chatty for someone who was terrified by the hurricane.

"We had a rendezvous with them in the swamp earlier. They had some very interesting things to say about you."

"What did they say? It's not true."

"They said you were responsible for Winston's death. They told us all about the phony kidnapping and the murder and said you planned the whole thing."

Darlene's face turned an unpleasant color of green. "I didn't. It was Sophia. She masterminded the plan."

"Now you know that's not true, but I thought you might want to know that Boris escaped, although we grabbed the sister, Sophia's younger sister, the one you said she hated so much. Anyway, Boris is probably just waiting for the storm to abate, and then he's coming for you."

Grandfather stepped forward. "I heard him say they were going to kill you anyway. That you were a troublesome woman."

Her color faded into ghostly white. She grabbed her throat and her eyes darted around the room. "I've got to get out of here."

"Don't be silly, Darlene. He can find you anywhere. He might not be a crack shot, but he's smart. He'll simply have Sophia take you out."

"She wouldn't do that."

"Why not?"

"She never knew a thing about the phony kidnapping. She thought it was for real. It was planned by Boris and the younger sister. Sophia is a real letter-of-the-law kind of person. She'd never have gone for the plan, so Boris thought up the phony kidnapping, and Sophia's concern made it seem real."

I thought about that. Sophia's concern? Well, I guess she was worried, genuinely so, but sometimes it sure was difficult picking that out from all the ice encasing her personality.

"Your only hope is to come with us and turn yourself in before Boris does what he threatened. I can speak to my friend, the one who's the detective here. I'm sure you can cut a deal if I tell her how cooperative you've been." I hated saying these things when what I wanted most was to put my hands around her throat and squeeze.

I heard a noise behind me. Both Grandfather and I turned at the same moment. Had Boris worked his way out of the swamps?

I turned. Behind me stood two men. The Hardy brothers, Digby and the bigger one, whose name I'd never heard, stood in the shadows. They stepped forward. Each carried a gun.

Grandfather tapped my shoulder. "His name is Darwin."

"Not now," I whispered.

"I told them the money was at your place." Darlene tried on a weak smile, which turned into a grimace of fear.

"We need our money," Darwin said.

I knew Frida was right behind us, but I wanted to do something to these two that they'd remember for a while.

I leaned over to Grandfather and whispered again in his ear. "Let them have it."

He looked at me, puzzlement on his face.

"Give it to them."

This time Digby heard me.

"You got something else for us?"

I nodded.

Digby stepped forward and held out one hand. "Don't try nothing funny."

Grandfather reached into his pocket and placed the snake gently into Digby's hand.

Digby yelped, dropped his gun and stumbled into his brother. Darwin regained his balance and leveled his gun at Grandfather. I think he would have fired it, but another deeper, more commanding voice came from behind him.

"Drop it." It was Mr. Napolitani.

Darwin did as Nappi commanded, and both brothers twisted their heads in all directions searching for the snake. Darlene had jumped onto a chair and stood there holding the hem of her nightgown. She was also scanning the floor. To my surprise it wriggled under Alex's sofa.

My mouth dropped open. "I thought that snake was rubber."

"No, this one is." Grandfather pulled the fake one out of his pocket. "That one was the real thing."

I thought I heard sirens in the distance. "Frida's right behind you."

Nappi nodded, but kept his eyes on the Hardy brothers. "I know. I saw her at an intersection where some debris had been blown into the road. I'd come through before the road was blocked. They had to clear it for her to get here."

"Well, then. It appears we have a nice surprise for her." I smiled at Nappi, hoping he would return the look. He did not.

"Eve, my dear. We need to talk. Meantime, I will keep these two for myself. They have some explaining to do to their bosses. I think it's better we allow them that opportunity."

Digby began to whimper. "No, take us to jail. I don't want to explain nothing. It was just bad luck."

"Take it like a man." Darwin slapped his brother, but I thought his face also seemed a bit drawn in worry.

Several of Nappi's men joined him, and they walked the Hardy brothers out of the house and pushed them into the vehicles waiting out front.

"Frida won't like that I let you take these fellows."

Nappi gave me a Mafia smile—one with no humor behind it. "How will you stop me? Threaten me with a rubber snake?"

"What about me?" Darlene was shaking, her red curls bouncing as if they were alive. "And where's that damn snake?"

The sirens grew louder. I looked through the window and watched the car with the Hardy brothers in it pull away from the curb as Frida's police cruiser pulled up.

"You'll go with her," I said and nodded at the police cruiser.

Darlene seemed relieved. I guess she worried I'd send her off with Nappi. I should have.

I found a piece of paper and pencil and scribbled Alex a note. It read, "I meant to get you a houseplant as a thank you present for doing all that work for me, but instead I found something more lively. Maybe you'd better call the exterminators. The upside is that there's a bounty on these things. You can collect on it."

I gave Grandfather a hug and thanked him over and over again for his help; then I drove him and Sammy back to their house. No one said much on the way there. The storm was over and the moon had come out, big and white as if it had been washed clean by all the rain.

"So now we know everything." Sammy unfolded himself from my car and helped Grandfather get out of the back seat.

"I guess so. It all makes sense now—horrible, greedy, murderous sense. At least I know what happened and who was responsible for my uncle's death. I don't know why he left me all that money or who removed it from his accounts. I still think he was at heart a good man. He tried to rescue a child he probably never met because he felt he owed it to her mother and her siblings."

I said goodnight then because I just couldn't think about this anymore.

On the way home, I finally felt able to grieve for my uncle. Tears filled my eyes. I reached in my pocket for a tissue and pulled out ... the rubber snake. Grandfather Egret had stuffed it in my jacket as a souvenir. I chuckled to myself. I loved that man.

CHAPTER 23

———

WHEN I STEPPED onto my porch, I knew something was not right. I always left a light on in the living room. It was a habit of mine, one I never broke. I was convinced it made it look as if someone was home, a deterrent to burglars. Alex said anyone surveilling the house would figure out it was a ploy. I did it anyway. It made me feel safe.

I was too tired and too sad to play heroine if my house was being burgled, so I did something all my friends had wanted me to do from the beginning of this murder/kidnapping case. I called Frida on my cell, inserted my key in the lock and stepped into the darkened living room. No one had to tell me who was there. I knew immediately from the earthy, moldy smell of the swamps.

"Did you manage to hang onto your money, Boris? Or was it gone with the wind, back into the swamp?" I reached for the switch inside the door and flipped it on. Nothing. Did I feel like an idiot! The bulb must have burned out. No. Wait a minute. I flipped the switch to turn it on. If the bulb had burned out, the switch would already have been in the "on" position.

"I get it now. You unscrewed the bulb. I know you're here,

Boris." I heard someone take a deep breath from across the room.

The table lamp beside the chair in the living room came on.

"You think you're pretty smart, but you're just another spoiled American woman. I have a passport, and I will go home with money. I come to take the money Darlene hid."

Now, how did he know it was here? Or did he?

"I followed Darlene here the other day and then to your boyfriend's house. She wasn't carrying the bag she arrived here with. It has to be the money bag."

I glanced around the room. It hadn't been searched yet, so Boris must have just arrived.

"You're lucky to be alive."

"I'm a strong man. No bunch of snakes or a swamp can do me in."

I thought about that old Russian joke, "Strong like bull, smart like tractor." I smiled.

"You think this is funny? I will give you your life if you give me the money."

I wanted to stall him more, but I could tell he was impatient to leave. I wanted to believe he would spare my life, but I couldn't count on it. I hoped the call I made to Frida had connected and that she was hearing the conversation. The one time I reach out for help, there's no one there. Where the hell was she? Where else? Home in bed, sleeping soundly, secure in the knowledge that the case was wrapped up.

No one was coming to rescue me.

"The money is in the bedroom," I said.

He gestured with his gun to indicate I should lead the way.

The only light in the bedroom came from the moonlight through the window, not enough to see well. I walked into the room and turned on the bed table lamp. "It's in the closet. In the duffel."

"Get it."

I went to the closet and fumbled around on the floor.

He came and stood over me. "Turn on the light."

"The bulb is burned out."

Boris reached up and pulled the cord. Nothing happened.

"It's in here someplace." I felt around among my shoes and boots until I located the bag, then zipped it open only an inch or so.

He heard the zipper. "Leave it. I'll look for myself."

I stepped back as he leaned down to get the bag.

"What is this, another one of your jokes?" He pulled out the rubber snake, shook it and threw it across the room. "You think that scares me?"

"It was worth a try."

He remained bent over and unzipped the bag its entire length.

"This might bother you more." I reached to one side, grabbed the bed table lamp, and slammed it down on his head. He dropped to the floor in a heap. Was he dead? I could only hope so. I heard sirens in the distance. I stooped over and picked up Boris' pistol, then spoke into my phone.

"What took you so long?'

Frida sounded put out. "The last time I came dashing to your rescue, you let the bad guys get away. You'd better have something for me this time."

"I gave you a bad girl. Call an ambulance. I think this one needs medical attention."

BORIS HAD A mild concussion from the lamp. The base was solid brass. The lamp had been one of Grandy's from her house in Connecticut. I'd asked for it when she and Max moved onto the boat. Boris' head had put a sizeable dent in it. I was sure Grandy would understand and forgive me for using it as a lethal weapon, and it would remain on my bedside table as a reminder of the evening's events.

Here I was again, down at the station, explaining to Frida why her prisoner was in the hospital for the night.

"You called me, sure, but you should have waited until I got there." Frida wasn't happy I'd taken things into my own hands.

"If I had waited, he would simply have bolted out the back way and been on his way to Mother Russia by now. You'd never catch him. We don't even know what the name on his passport is."

There was a ruckus in the front of the station. Sophia swept by two officers and rushed over to me. "You. You are a crazy woman. You've got it in for my family. You break my sister's nose and almost kill my brother. Arrest this woman."

"Sorry, Eve," Frida said. "I called her earlier when we arrested her sister and Darlene. She just got here from West Palm."

"Did you explain everything to her?"

Frida nodded. "I think she's in shock."

Yep. That would be Sophia's version of shock.

"Sit down." I shoved her back into a chair. As quickly as she had gone on the offensive against me, she deflated like a balloon and slumped into the chair.

"Your uncle was a good man," she said. "My mother loved him. I loved him, and I thought my brother did, too. Darlene, I didn't like so much. I thought she was after Winston's money. She told me he was leaving everything to us, but she knew that wasn't true, right?"

"Yes. And that's why she and Boris and your sister decided to stage the phony kidnapping to get his money. Then, when it was lost in the swamp, they came after me for money."

"It's my fault. I taught my sister how to shoot."

"Yeh, but you didn't tell her who to shoot."

Sophia looked up at me with something close to tears in her eyes. "I'm sorry."

I hadn't expected this from the ice queen. Was I seeing the spring thaw?

"It's okay."

"No, I mean I'm sorry that Uncle Winston didn't leave us more money. Maybe this wouldn't have happened."

Sophia's version of the crime. It only differed from her brother and sister's by the fact she didn't kill anybody for money. She may have loved Winston, but she was angry he didn't leave his estate to them.

"Take this away with you, Sophia. I didn't get any money from Winston. Nobody got any money from Winston."

She squared her shoulders and stood. "There's still his money in the swamp. What if someone finds it?"

"I think this time it's gone for good. But if it's found, I don't want it."

She looked peeved at my moral stance on the money. "You Americans are so goody-goody about things."

"Would you take it? Darlene said you were a letter-of-the-law person. It's money he made by working for the mob."

"I'd have to think on that."

"I'll call you if it floats in."

She gave me another look and strode out of the room.

"And she's the innocent one," Frida said as she rose from her chair and stretched.

"C'mon. I'll buy you breakfast," I said.

She put her arm around my shoulders and walked me to the door. "You mean like a real breakfast—bacon, eggs, pancakes—not just a stale pastry and lukewarm coffee in our break room?"

"Real, big breakfast."

CHAPTER 24

—

S EVERAL WEEKS WENT by before Alex finished his case in Pensacola. We talked several times each day by cell, and he came home on the weekend. The snake was located under the living room chair and returned to Grandfather Egret. I talked with Nappi, and he lectured me on going it alone into dangerous situations with only an old Indian and a bag of snakes as back-up, but he forgave me, then apologized for being out of touch. He broke down and gave me his cellphone number, but I suspected it was a burner and if I called it next month it wouldn't connect with him. I did appreciate the gesture.

The reason I couldn't contact Jerry that night was that he had given me the number of a burner phone he'd tossed that afternoon and forgotten to tell me the new one's number. There was no way I could have gotten in touch with my mob posse to assist me. Nappi told me he was punishing Jerry for his thoughtlessness by making him do the yard work on Nappi's West Palm condo. Anything that caused Jerry to break a sweat was anathema to him.

It was rumored that the Hardy brothers' airboat operation

was being taken over by a local. Nappi refused to discuss what happened to the Hardy brothers once he turned them over to their bosses, but I suspected the brothers were sweeping the floors of some casino in Las Vegas.

Frida called me frequently to lecture me on the same topic, adding a mini-lecture on endangering Madeleine's life by not letting the authorities know about her kidnapping.

"And don't push this one off on Nappi. You know better than to take advice from a mob boss."

Did I?

Between billing and cooing on the phone, Alex also lectured me about my propensity for getting myself into trouble and for thinking I could take on ersatz Russian mob members. Then he verbally flagellated himself for not being available to come to my aid. As quickly as he began blaming himself, he'd return to reprimanding me for my foolhardy behavior.

"And you took some crazy old Indian out into the swamps to meet with gun toting thieves? What were you thinking, Eve?"

Even Sammy lit into me about dragging Grandfather into this mess. But Grandfather put a stop to that.

"You weren't home to help. Anyway, I've never had so much fun in my life. Made me feel right frisky. Better than selling dresses to old ladies at your shop."

"Not all of them are old, Grandfather. And my customers liked you the days you were there. Madeleine and I are thinking about hiring you part-time. What do you think?"

He puffed on his pipe for a moment, then looked up at me. "How much do you pay?"

The evening Alex returned to town for good, we decided to go to Stuart and have dinner in one of the restaurants on the water.

"Dress up real sexy. This is going to be a night to remember."

Alex showed up at my door as I was getting dressed. I answered the doorbell in bare feet.

"I'll be ready in a jiff. I've got to find a pair of shoes to go with this dress."

Alex handed me a red rose and then swallowed. "You look good enough to take to bed."

"So do you, but if you don't stop ogling me like that the drool will stain your shirt front."

He did a pretend wipe of his mouth and grinned.

"Hey, buster, I paid a lot of money for this dress. I've just been looking for the right occasion to wear it. This is the night. C'mon with me. You can help me find the shoes I want to wear."

"It's a black dress, what there is of it. Won't any pair of black shoes do?"

I turned to look at him, shocked. "You've known me for over a year. Hasn't any fashion sense rubbed off on you yet?"

He had the good sense to lower his eyes and look repentant.

"That's better."

We both got down on our hands and knees on my closet floor.

"Wouldn't it be a lot easier if you replaced that bulb? Then you could see your shoes."

"I don't have a new bulb."

"They sell them everywhere."

"I know, but …. The shoes are a black pair with a wedgie front and five inch heels. I bought them last year and haven't worn them yet. I wasn't sure if the wedge would hit, fashion-wise."

"You were worried about whether you'd be 'in'? This is Sabal Bay, not New York City."

"I know, but …. Here's one of them." I reached farther into the closet. "And here's the other one."

I stood up and stuffed my toes into the shoes. "Ouch."

"What's wrong?"

"There's something in the toe of the shoe. What the hell?" I took off the shoe and pulled a folded piece of paper out of it. When I opened it up, it was one sheet with writing on it and signed at the bottom: *Uncle Winston.*

I scanned it, then handed it to Alex. He read it aloud. "Dear Eve, If you found this note then I'm dead. I wouldn't leave this for you otherwise. I don't know why I feel this way, but maybe as an old made man, my instincts are finely tuned to picking up on the possibility of death. I think someone will try to kill me. I've arranged with your friend and now mine, Mr. Napolitani, for me to leave the mob by doing a final job for them. I don't know if it will work, and I'm guessing you will be shocked to find that I have left everything to you in my will. Perhaps I'm just being paranoid, but I do not want my dead wife's children to inherit it, nor do I want to give it all to Darlene. Her past with men is too shaky. I know you will not want this dirty money, so I've arranged to make it "disappear" for a good cause. I've kept an eye on you since you were little and I am proud of what you've accomplished, having come through your parents' death and then that horrible marriage. Jerry isn't the man for you, but I hope you find someone who is. Forgive me for doing things in such a contorted manner, but it's just my way. Your loving *Uncle Winston*."

He handed the paper back to me.

I wiped away the tears that streamed down my cheeks and smiled. "I wonder what 'the good cause' was?"

"Have you read today's paper?"

I shook my head.

"Let me get it." Alex ran into the living room and came back with the *Sabal Bay Journal*. He showed me the headlines.

"Miccosukee Tribe Given More than a Million Dollars: Money Earmarked for Education."

"That is a good cause. I'm so proud of him. And he has such good taste."

"You mean giving it to education?"

"No, I mean hiding the note in a pair of shoes he knew I'd only wear on a special occasion."

"It's all about shoes for you, isn't it, Eve?"

"It must run in the family."

Creations in Fotografia by Rafael Pacheco

LESLEY A. DIEHL retired from her life as a professor of psychology and reclaimed her country roots by moving to a small cottage in the Butternut River Valley in upstate New York. In the winter she migrates to old Florida—cowboys, scrub palmetto, and open fields of grazing cattle, a place where spurs still jingle in the post office and gators make golf a contact sport. Back north, the shy ghost inhabiting the cottage serves as her literary muse. When not writing, she gardens, cooks and renovates the 1874 cottage with the help of her husband, two cats and, of course, Fred the ghost, who gives artistic direction to their work.

She is the author of a number of mystery series and mysteries as well as short stories. *Dead in the Water* follows the first book in the Eve Appel mystery series, *A Secondhand Murder*.

Visit her on her website: www.lesleyadiehl.com

Creature Kalhorn, she by Paine Perkins

Walter A. DiMantova loved his father for a lifetime of
...